I0572942

# Opportunity

## The Largest Cash Heist in American History

C.J.H. Moore

**Opportunity**
*The Largest Cash Heist in American History*

First Edition: 2023

ISBN: 9781524318338
ISBN eBook: 9781524328320

© of the text:
  C.J.H. Moore

© Layout, design and production of this edition:
2023 EBL

# Table of Contents

# Foreword

I would like to encourage everyone to read this amazing novel. Author C.J.H. Moore did a masterful job in the Dunbar Heist story. I was able to read a soft-release-date copy in the LAX complex waiting to catch a plane to Dallas. I was so enthralled in the story that I missed my plane. I met the Author in Starbucks in Compton while he was writing one of his other Novels. I told him that I had Rights to the Biggest Cash Heist in American History. He said he was born to write the book. I gave him the opportunity and he delivered. Bravo. Thanks to Mr. McCrary for trusting me and granting me the Rights to tell his story. My next endeavor is to produce the movie. Any questions about joining me, I can be reached @ Vince D Productions.

comedianvince@gmail.com
Vincent T Devereaux

# Acknowledgements

We would like to thank Adriane Hopper Williams for conducting the interview with Mark Mcrary in the form of question and answer sessions, and Allana Botley for listening and preserving the transcribed transcript of the interview. We would also like to thank producer Joey Wells for believing in the story of the Dunbar Heist, and presenting it enthusiastically to his colleagues. We would also like to thank in memory of John and Princella Moore and Joseph D. Devereaux Jr. and Bettye Jo Webb and Dennis Harris and Skip Mullen. We would also like to thank the Devereaux family and friends and everyone else who contributed to this book for your contributions, love, and support along the way in the twelve-year process in an effort to share the Dunbar Heist's story, the largest cash heist in American history, with the world public.

# Prologue

The true story of the September 12, 1997, Dunbar Heist in Los Angeles, CA, the largest cash heist in American history, as told from the Q&A interview of Freddie Lynn McCrary, Jr. aka "Mark", an integral member and childhood best friend of Allen Pace III, who conscripted and conspired with five friends to rob $18.9 million in cold, hard cash without a single shot being fired.

Some names have been changed to protect the contributors and the $10,000,000 unaccounted for. This material is based on the true story of the historical September 12, 1997 Dunbar Heist that shocked and snubbed the smartest criminal investigators in America for two years. Adriane Hopper Williams and Vince D. collaborated with "Mark" in an eighty-page interview to give a true account of the happenings leading up to the historical Dunbar Heist, the participant's arrest, and the rest.

# Chapter 1

*Fate, friendships, and love make poor bedfellows in a world of wealth, laws, and justice.*

In early December in 1978, the Los Angeles skyline melts like butter over hot cakes. The Palos Verdes Hills blink at the San Gabriel Mountains as a thousand eyes seemingly overlook the Inland Empire in the form of distant lights. A black Viet Nam vet stands outside of a Nix check cashing facility on the corner of Compton and Wilmington in the city of Compton wearing a filthy Santa Claus hat and livery and has a sign hanging from his neck that reads: **VIET NAM VET – I GAVE MY ARM FOR YOUR FREEDOM – WHAT HAVE YOU GIVEN ME?** His left hand is holding a decorated stainless-steel cruet; his right hand is shrouded by a dirty blanket while the horrors of war are hidden from view.

A woman and a small child walk by.

"Merry Christmas," greets the vet holding out the container covered by Christmas wrapping paper.

"Grandma, it's Santa," said the child excitedly.

"Don't make eye contact," she tells the child pulling him hard.

"Cheap ass motherfucka," the vet mumbles under his breath.

A Dunbar truck rolls up with two employees looking hard and tired.

Speaking into a small microphone attached to his collar, the vet says, "The prize has arrived." Standing in line are three men dressed as The Three Wisemen seemingly waiting to cash their checks. Children stand with their mothers while a man dressed as Jesus is at the front of the line. Jesus turns his head and looks towards the door.

Outside, a Dunbar employee pops out the back of the truck carrying two bags in either hand, while the driver stays in the front driver's seat of the Dunbar truck. The other Dunbar employee walks behind the counter and gathers the cash, stuffing it in the bags. The Three Wisemen and the white man dressed as Jesus patiently stand in line. The cashier with a bodacious booty sporting a wedding ring big enough to break her arm makes small talk with the Dunbar employee.

"You get me anything for Christmas this year?" asks the cashier.

"Just because I'm surrounded by money doesn't mean I actually make any of it," replies the Dunbar employee smiling nonchalantly.

"You're too funny," said she, and as she turns all of her attention back to her customers as Jesus approaches the counter.

She takes the check—*it's blank.*

"Sir, I'm sorry, but this is not a valid check," said the cashier with perplexity.

Jesus grabs her hand, looks at her ring, and then says, "I will seek opportunity; if not given opportunity, I shall create opportunity."

She is about to respond when he pulls her forward, slamming her into his forehead. She falls to the ground, knocked out cold. The Three Wisemen pull out guns and overpower the security guards and detains the Dunbar employee.

Jesus pulls out a sawed-off shot gun from underneath his robe and shouts in a horrific voice, "Everyone freeze, everyone freeze!!!"

"Please don't hurt anyone," squeals the Dunbar employee.

Wack! A wise man hits the Dunbar employee on the head and blood oozes out in a thick mass as women cry and men moan, and children look on in ignorance.

"Shhh! Shhh! Shhh! Relax, I have come, so that you may have life more abundantly motherfucka—now shut the fuck up!" Jesus roared addressing people in the lobby.

Outside, the Dunbar driver waits patiently. Knock! Knock! Knock! The Dunbar driver jumps, "Fuck!"

As he looks towards the window, the vet stands there with puppy dog eyes pointing towards his sign written in red: "VIET NAM VET – I GAVE MY ARM FOR YOUR FREEDOM – WHAT HAVE YOU GIVEN ME?"

The Dunbar driver exhales in relief, "Man I can't help you," as he motions for the vet to walk on.

Inwardly anxious, the vet thinks, *Please, c'mon cocksucker, open up!"*

The Dunbar driver shakes his head from side to side, holds up his hands, and says, "I can't hear you, you dumb fuck!"

The vet walks closer, and says, "Please!"

The Dunbar driver shakes his head NO.

The vet shrugs his shoulders in an oh-well manner. A sinister grin grows large across his lips and he throws off the blanket.

The Dunbar driver screams, "Man, back up!"

The vet motions towards his own ear in an I-can't-hear-you manner and jumps back revealing a M2 rifle in his right hand and a fully intact left hand.

The Dunbar driver sees the rifle, but ducks too late. The vet pulls the trigger, an inaudible "fu" could be heard. The rifle shot obliterates the glass and the vet reaches inside the truck and hits a button on the dashboard and the back door of the truck flies open. Blood and gore is everywhere, the driver convulses trying to hold on to his last breath of life.

The vet screams at the Dunbar driver, "Can you hear me now motherfucka!"

The vet runs to the back door of the truck as two masked men pull up behind the Dunbar truck in an unmarked van. They keep the van idling and unload the money.

Concurrently, inside the Nix check cashing place, one of the wise men zip ties the other Dunbar employee while the other two wise men load the loot up on the other side of the counter.

Jesus enjoys the show as he looks at his wristwatch. The guys outside finish loading the van. They jump in and peel rubber as they leave with sirens blaring in the distance.

From outside, the vet speaks into his mini microphone, "We've got heat."

Inside, Jesus touches his earpiece, vibrating with the message. He looks towards the sound of the approaching sirens and cautions the wise men, "Let's Go!"

At that moment, the cashier comes to. She lifts her head up and sprints for the door when Jesus says, "Where you going beautiful?" She reaches for the door—BANG!!! Jesus shoots the cashier in the head. As brain fragments fly everywhere and splatter on some customers, she falls limp, thud, and dead right in front of eight-year-old Mark while blots of blood stain his glasses. Grandma Pearl, fifty, dark-skinned, salt and pepper short Afro hairdo, squeezes and hugs young Mark tighter. Sharp shrilling screams fill the Nix lobby. Jesus reaches down and takes the ring from the dead cashier's finger and momentarily locks his flaming eyes with Mark's eyes, and says, "I will seek opportunity, if not given opportunity, I will create opportunity." The man's eyes reveal something deep, mysterious, and alluring in them—dangerous. The menacing sirens get closer and louder, breaking the trance.

"Let's get the fuck out of here!" shouted one of the wise men. They run hard. They jump in a van and speed off peeling and burning rubber so hard that Mark smelt the burnt rubber inside the

Nix lobby. Minutes later, the blaring sirens pull up and cease right outside.

"Shhh! Shhh!" said Grandma Pearl as she soothes him, and wipes clean his blood-stained glasses. But Mark is not crying, upset, or scared.

Mark is more caught up in a daze than scared when Grandma Pearl begins to pray, and people start screaming louder. Cops and EMT's flood the scene. EMT's carry the dead cashier away in a body bag.

# Chapter 2

Five years earlier, Mark knocks on Allen's door. Allen answers the door, "I can't come out and play right now, I'm watching Inspector Gadget, Tom & Jerry, Schoolhouse Rock, and Conjunction Junction. I'll come out when they're off in two hours." Allen slams the door.

"Who was that?" asked Allen's mother, Queenie, who was pretty, light-skinned, soft-spoken, and marvelous cook. Mark thoroughly enjoyed eating the different snacks and pastries she offered him from time to time.

"My friend, Mark," answered Allen, "He wants to play Cowboys and Indians outside."

"Invite him in, Allen. It's okay," said his mother.

"That's okay, mom. I'd rather watch TV by myself," said Allen with good diction for a four-year-old.

When the cartoons were over, Allen grabs his shiny cap gun and black holster with a whole roll of caps and heads across the street to Mark's house.

Marks's mother answers after Allen knocks on the door, "Can Mark come out to play?"

"Maaaarrk, Allen is here!" screams his mother from the front door towards the inside of the house.

Mark comes running with his cap gun bouncing inside his holster. He fired three caps, "I gotcha Allen." Allen played like he was shot, held his stomach and fell to the ground prostrate and motionless for a few seconds, then got up and ran across some neighbors' front yards with Mark running after him. They hid behind bushes, tree trunks, parked cars in driveways, and the sides of neighbors' houses. Each head appeared and disappeared, popped up, and ducked behind the obstacles they chose for protection. They shot popping caps as if they were firing real bullets and making ricochet sounds like they heard in cartoons and movies. Deep into play, Mark loses sight of Allen and races for better position in the play battle. Allen pops up outta nowhere and fires his cap gun several times. Mark is caught in the open and plays dead, acting the scene out like he saw on television. Allen runs over and shakes Mark back to normal; they smile at each other.

"You wanna play concentration?" asked Allen.

"Yeah, let's go," said Mark happily.

They ran side by side over to Allen's house where he found a deck of cards in the kitchen drawer. They pulled out chairs from the kitchen table and placed the entire deck face-down with both of them spreading the deck evenly around the round tabletop. The small boys walked around the table finding matches until Allen won with the most matches.

"Let's go play some baseball," said Allen full of excitement after winning concentration.

"Okay," agreed Mark.

Allen ran into the garage and grabbed two gloves, a baseball bat, and a little league-sized softball. The boys started playing catch from a few feet apart then widened their distance to several feet in the street. Other kids came over to play, until they had enough to play a game. They made bases out of squashed soda and beer cans, chose teams, and Allen and Mark were on the same team with two other boys. Allen was the best hitter and catcher out of them all and their team won.

"Let's play some football," said Allen. Everybody agreed, so Allen ran over to his garage and found a Voit football. Again, Allen was the best athlete in catching and throwing with Mark on his team, they won. Each time they won, Allen and Mark shook hands.

"You wanna go play some battleship?" asked Allen.

"Yeah!"

Allen had a computerized version and a plastic board game version of the battleship game. Both boys preferred playing with the plastic board and pegs.

"These small plastic ships are cool," said Mark placing it in position on the board.

"This one of the coolest games in the world," said Allen in agreement.

"You sunk my battleship," said Mark several times as they played.

Allen's "tracking" grid was replete with red pegs before Mark's, and the game was over.

Since Allen was older, Mark always accepted defeat because of the age difference and not personally. He always longed for the day when he announced himself the winner. He enjoyed being on teams with Allen because they won most of the time. For some reason, thought Mark, since a very early age, Allen was always in the right place at the right time.

"Let's go in the backyard and play some marbles," said Allen.

"Okay, I've got to run across the street and get my marbles."

Allen and Mark played a lot of games together, but this was Mark's favorite because, one-on-one, Mark was successfully competitive. He played .500 marbles against Allen, which compelled him to practice a lot in his own backyard. Most of the time, they'd carve out a corner in Allen's backyard and play hot-box and circles. Mark's favorite marble was a yellow cat's eye, his shooter; the boulders, solids, clears, pearls, snakes, butterflies, and creams he would keep for patsies. He had a collection of one hundred marbles that he carried in a blue Crown Royal liquor bag with a yellow drawstring that his Uncle Phillip gave him after watching him practice in the backyard one day.

Mark showed up in minutes trying to catch his breath, "Let's play circles first."

"Okay," said Allen.

Whenever the boys played marbles, they wallowed in the dirt like puppies with dusty-looking shirts and dirt-dotted knees. Since the match was taking place in Allen's backyard, he drew the circle a little larger than usual and the boys dumped ten marbles a piece of their choice into the circle. They lagged the line for first shooter; Mark won. Mark took his yellow cat's eye shooter and started firing away focusing on Allen's marbles first. Whenever a shooter's marble stayed in the circle knocking out the subject marble, the shooter himself would get another turn. Mark practiced on sticksies—knocking the subject marble out of the circle while the shooter marble would stop in its place sometimes spinning in inertia. Mark had knocked eleven marbles from the circle when his yellow cat's eye trickled just across the threshold of the circle. Allen flushed the remaining marbles. Mark happily added one more marble to his collection.

"Let's play hot box now, you wanna?" asked Allen.

"Okay," replied Mark stuffing his winnings into the blue Crown Royal bag just before he drew the yellow string.

Hot-box was a square-configurated marble game that featured peaksies. The two boys agreed on putting five marbles of the opponent's choice in the box. Sticksies was always good because if the shooter's marble stayed within the drawn parameters, the shooter himself could shoot again. Both players could remove any marbles they chose from their bag. Mark never put his cat's eye in jeopardy.

Allen's favorite marble was a blue pearl and he never put that one in the hot-box either. Allen kept his marbles in a Kerr preservative jar with a gold twist cap. Allen's mom, Queenie, maintained several fruit trees in their backyard—

apricot, peach, lemon, and plum. She preserved the fruits in Mason, Ball, and Kerr jars, eating the preserves daily with meals. The boys made their selections. Since Mark won circles, he was first to shoot.

Mark called peaksies and formed a small mound of dirt for an easier shot. He executed sticksies until six marbles were shot out of the box. On his sixth shot, two marbles were kissing so he had to fire a combination shot, and his cat's eye flew out of the hot-box. Allen easily shot the rest of the marbles out of the hot-box.

"Allen and Mark, come inside and have some lunch," said Queenie from the back door.

"Good," said Allen, "I'm hungry. When lunch is over, we can watch Conjunction Junction together."

Mark's eyes lit up because he knew Allen liked watching cartoons alone. Besides Conjunction Junction, Schoolhouse Rock was one of Mark's favorite kid shows. Even at his age, he knew the lyrics and each time he would sing along:

Conjunction Junction, what's your function? (CHORUS)

Hooking up words and phrases and clauses.

Conjunction junction, how's that function? (CHORUS)

I got three favorite cars that get most of my job done.

Conjunction junction, what's their function? (CHORUS)

I got "and", "but", "or", they'll get you pretty far.


"And" that's an additive, like "this and that."

"But": That's sort of the opposite, "Not this but that."

And then there's "or". O-R, when you have a choice like

"This or that". "And," "but," and "or," get you pretty far.

Conjunction junction, what's your function? (CHORUS)

Hooking up two boxcars and makin'em run right.

Milk and honey, bread and butter, peas and rice.

Hey that's nice! (CHORUS)

Dirty but happy, digging and scratching,

Losing your shoe and a button or two.

He's poor but honest, sad but true, Boo-hoo-hoo-hoo-hoo!

Conjunction junction, what's your function? (CHORUS)

Hooking up two cars to one

When you say something like this choice:
"Either now or later" or no choice:
"Neither now nor ever"
Hey that's clever! (CHORUS)
Eat this or that, grow thin or fat, never mind,
I wouldn't do that, I'm fat enough now!

Conjunction junction, what's your function?
(CHORUS)
Hooking up phrases and clauses that balance,
like:
Out of the frying pan and into the fire.
He cut loose the sandbags,
But the balloon wouldn't go any higher.
Let's go up to the mountains,
Or down to the seas. You should always say,
"Thank You"
Or at least say, "please."

Conjunction Junction, what's your function?
(CHORUS)
Hooking up words and phrases and clauses
In complex sentences like:
In the mornings, when I'm usually wide
awake,
I love to take a walk through the gardens and
down by the lake,
Where I often see a duck and drake, and

I wonder, as I walk by, just what they'd say
If I could speak, although I know that's an absurd thought.

Conjunction function, what's your function?
(CHORUS)
Hooking up cars and makin'em function.
Conjunction function, how's that function?
(CHORUS)
I like tying up words and phrases and clauses.
Conjunction function, watch that function?
(CHORUS)
I'm going to get you there if you're careful.
Conjunction function, what's your function?
(CHORUS)
 I'm going to get you there if you're careful.
Conjunction function, what's that function?
(CHORUS)
I'm going to get you there if you're very careful.

As little Mark sang along reciting every word in the song, he clapped and patted his feet on the brown linoleum floor. Queenie was impressed and spellbound watching the three year old perform. When the song was over, she hugged Mark and said, "Good job Mark. You want some more cookies and milk?"

"Yes, can I!" he said bouncing up and down sitting on the couch.

Through the whole program Mark had his eyes glued to the television set as did Allen.

Then Allen's father walked into the room, "Go pick some apricots and peaches for your mom, Allen." Mark froze inside whenever Allen senior came around. He looked mean to Mark, hardly ever smiled, and had a deep menacing voice. He never made Mark feel comfortable, so Mark wanted to go home every time he saw him.

"Come and help me, Mark."

Allen's father eyed both boys, "You can have one fruit a piece. Pick about a dozen a piece and put them in this bag." He handed Allen an Alpha Beta brown grocery bag, "Your mother wants to make an apricot/peach cobbler for desert tonight."

Picking fruit was always Allen's passion. Sometimes he'd eat peaches and apricots until he got sick and his teeth would hurt. Of Course, his father knew it, and whupped Allen on occasion for overeating the fruit until Allen learned his lesson. Allen loved to see the fruit trees blossom in the spring with the pink, yellow, white, and green ragout mixture of colors. Often, he would examine the tiny fruit buds that grew into voluptuous, juicy balls of eating pleasure. And his mom's pies were so good, he thought, that no cook in the world could bake pies better. Picking fruit with Mark was one of the funnest things he'd ever done. For Mark's size he had a better-than-average vertical leap, higher than his own, studied Allen, but it was still fun challenging each other in the jumps. Mark was also a good climber. Like a crab, Mark could cling to a tree trunk and crawl upwards and hang like a monkey from a low-hanging branch, then catch the branch with his legs, pull himself up and balance himself aplomb on a supportive branch.

Allen wasn't athletic, wiry, and strong as Mark, but Allen noticed talent when he saw it. In fact, he noticed a lot of things that others took for granted at an early age. Whenever he wanted something, he would use these skills often without the participant's knowledge to gain his objective as if they wanted it anyway for themselves. So, he would coordinate and manipulate people and situations like a fine manager on an unprecedented level to supervise a team of individuals to win.

That day, Allen and Mark carried a lightweight aluminum step ladder and placed it under the trees and picked apricots, peaches, plums, and lemons as his father ordered. "We're almost finished, Mark. We got lots of stuff. Which one do you wanna eat?" Allen asked.

"I wanna a peach and two apricots," said Mark. "Can I have two apricots?"

"No, you can only have one. My father is watching. If you want two, put one in your pocket for later, go ahead."

Already afraid of Allen's father, Mark didn't argue. "Okay," he replied.

The boys brought the Alpha Beta shopping bag back in the house after replacing the ladder. Queenie was in the kitchen applying pie crusts in three large pans.

"Allen, go see if your sister's awake and if she is, warm up her bottle in the bottle warmer." She smiled at Mark, "You ever had apricot/peach cobbler, Mark?" asked Queenie.

"No, but it sounds good," answered Mark smiling.

Allen returned, "Velvet is still sleep." Allen ran out again.

"It'll be ready in a few hours," said Queenie, "Would you like a piece before dinner."

A broad smile grew on Mark's face, "Boy would I!" Then Mark curiously looked at the large shopping bag pointing at it, "What does A-L-P-H-A B-E-T-A mean?"

Allen returns running cautiously, "Velvet is still sleep."

Queenie was an elementary school teacher at Ralph Bunche Elementary School in Carson, and she admired inquisitive children. "Do you know your alphabets, Mark?"

"Yes, my mother, Lady Sue, taught them to me."

Mark starts singing the alphabet song in different notes, "A-B-C-D-E-F-G-

H-I-J-K-

L-M-N-O-P-

Q-R-S-

T-U-V-

W-X

Y & Z

Now I know my ABCs tell me what you think of me."

Queenie smiled, "There's a Greek alphabet, too. Alpha and Beta are the 1st and 2nd letters in the Greek alphabet. There are twenty-four letters in the Greek alphabet, seven vowels, and twenty-six letters, and seven vowels in the American/English alphabet. Unlike the English alphabet, the Greek alphabet gives its letters names. I'm going to tell you what they are in case you hear them again or want to study them later. American English refers to them a Iot, and you should at least know what you're hearing. Please listen: Alpha – Beta – Gamma – Delta – Epsilon – Zeta- Eta- Theta- Iota – Kappa- Lambda – Mu – Nu – Xi – Omicron – Pi – Rho – Sigma – Tau – Upsilon – Phi – Chi – Psi – Omega. To answer your question Mark, Alpha Beta is a chain of grocery stores that stock all the items in the store in alphabetical order.

Sitting at the kitchen table restless, Allen blurts out, interrupting the lesson, "C'mon Mark, let's go play."

"Don't be rude, Allen," said Queenie.

"Thank you, Mrs. Pace," said Mark. "Can I go out and play now?"

"Sure, honey," said Queenie. "And Mark, you can call me Queenie."

Allen and Mark ran outside. The boys played army, checkers, and other board and card games until dinner. Pinto beans and ground beef was one of Allen's and Mark's favorite meals.

"Marie Callender's ain't got nothin' on this pie," said Allen's father stuffing a spoonful in his mouth.

"Who's Marie Callender's?" asked Mark, being more inquisitive than afraid.

Over the years, 10 years to be exact, Queenie had developed outstanding patience with pre-school and school-aged children. She developed the philosophy that no question was a silly question or too hard. She was a practicing educator who took her job seriously in and out of the classroom. She believed that a child could and should be taught from conception. She understood that people retained 80-95% of whatever they experienced or taught. Although she knew that this procedure sometimes backfired with older people (who think they know everything), adolescents lapped it up like hungry animals.

"Marie Callender's is a restaurant chain where people go out to eat. Marie started the business in the '30's with her son, Don. She baked pies and her son, Don, delivered them to customers on his bicycle. Later, Don opened up a restaurant in his mother's name not too far from here in Orange County. As the restaurant grew, they added food and alcoholic beverages. They developed an antique theme with early American furniture, pictures, and photos. The business has grown in worth to cover millions of dollars per year."

Even at his age, Mark thought how lucky Allen was to have a mother so patient and smart. Mark loved being around Queenie but was scared to death of Allen senior. Unlike the McCrary household, Allen had the perfect two-parent household—a loving, compassionate, and smart mother and hard-working and disciplinarian father. It was Queenie who satisfied Mark's deepest desires for knowledge, and his father who kept him on the straight and narrow. As Allen and Mark grew together from year to year, they developed a bond of friendship where they both used their God-given skills to help each other even in the direst situations.

Saturdays were fun for Mark and Allen because on Sundays Mark's family would be in church all day and sometimes all night, too. Mark's grandmother, Grandma Pearl, was a bishop at Greater Ebenezer Baptist Church in Los Angeles. Grandma Pearl would often visit various churches after regular service on Sunday evenings till 1 AM, which made it hard for Mark to get up Monday mornings and many times through the week throughout Mark's grade-school years. Sometimes, Allen and his family would go, too.

Mark lived in an eight-person household with his mother, grandmother, two uncles, two sisters, and an auntie. Mark lived in a loving and nurturing environment, but he was never claimed by his biological father. Mark was the youngest, the baby of the family, so, his family claimed the position of him being spoiled, a cultural stigma adopted and nurtured by black families although happy families are all alike; and every unhappy family is unhappy in its own way. But Mark himself never thought he was spoiled like rotten eggs or neglected fruit because he never ever got everything he wanted and when it was time to get whuppings, everybody got an ass whupping. Only Lady Sue, Mark's mother, and Grandma Pearl were the two that ever really whupped the kids. In fact, many times he was first, and the belt swung harder. Mark always thought his grandmother was the fiercest whupper. Auntie Robin was gone with her boyfriend all the time. Uncle Phillip liked to dress sharp and go to clubs and concerts and Uncle Paul was only five years older than Mark. Monique, his eldest sister, was five years older, and his sister next to the oldest sister, Anna, was three years older.

A ringing doorbell—Ding-Dong-Ding-Dong-Ding-Dong—sent musical chimes throughout the dining room.

"Go get the door, Allen," said Allen Senior.

Allen slid from his chair and ran to the door. "Who is it?" asked Allen through the closed door.

"Anna! Is Mark over here?" she asked trying to catch her breath. Anna was a pretty little girl with light-brown skin, long black hair, and light brown eyes.

"Yeah!"

"My momma says he has to come home," said Anna, then she ran away quickly.

Allen ran back into the dining room, "Mark, your momma wants you to come home."

"Thank you, Mr. and Mrs. Pace, for the dinner," said Mark. "I'll see you later."

Mark slid down from the chair with Allen following, and Mark cautiously ran across the street.

Allen watched Mark leaving and hollered after him, "I'll see you tomorrow."

Before Mark could get across the street good, his grandmother was standing in the front door smiling. "Mark, put some clothes on, we're going to church."

Sometimes three-year-old Mark wore a tie, and he liked it better when he wore a tie because he would get more attention from the older ladies saying how cute he was. At three years old, his Uncle Phillip had already taught Mark how to tie a tie, and to properly tuck in his shirt instead of just stuffing it down in his pants. He would curl his shirt in swaths and place the neat swaths under his belt. And his black penny loafers kept a spit shine that many grown-ups envied because, again, Mark's Uncle Phillip was one of the smartest dressers around.

If Mark wasn't playing with Allen, he basically kept to himself. He hardly played with his Uncle Paul, who was five years older, primarily, because of their age difference, but he didn't like what Uncle Paul liked anyway. Uncle Paul spent a lot of time riding skateboards and playing video games. Mark liked reading children's books, playing board games, collecting matchbox cars, and watching children's programs on TV in his spare time when he was alone. Often, Anna would ask Mark to play house, but he thought that was a silly game to play with his sister, although sometimes when he agreed to play house she'd play with her dolls most of the time.

Young Mark had to live with the fact that he didn't have any brothers close to his age; so, he developed introverted tendencies and lived out being comfortable with himself. Uncle Paul, his older uncle, was five years older than Mark, and he spent a lot of time with his friends. Besides, Mark was the shy type, and he really didn't like being in the limelight, but he liked being noticed.

Grandma Pearl drove herself around town most of the time, and she liked taking Mark with her whenever she could. "Mark, are you ready to go?"

Mark appeared from his unshared bedroom in his little blue suit, white shirt, and blue tie. "I'm ready grandma, let's go."

Although the church had a good choir, Mark liked Pastor Jones' sermons more than anything. In fact, he liked all of the pastors of the churches they visited. Oftentimes, he'd ask Grandma Pearl what they preached about. Grandma Pearl thought that it was so cute and grown up the questions that he'd ask: Who is God? Who is Jesus? Who made the angels? Who is the Devil? Is money the root of all evil? And many other questions he'd ask all the way home from services.

Many times, Mark would sit in the pews on a sister's lap while Grandma Pearl ushered and directed the congregation. He really liked sitting on Sister Jones' lap, the Pastor's wife, because she had big breasts that were softer than a pillow when he leaned back during the sermons.

When they made it to the church, a preacher was already in the early stages of introductions of other preachers. Mark and Grandma Pearl found empty seats on the front pew. It was awkward enough attending church on a Saturday night, but at least he didn't have to go to school the next day. Many of the people he hadn't seen before, and he was sitting with Grandma Pearl for a change. Mark recognized the preacher speaking now, he listened., "Let the church say, Amen. Isn't God good." A bevy of amens flowed from the congregation. "Look to the person next to you and say God is good." Every head in the church turned, about two hundred including his.

The pastor continued, "The creator has blessed you tonight to make it here, and we've got to give Him thanks. In the book of Ecclesiastes written by the wisest man of all time, King Solomon, and he says that we are never satisfied. The more we get the more we want. Greed is the sin of sins. Let's turn our bibles to Ecclesiastes 1-11 and I quote:

'1 The words of the Preacher, the Son of David, King in Jerusalem. 2 Vanity of vanities, saith the Preacher, vanity of vanities; all is vanity. 3 What profit hath a man of all his labour which he taketh under the sun? 4 One generation passeth away, and another generation cometh: but the earth abideth forever. 5 The sun also ariseth, and the sun goeth down, and hasteth to his place where he arose. 6 The wind goeth toward the south, and turneth about to the north; it whirleth about continually, and the wind returneth again according to his circuits. 7 All the rivers run into the sea; yet the sea is not full; unto the place from whence the rivers come, thither they return again. **8** All things are full of labor; man cannot utter it: the eye is not satisfied with seeing, nor the ear filled with hearing. **9** The thing that hath been, it is that which shall be; and that which is done is that which shall be done: and there is no new thing under the sun. **10** Is there anything whereof it may be said, See, this is new? It hath been already of old time, which was before us. **11** There is no remembrance of former things; neither shall there be any remembrance of things that are to come with those that shall come after.'"

The pastor paused and looked across the congregation.

"May the Lord bless the reading of the scriptures. You have a refrigerator and a freezer full of food and your neighbor or a guy on the street is hungry and you don't help to feed them; yet you want more. You have two running cars in your driveway and yet you won't give your neighbor a ride to the grocery store. You have a houseful of furniture and yet you won't let your neighbor rest when he is tired. You have an abundance of things and yet you won't share. You know a lot of things and yet you won't teach. Solomon says all is vanity and vexation of spirit. Weigh what you have against what you don't have and know when you increase in knowledge you also increase in sorrow. Pride increases pride and sharing increases sharing. You cannot take anything with you, but your soul. Greed is manufactured by the devil and is a proponent of evil. When you are blessed, it is best to share. And may the congregation hear the words of Solomon who is a servant of the Lord. Let us bow our heads and pray."

Other preachers rose to preach as young Mark listened trying to understand every word. Each time Mark listened to a sermon, he grew mentally just as fast as he was growing physically. On the way home, Mark thought about the sermons. "Grandma Pearl, what does vanity mean?"

Grandma Pearl smiled a wide smile, thinking: *this child is so inquisitive, God bless his heart.* "Vanity means pride, and it means a lot of things, baby. It could mean something good or bad. When you want too much of something and only think of yourself and think you are the best at something and you don't listen to better ways of doing things, that's too much pride or bad pride because there's only one "best" and that's God.

There is good pride, too—feeling good about yourself and doing your best to make another person feel comfortable so they can do their best, especially if they're a friend."

"Allen is my friend," said young Mark. "I should do my best so he could do his best and think about his feelings, too, because God is the best."

"If you could do that baby, you will give respect and get respect back."

"What is respect, Grandma," asked young Mark.

"When you like yourself, and others like you for who you are and not who you wanna be or what you got."

"I like you for who you are, Grandma. You don't have to change for me to like you, and you don't have to have a million dollars."

"Baby, money is good if you spend it on necessities like paying basic bills like gas, light, rent, and food. It is easier to love someone if you like them. You feel more comfortable around them."

"Well then, I know that I love you, Grandma," said Mark.

Grandma Pearl blushed. "I love you, too, baby."

# Chapter 3

As Mark sat on the floor by Grandma Pearl hugging her not noticing the splotches of blood on the rims of his glasses, a young Caucasian cop in his early twenties, handsome with a hungry look in his eyes, takes charge of the room.

"We're here now, and we're going to take care of you."

Mark looks up through rim-stained glasses and manages to say in a low voice, "They got away."

"My name is Officer Warren, and everything is going to be okay," he said kneeling down as he cleaned the rims of Mark's glasses with a tissue, he picked from his suit coat pocket. "Don't worry little man, we'll catch these guys—everyone gets caught," officer Warren paused for a second locking his eyes with Mark's eyes like looking through a glass window to his soul. "How old are you, son?"

"Eight," said Mark looking back at Officer Warren in the same way.

Mark watches Officer Warren take control of the moment and the whole place seems to move in slow motion, all except for Mark's thoughts. He couldn't stop looking at the door. The sun seems to get brighter as warmth blankets his face. Those words that Jesus spoke burned into the fabric of his being because after that day, after he saw what he saw, he would grow up thinking: *I will seek opportunity, if not given opportunity, I will create opportunity.*

That night after the robbery, while lying in bed, Mark fixed his mind on Jesus' burning eyes and said with a low audible voice: *Yeah, I know what you're thinking. That I learned one of my most valuable lessons from a white dude dressed like Jesus—but that was a minor detail—the thing he said today was full of truth. The other lesson is that life is 'all about strategy,' he'd say, 'It's all a game of chess,' he'd say. I met and realized him that same year in the fourth grade.*

The very next day after school, Mark runs for his very life with his backpack slamming against his torso. The chasers were three bullies ranging in age from 10-11.

In their childhood, Allen and Mark became the best of friends or, from the words of the times, they were homeys. Allen possessed leadership qualities as early as eight years old or younger, when he drove some bullies away from Mark after school was out. Allen carried around a sack of marbles for days, waiting and planning for an opportunity to use them. One day in early October, Allen, sees his chance. Allen strategically put himself in the perfect position to execute his plan. Three bullies begin their assault on Mark in an isolated area on school grounds as Allen watched from afar.

"When I catch you Cuz, I'm gonna fuck you up," one of the bullies cry out.

Mark's glasses bounce around his nose and his eyes fill with tears as he rounds the corner and... SLAM! Hidden behind a building, one of the bullies jump out and Mark runs right into his chest; he punches Mark in the face and blood spews out his nose like a running faucet.

"Oooo damn," said a bully. "Lil homey is a bleeder."

Mark slams to the ground and another bully is getting ready to clean his clock with a haymaker. Mark looks up and his eyes widen in terror when from behind a tree an unrecognizable boy appears, tall, lean and a bit goofy looking slams a sock of marbles—CRACK!—upside the bully's head. The bully screams writhing on the ground in profuse pain. Surprised by the courageous attack, the other two bullies hightail it away and Allen and Mark start running. After, Mark recognizes Allen through the commotion as the wind whips against their faces. Mark and Allen run in the opposite direction until they collapse on the grass in a nearby park in Carson.

"You saved my life," Mark said breathing hard.

Then Allen extends his arm and the two boys shake. Do you play chess? Asked Allen.

"No!" replied Mark. "I owe you one," Mark laughed hysterically with tears of joy in his eyes.

"You wanna learn."

"I don't know," Mark answers as they rise to their feet and head toward home.

"Chess is a game of strategy. It's like carrying around a bag of marbles knowing that one day you may need to use them as pawns in order to protect the king."

"You talkin' about that game with kings and queens and stuff; it sounds too hard," Mark said.

"That's the same thing I thought. But my father taught me when I was about four. It only looks hard. It's easy, you'll see," said Allen.

"Okay, I'll try," whispered Mark.

Later, in Allen's Garage, he pulls out the chessboard.

The red and black squares on the board reminded Mark of a checkerboard and carom board. Allen took each piece in hand, named it, and described how it could move: "This is the pawn—the first time you move it, it can move one or two squares straight ahead, but after the first move, it can only move one square at a time. And the pawn can take any opponent's piece diagonally—I like that word opponent, my dad taught it to me when he taught me this game, it means your enemy. This is the rook or castle, it can only move horizontally or vertically, that means up and down or from side to side. This is the knight or horse; it can move either one square up and two squares over or two squares up and one square over in both directions. It's the only piece that can jump opposing pieces or your own pieces and take pieces within its range. Just think of the letter L in all directions. This is the bishop; it can move diagonally on the red or black squares only or the same color square it is sitting on. This is the queen, the most powerful piece on the board—so always treat your woman right—that's what my dad taught me. It can move in all directions along the same color squares only—and this is the king. It can only move one square at a time. The main object of the game is to protect the king. Let's try a game," explained Allen.

Allen and Mark played chess until Allen won. Mark saw a lot of interesting possibilities as he learned more and more about the game of chess. He had to practice on his own like marbles. After the game was over, Mark was still studying the board.

"But what if you never get to use the bag of marbles? You'll get stuck carrying that shit all around each day?"

"There are some people who wait for an opportunity to happen, while others create an opportunity," said Allen.

Then later, Allen puts his arm around Mark as the boys walk happily down the street directly into the setting sun. Later that evening, while Mark and Allen were having chicken at Kentucky Colonel, Allen reflected to Mark that he had seen them bully Mark for days and planned on the perfect attack moment. He had planned and created this opportunity.

And I thought he was smart and brave, and I wanted to be like him, thought Mark. I knew we were brothers for life. But life has a way of testing even the strongest bonds.

# Chapter 4

At an early age, Allen had a knack for being amicable, organizing people to get what he wanted, and being at the right place at the right time. Allen not only learned at an early age how to be a clean-cut fop and sharply dress, but he also learned how to psychologically manipulate the toughest-minded-people. He had cognitive skills where he picked up mastering mathematical and language skills quickly. His learning curve was as steep as they come, considered by those who understood, an aplomb or almost vertical curve. Showing these abilities at an early age, his biological father taught Allen chess concepts as early as four years old. He could read, write, and verbalize before he attended kindergarten. His attentiveness and focus-bearing skills were unprecedented because at an early age he was a cartoon-watcher, and his ability to sit for hours in one place far exceeded that of the average kid.

Allen not only watched cartoons, documentaries, and sports, but he also liked watching movies. A lot of his psychological and philosophical techniques he learned from studying movie story lines—the beginning, middle, and the twist. It didn't hurt that his mom was a grade-school-teacher for oftentimes she outwardly, in public, corrected his English and math skills on the fly and helped him with his homework. It also helped that his dad was the ultimate disciplinarian but inwardly kind and sweet to his children. Allen grew up in a balanced family structure because both parents worked in professional environments, of course, his mom an elementary school teacher and his dad an engineer for Northrop, and his sister, Velvet, naturally taught him the female version of life's intricacies and values. Allen constantly manipulated situations to his advantage in all areas. Whoever fell into his whimsical web of successful maneuvers were happy they knew him.

Allen and Mark were a perfect match. Their childhood physical and mental matches spurred each other on as they grew. They rubbed off on each other because Mark had the heart of a fighter, competitive, and smart to ask the right questions. Yeah, that's why they were childhood buddies, thick as thieves.

As the life of young Mark carried on, he wondered if he was really loved and cared about by more than just his grandma, Queenie, and Allen. One day, he was left at the church on Normandie and 90th when they still lived on 169th and Avalon in Carson. The whole family attended church that Sunday. His Grandma had to leave early in the morning to help prepare for early services. Mark rode with Uncle Phillip, Anna, and Auntie Nicki. Mark fell asleep during services and when he woke up, everybody was gone. Somehow, they all thought each other had gotten him, so he ended up having to start walking home. On the way home, his Uncle Phillip searched and found him. "Y'all was really trying to leave me. I'm only eight. Y'all really trying to get rid of me cause—," said Mark sobbing.

"We—we—we thought your grandma had you," said Uncle Phillip nervously trying to remain calm.

After that incident, Mark really had second thoughts about how much his family wanted him, so he got more stand offish, more to himself, more introverted.

As time went on, two years to be exact, Mark was ten. His Uncle Phillip and his sisters wanted to go swimming and Mark didn't want to go, so he played by himself in the park on the playground. They thought Mark had walked home. The park wasn't that far from home. When Mark came later, they thought he was around the house playing.

Uncle Phillip was in the front yard cutting the grass when he saw Mark walk up with sweaty clothes. "We thought you walked home."

"Look at me that was a long walk," Mark said angrily. "Now that I think about it. I think y'all trying to give me a hint. Instead of dropping me off, y'all, uh, just left me."

"C'mon Mark," said Uncle Paul. "It was just a mistake," he said walking into the conversation.

Another time that same year, Uncle Paul was in a hurry to meet some people to go to a concert and Mark started playing with some other kids. He saw Monique and Anna, but Mark was nowhere around, he left without Mark. Mark started walking home after he looked for his sisters after it started getting late, too late. Some people at a church on the corner of Avalon and Victoria saw a little boy walking by himself.

"Where are you going little boy?" asked one of the church people.

"I'm going home," replied Mark.

"No!" said one of the church people. "Come in here." They called Mark's mother and the police. His mother came first.

"Why are you out here by yourself?" asked his mom.

"I don't know, they left me again," said Mark.

"Mark," said Lady Sue. "Don't ever think that we don't love you. You've been spending a lot of time by yourself lately. Just try to stay closer to your family next time."

Because Mark was the baby, he did receive a bit more attention when the entire family was together. It wasn't until Rayshawn, Auntie Nicki's baby, was born that Mark didn't receive as much attention.

When Mark was thirteen, because of the growing family, his mother, grandmother, and Uncle Phillip moved to Edwards, Mississippi where Lady Lucy lived, grandma Pearl's sister. Mark always thought the move was because it was too many people in the house in Carson, but his mother told him that they moved so Grandma Pearl could better serve her church responsibilities because she had to travel to Chicago and New York so much. Mark and Uncle Phillip had to move, too, since they were not babies.

***

I hated Edwards, Mississippi. It couldn't have been more than a thousand people living there. It was the most boring place on earth, a small town of a thousand people. The middle school two houses down from our house in Mississippi was a mimesis of Carson schools and the tiny downtown civic center was right around the corner. Again, I really hated living there with a passion and I told my mother one day—if I ever leave Edwards, I'll never come back. I'll do anything not to come back here. I liked being alone, but not that alone.

One of my scariest memories in Mississippi was when Uncle Phillip had to take one of Grandma Pearl's friends home. The man had just popped up and stayed for about a week while grandma was gone on a church trip because he didn't want to go home, so my Uncle Phillip finally took him home and left me in the house by myself; I was fourteen.

"Can you stay by yourself while I take Grandma Pearl's friend home?" asked Uncle Phillip.

"Yeah," said I. "I'm cool."

When I was alone that time, it was the first time I drank beer. It was so nasty I tried to put sugar in it and the sugar made it nastier. I wouldn't drink beer again without some kind of chaser. Everything they taught in middle school I had heard it before. It was like repeating grades.

# Chapter 5

Two years had lapsed, and his mother, Grandma Pearl, Lady Lucy, Uncle Phillip, and Mark moved back to Southern California. Mark lived with his granddad in Compton, and after a few months they both moved back to the old house in Carson. A month after he moved back to the old house in Carson, Mark got into a physical confrontation with another uncle named Johnny, who just moved in. Feeling like he was the man of the house, he wanted Mark to graduate.

Like many high school students, Mark had lost interest in school. The Edwards, Mississippi experience didn't help increase his interest either. He wasn't involved in any extracurricular activities in terms of service or sports. His mother having to work as a waitress at Coco's restaurant on Central and Artesia, adjacent to the 91 Freeway, was hardly ever home to make Mark go to school. His interest in matchbox model cars grew into working on real cars.

Ben, a play uncle of Allen and Mark, had retired from the city of L.A. as an automobile and truck mechanic. He was an older, dark, white-headed, senior-aged man who lived down the street on Moorhaven Drive in a two-story, quasi-mansion, who moonlighted under the shade tree as a mechanic fixing on neighborhood cars. He invited Allen and Mark to help him install and rebuild engines, replace and rebuild transmissions, and conduct minor and major repairs on foreign and domestic cars.

One Saturday morning, Ben, Allen, and Mark were working on a 1963 black Lincoln, like the one JFK was assassinated in, with suicide doors hinged at the rear panel.

"Damn, this baby is nice," said Allen. "I want one like this for my first car."

"If you keep getting good grades in school, something like this would be easier to get," said Ben.

"This is nice," said Mark. "But I'm in love with that Dodge Charger."

"By the time you guys get your first car, your taste will probably change," said Ben with his head under the hood. "Allen, hand me that five-eighths boxed-end and a three-quarters socket wrench. After we get this radiator replaced, we've got to replace the generator."

"How many cars we got today, Ben?" asked Mark.

"We got five and two more coming in tomorrow," said Ben loosening a bolt. "You boys can ride with me in the tow truck later to go pick them up."

Allen and Mark liked riding with Ben to pick up cars in his 1988 Ford F-350 tow truck. Allen thought it was the nicest tow truck he'd ever seen with its ruddy red metal-flake color and black plush leather tuck 'n roll seats.

Oftentimes, they would stop by McDonalds and get Big Mac combos. Although Mark loved cars since early childhood, Allen loved nice things like a genuine fop on Sunset Strip in the figurative sense, because he was no foolish boy. Allen and Mark talked a lot about how nice Ben's tools were. Ben's 2-ton cherry picker engine hoist worked as smooth as silk for replacing engines and his hydraulic pro-lift 2-1/2-ton floor jack made replacing transmissions a breeze and his stalwart massive and mobile 3 – part stainless steel tool chest with two drawers and casters wheels carried every tool in the book. Allen and Mark learned more about building, fixing, and car maintenance from Ben than they could ever learn in school, although mechanic shop was provided at Carson Middle and Carson High.

Allen always found school a piece of cake for on many report cards he'd get straight A's and many times he'd rush home from school before time for homework and then work on all models and types of cars with Ben and Mark. As a team, they had a good working relationship, because many times after school and on weekends, they'd fix broken down cars and they were well-paid by many satisfied customers.

Mark's passion for cars and the money kept him from his school efforts until all he thought about was cars. Ben knew the importance of Mark's education.

"You know Mark, I really appreciate all yo' help around here, but a young man like you should get a high school diploma. Cars will always be around, but the older you get, the less you'll have interest in school. Your friend Allen aces school. He can help you through. I ain't no genius but I'm willing to bet homework and tests are a big part of yo' grade and just sittin' yo' ass in that classroom seat. If school is that boring to you, just get yo' GED like I did. Trust me little bother, you'll be glad you did. Life is a lot easier when you build a foundation."

"Uncle Ben, I like the money. I can buy hamburgers and clothes."

"Every man has to make a livin' and it ain't no joke when a man is broke, but you're young little brother. Believe me food will come, but that basic education can get away from you for the rest of yo' life. You're a smart kid, Mark, and I wanna see you healthy and happy. Get a basic education, even if you have to sacrifice a few dollars right now in comparison to the rest of your life because it will be worth it in the long run."

Eventually Mark's love for cars came to a head. Oftentimes, he'd ditch school to work on cars with Ben. Ben would accept his help, but Ben knew it wouldn't last long. Ben surmised that cars were a child's fetish with Mark and would soon blow over; besides, he'd rather have him in the shop than getting into some other foolish activity, especially at his vulnerable age. Moreover, Mark really didn't like school that much, but he knew he'd get his high school diploma one way or the other. Ben had faith in Mark's ability to eventually finish high school. Receiving pressure from nobody else, one day after working with Ben, Mark came home early, and his uncle was waiting for him. Before Mark could get to the kitchen to get something to eat, Uncle Johnny was waiting with a little league baseball bat in his hand, "Where you been all morning, boy?"

"I was with Ben making money fixing on cars," spoke Mark honestly.

"Didn't your granddad tell you to go to school," gabbled Uncle Johnny.

"Granddad ain't told me nothin'," said Mark with a slight attitude.

"You're gonna mind your granddad," said Uncle Johnny while hitting Mark with the little league bat on his legs. "And take your sorry ass to school."

"Why you so worried about it," said Mark holding back tears. "You didn't graduate."

"I couldn't graduate because I had to work to help with the family," said Uncle Johnny between strokes.

"Damn, Uncle Johnny," cried Mark with tiny tears in his eyes. "You didn't graduate and you're doing okay, and I do mind granddad."

Uncle Johnny kept swinging, "I'm not okay, why do you think I'm here?"

Mark couldn't make sense out of the whole scene because the uncle who was confronting him never graduated from high school himself. On the day of the confrontation, Uncle Johnny grabbed a bat and beat Mark on his legs till they were swollen and sore. Mark always thought he chose the bat because Uncle Johnny was a little man and at seventeen Mark was bigger in stature. Upset, Mark went to Ben's house and made a couple of phone calls, caught a bus and went to the Carson Sherriff Department on Avalon and Carson Boulevard to file a report. Two black police officers showed up. They had a conversation with Uncle Johnny, then left. Uncle Johnny, acting as the authoritative figure in the house, caused Mark to move out. He wanted to move in with Monique in Long Beach.

Mark felt like the police and Uncle Johnny were ganging up on him, so he returned to Ben's house and called his sister, Monique.

After the phone call, Ben asked Mark to sit down in the living room before his sister came. "Listen son, I knew this day would come and I've already given you my advice. I just wanted to give you some place to go and keep you off the street. Take this hundred dollar bill; you've earned it. You don't have to pay me back. Again, I'll say, go to school and get yo' paper. If you can get back on the weekends and help, you're always welcome. I heard the conversation you had on the phone. You can wait here until yo' sister come. I got lucky 'cause I always been good with my hands and I got lucky passin' that test for the city. I done the best I could do. Now I'm askin' you to do the same."

"Alright Uncle Ben, I hear you. I promise you, I will," said Mark fighting back tears.

Monique came within an hour. She drove down the street, went in the house, stayed a little while and came out traipsing with two suitcases and slammed them in the trunk. They drove back to downtown Long Beach on Lime and Atlantic and settled in the apartment.

"Mark, you can live here, but you've got to help out with these bills," said Monique. "You either go to school or find a steady job."

"They need my school records and transcripts from Mississippi," countered Mark. "Grandma Pearl said they'd be here shortly."

"Why didn't you tell Uncle Johnny that?"

"I don't think it made a difference to him, he just wanted me out," reasoned Mark.

"Alright, for starters, Mark," said Monique, "We need some money coming in or food stamps. I'll take you down to the county building tomorrow. Just do what they say and you'll be okay."

The next day, Mark stood in a long line at the county building on Alondra between Santa Fe Ave. and Alameda Street in Compton and was finally seen at 3PM after Monique dropped him off at 8AM. He kept thinking during the wait in the queue that there's got to be a better way than this to make money. All sorts of ideas kept popping up in his head—even robbery by trick or strong arm. It was then that he made up his mind to at least finish high school.

When they called him, he was tired as fuck. "Fill out these papers," said the clerk.

As Mark read through the information they wanted, he paused, "I don't have a birth certificate."

"We can't process your application until we get your birth certificate," said the clerk. "We need proof of age and citizenship. Just go down to the Hall of Records on 12400 Imperial Highway in the city of Norwalk and request it."

Mark caught the bus back to the Long Beach apartment later that day. "You need to fill out these papers and get my birth certificate."

Monique took the papers, "You know Mark, it'll be a lot easier if you just go to school."

"I think you're right," agreed Mark. "Carson High here I come."

In the meantime, Monique pursued the county assistance to make it easier to pay rent. When the notice arrived that Mark McCrary does not fit the descriptive name on record, Monique told Lady Sue and she said the right name on the birth certificate is Freddie Lynn McCrary, Jr. Everybody but my mother was shocked because all they ever knew was Mark. He heard his sister ask his mother why they called him Mark.

When she got off the phone with Lady Sue, Mark asked Monique why Mark instead of Freddie. "You're not going to believe this, but Grandma Pearl thought your dad didn't want you, so she insisted that we call you Mark. Your dad insisted when you were born that you wasn't his. So, since he felt that way, your grandma started calling you Mark, and we've been calling you Mark ever since. Besides, every boy's name, if grandma had anything to do with it, would be a biblical name. Believe me, when you were born, grandma had a very strong presence in the house."

"That explains a lot," said Mark. "That's why he barely came around."

This new revelation riled Mark a little tight, so he picked up the phone and dialed. "Hello momma, this Mark. You know I love you momma. If my birth certificate reads Freddie Lynn McCrary, Jr., how did you get me in school under the name Mark?"

Mark listened for a while changing his facial expressions, then he said, "I love you, momma, see you later." He placed the cell phone down gently.

"Well," said Monique, "What did she say?"

"She didn't remember."

At that moment, a flood of memories and calculations filled Mark's mind and the connections came crystal clear. Of course, he was growing up; and above all doubt, he had to live with himself even if nobody else really wanted him. He had to want himself. He recollected the visits that he had made to St. Louis during the summers when he was between five and ten. Mark's god dad, O. C. Tolson, had an older daughter and two of Mark's uncles and Freddie Sr. worked at Busch Stadium and Mark went to a lot of baseball games free. Mark figured that his mom met his god dad in St. Louis while Freddie and his mom were playing around, and O.C. was the main reason she made the visits. His mom got pregnant with him during this uncertain time and went back to California. But he understood the old saying, "Momma's baby, Poppa's maybe," however true or untrue that old saying is, it is truer that the momma really knows who the father is more than not and that's why Freddie Lynn McCrary was on the birth certificate.

But Freddie Sr. was unsure for two reasons: Lady Sue didn't stay in St. Louis to have the baby and Freddie had an idea that Lady Sue was seeing another man. Could he really blame him? For now, his god dad, in his mind, was his real father, because he was there, and Freddie was not.

Mark vividly remembered that O.C. taught him how to fish, golf, and bowl during those long, hot summer days. Aside from what his mother was doing, O.C. was there in the flesh hanging there in Mark's mind, hanging like a rock, and if blood is thicker than water, love is thicker than blood. Although O.C. never talked to him about the birds and the bees, maybe because he was too young, nobody else did either. He learned about that like most kids in the black culture during the times of the '70s—from their friends. But Mark truly believed if anyone would have had that conversation with him, it would have been O.C. Tolson.

The memories kept flowing and he thought deeply about Freddie when he came to Carson once to help celebrate Grandma Pearl's birthday. Mark was fifteen, Freddie walked into the house, and everybody said here's Freddie not here's your father. Mark also remembered one time Freddie was supposed to take him shopping for school clothes but Freddie showed up and said that he didn't want to go to no boy store. Mark thought that was a gay move. At sixteen, the whole Freddie thing was a dead issue because Mark finalized with the thought *the thrill is gone* and he would never come back.

# Chapter 6

Five years later at the tender age of twenty-three, Allen captures Mark's queen diagonally. As Mark studies the board, Allen grins as The Godfather Part I blare in the background. Allen and Mark watched gangster movies together on DVD many times at Allen's request. Allen had been working for the Kentucky Fried Chicken store for six months now. He recommended Mark for a job there and Mark was hired. Mark had gone back to adult school for four months to earn his GED at 19. Being on the county for three years had taken its toll on Mark, but his sister got the bills paid while he concentrated on school. He hadn't spent that much time with Allen or anyone else over a two-year period while studying for his GED and going back and forth to school after regular graduation and not having enough credits himself to graduate on time took up most of his time. After working for Kentucky Fried Chicken for a month now, he had started meeting some of Allen's new acquaintances.

Travis, mid-twenties brown-skinned, brown eyes, petite nose, fast-talker, smart as a whip; Henry, late twenties, dark brown-skinned and handsome; Gene, late-twenties, light-skinned, cute to the hilt–all are lounging around smoking weed and having a few beers at Allen's apartment in Carson before work at the KFC on Avalon Boulevard by the Victoria golf course where Allen and Mark had eaten for years.

"Man shut up, they just fruit," said Gene commenting on a bowl of fruit sitting in the center of the dining room table.

"The oranges symbolize life and vitality; the apples symbolize knowledge, immortality, temptation, and sin; the bananas symbolize fertility, sex, and a blow job," said Henry, who was the oldest of the group and sported a set of rotten and crooked teeth. "That's how I'm going to do it when I make my movies."

"Movies?!" said Gene. "What you need to make is a dentist appointment to get that shit fixed." Gene and Travis laughed out loud and exchanged high fives.

Allen looked down at the chessboard, "I won three moves ago." he said.

Mark looks at the board determined to move. "You can't win all the time, Allen."

"The dude is unbeatable, Mark," said Travis.

Allen rises, buttoning up his fast-food KFC uniform getting ready for work after he puts Mark in checkmate.

"How do you always win?" asks Mark with a befuddled look on his face.

"Simple," said Allen smiling. "I had a plan and I stuck to it." He continued, "C'mon, I'll let you drive," as Allen throws Mark the keys.

Minutes later, Allen and Mark pull into the KFC parking lot and park, and both notice a license plate that reads 'DELILAH.' The 1964 metal-flake baby blue Chevy Impala had hydraulic lifts and deep 6-inch Cragar Super Sport Chrome Wheels, a real classic. Mark turns the key off in the 1969 Dodge Rambler as it coughs and spits some exhaust out of the tail pipe before it came to a complete stop. They sit outside for a while, mesmerized, wearing KFC silly hats and uniforms watching the '64 Impala roll down the street as loud music pours out vibrating the street. Everything slows down a bit as Allen and Mark watch the '64 Impala roll by. They both admired a beautiful woman sitting in the passenger's seat.

"Damn!" said Mark.

"Rome wasn't built in a day," said Allen. "Feel me? We just about to get ours," as he gives Mark a goofy smile. "Plus, this job has undeniable perks."

In anticipation, Allen imagines while he and Mark work cash registers side by side that everybody needs to eat. A variety of honeys breeze in the store, then she walks in, and he's gotta take this order.

Mark turns towards the honey, "This whole place just lit up brighter than the sun. What may I ask is the sun goddess's name, and I know you can't be as old as the sun, or are you?"

"My name is Florence," she says as if she knows she's sexy and beautiful. "And I'm 19."

"My name is mark, I'm 22, and who are these fine young ones?"

Florence smiles beautifully, "This is my sister, Janine."

"And I'm 16," Janine blurts out. "And this is my little brother Barry, he's 14," she says as they stand next to Florence hugging her, "I'm too old for a happy meal; I'll just take some fries."

"You just wanna pocket the extra money for your nails. I'm gonna tell mom," said Florence.

"I'm hungry, I like happy meals," cried Barry.

"Shut up! Barry, mind your own business," said Janine.

"No, you shut up, Janine," said Florence. "Or, I'll tell mom how you're acting when we get home and then she can deal with you. Who do you think she's gonna believe?"

Janine storms out in a huff. Victorious, Florence moves her bangs out of her face with her long, red manicured nails.

"You like Al Capone with little sis," said Allen.

"Huh," said Florence rolling her eyes.

"Watch out!" quips Allen. "You gonna get your eyeballs stuck."

"Excuse me?" responds Florence with a sneering smile.

"Let's start over, shall we?" said Allen in a regretful tone as he extends his right hand. "My name is Allen, and this fine, well-built, fast-food soldier is my boy Mark."

Florence doesn't shake his hand and Allen plays it off.

"Your boy," said Florence. "What, you like his daddy or something?"

"It's an expression," said Allen. "What might your name be, pretty lady?"

Florence looks away from Allen and at the menu. Mark gives Allen a you're-not-running-this look, while a cute woman with a big ol' juicy ass walks up to Allen's register with an empty cup and a straw.

"The future Mrs. Pace approaches," Allen says to Mark as he goes back to his register.

With a charming look on his face, Allen says, "What in God's creation is your name?"

She smiles, "Monique."

"You want me," said Allen.

"I want a refill or are you just the middleman," said Monique.

Allen stands at attention and salutes, "I'm the man with the plan."

Mark eyes and studies Florence up and down, "You ready, Florence," demands Mark.

"Why you rushing me?" asks Florence.

"Take your time."

"I'll do what I want, I don't need your permission," said Florence.

"That's funny; I think you're cute when you're angry," said Mark with a smile.

Florence tries to bite back a smile and then said, "I think you're cute, too, I'd like to make up for our little spat. I'll be back later. What time to you get off."

"Ten!"

Florence shows up at nine. Allen senses the situation and assures Mark that he'll wind up the night's activities by 11.

Florence is prompt. They sit in KFC's lobby enjoying some chicken popcorn nuggets, coke, and a lemon mini cake. "That was good, baby boy," said Florence. "Let's go pay 'DELILAH' a visit to have more privacy."

"I think I'll like to meet her," said Mark.

"I think she'll like you, too" she cooed.

In the back seat of 'DELILAH' Mark and Florence kiss passionately for a while, and then Mark reached under her skirt and felt the moistness of Florence's crotch. She shivered. That move made Mark bone hard. Then Florence caressed his hard flesh with her fingers and rubbed it with her palm, unzipped his pants, unfastened his belt, and slung his pants to the floor, while she panted and moaned. She stretched her legs and dropped her panties on the back seat, slipped out of her red dress that revealed no bra. Her firm titties bounced like water-filled balloons. She gently pressed him in a supine position with the palms of her hands, and then climbed atop a hard mountain of flesh. They both sang with deep guttural and high-pitched moans as Florence took control, moving her hips with circular and up-and-down motions.

The windows and Mark's glasses quickly fogged up. Florence slid her fingers up and down her body accentuating and revealing her naked body and her firm titties, riding Mark like a cowboy rides an unbroken feral-wild stud. The rhythm of the motion beats up. Mark tenses his ass muscles like he was trying to poke his dick through concrete. Florence and Mark release sensual moans that echo through the car escalating to a loud boom. Florence collapses on Mark's chest breathing frantically.

"God damn," she cried, "That nut was a motherfucka. Nigga, I love you."

The license plate 'Delilah' rattled vigorously from the motion.

Later, Mark cleaned off his fogged-up glasses.

"Oh Delilah!" said Florence as Mark rubs the interior of the car in a gesture of thanks for the fun.

"Every man loves a woman who makes him wanna sin a little," said Mark.

"Cute!" said Florence as she eyed Mark's fast-food hat lying on the seat. She tried to put it back on his head. He blocked the move and crumpled the hat.

"This shit is transitional," said Mark.

"Oh yeah," said Florence, "How's that?"

"Yeah," he said. "Me and my boy Allen 'bout to open up our own security company—make some real money—we gonna call it "AMT.""

"What's that stand for?" asked Florence

"Allen, Mark, and our boy Travis, he grew up in the neighborhood with us."

Florence kissed him, "Why is Allen's name first?"

"It's alphabetical."

"You sure it's not because he's the boss." Florence said.

The mood changed a bit, so Florence sweetened him up with another kiss.

"I like that you have dreams. I'm gonna be a nurse one day."

"Dreams live in your head, baby, but this shit is about to come to fruition. Real life. We gonna be moguls."

She watched him, taken by his drive. He grabbed her hands, and kissed her fingers, arms, and neck as he talked to her, "You stay with me and don't forget about me, then I'll make sure you get everything you ever wanted."

"I don't want nothing," said Florence.

"Nothing?" he repeated.

He looked down at his groin and hers. They lock eyes. Florence grins, "Round two."

Later that night, Mark tip-toed in the front door and walked towards his room as Grandma Pearl sat in the darkness.

"Why you sneaking around like a hound dog?" she asked.

Mark spun on his heels and walked over to his grandma, "I met the woman I'm gonna get married to Grandma."

"She go to church?"

Taken off guard by the question, Mark stammers, "I – I don't know."

"You don't know?!"

"We just met, Grandma," said Mark quickly without hesitation.

Grandma Pearl came closer, and Mark noticed the twitch in her top lip that he saw so many times growing up when she really meant business, "You talking about marriage already—you should know a few more things about her."

"I know she believes in me." said Mark with conviction.

# Chapter 7

Four years later, Mark and Florence step out of church, bride and groom, on a sunny Sunday in June as people throw rice and cheer. Allen and Monique stand close to each other as Monique holds a baby girl in her arms. Allen eyes a woman in the crowd and winks unnoticed by Monique. Mark and Florence passionately kiss in the back seat of DELILAH. They part lips and Florence rests her head on Mark's shoulders looking content as Mark gazes out of the back window watching his friends and family get smaller and smaller. He compares his dreams to the moment and scene as he thinks to himself: *Time is like that, the more it passes, the smaller and smaller your dreams seem to become.*

Allen and Mark still worked for KFC for a few years before Anna started working for armed security companies. That's when Mark saw the opportunity to improve his salary a little. Anna got Mark in, and then Mark got Allen in. Anna had hook-ups with L A and Excalibur Security

Company where Allen and Mark got some valuable experience many times working side by side on various assignments all over L.A. They both applied for and received gun cards with no problem. After a couple of years working with L A and Excalibur, they began working for Haze, a black-owned security company. Haze had multiple Armed Security Contracts, including the entire South Bay area and the San Gabriel and San Fernando Valleys. When Allen and Mark started working on the 105 Freeway project and the expansion of the Downtown L A Convention Center, and various shopping centers, they would begin gaining the experience to seize the opportunity to eventually do the Dunbar Heist.

Their job duties entailed patrolling construction sites. They worked with Travis Tollson, an amateur writer/singer rapper with loads of talent—brown-skinned, brown eyes, petite nose, fast-talker, smart—at a shopping center job on Vermont and Martin Luther King Blvd., where they continued talking amongst themselves about their business dreams. Tyronne Johnson, an unseen savvy friend of Allen's, was a no-nonsense sort of guy, serious about his future, and it was then Allen decided to start pooling funds for their own Security Company— "AMT"—Allen, Mark, and Travis and investors in big fat capital first letters on the front of the building on a billboard on Avalon Blvd. across the street from the Carson Mall. They worked together at a golf course on Western and 122nd named Chester L. Washington and that's when they talked a lot about AMT to Gene. They also worked a lot together at a strip club on Florence and Hoover and got to know each other very well. They constantly talked to Gene about the business, AMT, but they wouldn't make him a partner although he wanted to be. While they all were still working for Haze they got a lot of AMT business on the side, on the sly so to speak. So, they wouldn't bring Gene in as a partner and kept on working at the strip club, that's how the five got together. They already knew Henry because he was Velvet's boyfriend. After that, the five spent a lot of time together getting tight—playing baseball, basketball, chess, going to dinner, and that sort of stuff. Then, Allen applied and got the job for Dunbar.

Dunbar Ulmer Truck Company is a family-owned business since 1923, providing organizations with cash and valuable management solutions for their ever-expanding business needs. Whether businesses require one service or ten, the Dunbar team of experts work directly with the customer to customize

Dunbar's services to the customer's needs. Meetings and training for logistics and cash management took up a lot of Allen's time in the early months at Dunbar. Allen noticed early that Dunbar was a highly professional organization where safety, protection, and cash management were their delights and strengths. 'The Dunbar difference' was a slogan that rang out throughout the company. Allen was surrounded by cash and responsibility. He eventually learned everything about the Dunbar system and the people who ran it.

Allen still moonlighted with AMT, filling in the gaps when they needed an extra body. Working for Haze was like a stepping-stone-job for all of them, thought Allen. The job gave them unlimited experience in the security field and the potential use and the correct handling of firearms. Allen, Travis, Gene, Henry, and Mark had all gotten fired from Haze because they all liked going to WindBa in Costa Brava. They went to WindBa every year because it had everything they liked and it gave them ideas for future business investments—extreme sports equipment, hair and beauty shows, house cleaning and laundry advice and equipment, massages, how to store and preserve food, rent safe deposit boxes, medical services, camping equipment, vending, and ATM machines.

Velvet and Anna turned them on to WindBa three years ago, and they'd gone as a group every year. In '94, WindBa was held in L.A. at the Disneyland Hotel. They'd asked Haze if they could go, and he said no. Haze put them on the schedule, but they all went to WindBa anyway. But during that time, Mark's gun card had expired, and he told PG, the Director of Operations, to not schedule him but he did anyway. He must have forgotten, and Haze fired all five guys. Later, PG, Haze, and Mark had a meeting to clear up the misunderstanding, so they went to lunch. Mark was fired and hired back. Everybody else was fired because they were on the schedule. Allen moved on and started working for Dunbar as supervisor of security, and in a year and a half, he was promoted to Regional Safety Inspector.

Mark always thought that Allen got lucky with the good job at Dunbar because a guy named Mr. Shreekin, a former manager for Haze, also got fired from Haze, and hired Allen as a supervisor for Dunbar. He pulled Allen in. Mark also applied at Dunbar, but Shreekin didn't like Mark because in an earlier incident, he tried to get Mark fired from Haze. Mark thought, at Dunbar, Shreekin would have had too much power, and he would eventually find a way to fire him. So Mark continued working for Haze without the company of his friends, but Mark still saw them often at LAX where they had a solid contract with AMT as did First AME Church on 2270 S Harvard in Los Angeles on a six-day schedule. They all still hung together after Allen got his job at Dunbar. They worked together, played together, and bonded as a team.

# Chapter 8

One year later, Allen walks through the hallway of the Dunbar facility concealing something behind his back as he checks his watch which reads: Thursday, June 13, 1996. Then, he fixes his eyes to the end of the hallway. He walks towards the vault. The vault is wide-open as Dunbar employees unload large quantities of dollar bills onto steel shelves.

Playfully, Allen pulls a gun from behind his back, stands his ground like a Wild West gunslinger, "Hey," he loudly screams, "Give me all that shit or die."

The employees freeze and turn around as terror crosses their faces. Allen grins, pulls the trigger, and drenches them all with water.

"You scared the shit out of us," cried an employee, as Allen put his hand on the guys' shoulders.

"Guys," said Allen," As head of security, it's my job to make sure that there are no holes in our system."

Miles, in his 50's, the boss walks in and Allen hides the water gun, "We appreciate your—" He eyes the water gun, "—creative tactics, Allen, but please, don't get the goddamn money wet."

Later that same night, Allen sits at his desk taking notes as a nearby clock ticks like a metronome. A chime gonged when the clock struck twelve midnight.

Molly, an accountant/secretary for the Dunbar firm, a bit too skinny; pokes her head in Allen's office door. "Knock, knock, knock workaholic motherfucker, you hungry? Everyone's taking a lunch."

Allen leans back rubbing his nonexistent belly, "I'm trying to watch my girlish figure; gotta stay taut for the ladies."

"For the ladies," repeats Molly.

Allen grins and winks, "You know I meant, for you."

"You're silly," reasoned Molly as she leaves in a huff.

Allen jots down in his notebook: Lunch 12PM and everyone and everything that matters. He looks at the clock on the wall and sets his Longines wristwatch to it.

Around a year now, Allen had been thinking for a whiles now about a way to secure his future and he needed cash to do it. With AMT in mind, he had a strong foundation to build on and a large cash infusion into his own business interests that could only make AMT grow. He knew that he didn't want a career at Dunbar and each day his planned unfolded until he mentioned his plan to his friends.

Allen and Gene had been talking and planning to capitalize their business interests by some scheme unbeknownst to the rest of the crew, so they took their ideas to Mark and Travis one day outside the strip club on Florence and Crenshaw where Mark and Travis were working. The warm Santa Ana winds winnowed through the aspens, reflecting intermittent light from the buildings' lights and signs. It was a usually clear night, and the air was as fresh as a morning breeze.

"Gene and I were discussing a job on how we can capitalize our business interests without applying for a loan from Bank of America, Chase, or Wells Fargo," said Allen.

"Our business is doing okay," said Mark. "Do we really need to capitalize right now?"

"The way I see it," said Allen, "We can't grow without cash, and we can't attract the big acts."

"How big do you wanna get?" asked Travis.

"The biggest in the world," said Allen.

"We want to move into entertainment," said Gene. "Security is cool, but the big dollars is not in security. Besides, security is dangerous. One day, we'll be shot at, or we'll have to shoot somebody. In entertainment, we can stay away from guns and rake in the cash."

"If we get a loan," said Mark, "All we have to do is pay it back, and besides, we'll be building up our credit."

I don't like credit," said Allen. "Credit is a form of slavery, and our people have been in slavery far too long. Opportunities don't come along too often. If we can seize this opportunity, the sky's the limit."

"Okay," said Travis. "What is the job?"

Allen paused and peered into the starry skies, "Hit the ATM machines at the Dunbar fields."

"That's strong-arm robbery," said Mark. "They'll throw us under the jail for that shit."

"Mark," said Allen, "We used to play baseball in the streets as kids. Remember how you used to strike out all the time because you were pulling your head out at the last second and how happy you were when you started hitting the ball. You started hitting the ball because you saw it hit the bat. They can't hit or catch what they can't see and besides nobody gets hurt. We coordinate it where we hit three locations at once and I know every location and time of every drop-off in southern California. Two of us per location.

I can get another guy, and we can communicate via short-range electronics."

"How much money are we talking about?" asked Mark.

"One-hundred thousand," replied Allen.

"Sounds like peanuts to me," said Travis. "I don't think it's worth it."

Allen's eyes lit up; *this is going somewhere.* "Fuck it then, let's hit the whole damn facility."

The four stood in silence looking at each other for a while like they were polarized by their very body language.

Allen spoke a paralyzing blow, "Think about it fellas. Opportunities come and go and some opportunities never come back. In the meantime, I'll put all this shit together, so you can get a bird's eye view of what the fuck is really going on."

The next twelve months, Allen met with the group showing pictures and drawings of all the employees and important plans of the layout of the whole facility. What started out as a plan was starting to materialize into potential reality. It wasn't until the meeting at the parking lot around the corner from the AME Church while Mark was patrolling that the talks really started getting serious like Allen and Gene really wanted to go through with the plan. Allen emphasized the sequenced bills, that they should not be taken because they could be traced and not to take anything without his approval. As a group, they would scout the Dunbar facility from the exterior to familiarize themselves with potential escape routes, sewers, tunnels, and hideouts in case they were chased or needed a place to lay low. This way, the group had plans A, B, C, and D.

One of the initial plans was to have Allen call the office and have one of the guards to look for his keys because we had to know what door the guard came out of, so they could know what door to go in. Allen knew, from his inside knowledge, that the guards didn't lock the doors for a while and they would have to be buzzed back in. The other plan was to use his own keys to get in and break the lock later to at least have them guessing. So, after they got in, they had to escape, and the group came up with several plans. The first plan was in case we were being chased, we would hideout in a sewer. The second plan was to go to Travis's family's warehouse and count the money. The third plan was not really no plan at all. Beyond the two plans, it was like a dues ex machina that fell from the sky—a happy or unhappy ending.

# Chapter 9

The next day at dusk, the sky was a reddish-brown as distant clouds planked the western horizon just above the Palos Verdes skyline. In the plush green manicured front lawn of the McCrary's residence, Freddie, age seven, and Malcolm, age five, played kickball. Mark opened the front door, exiting with Florence who carried two-year-old Nadine. Mark kissed Nadine and walked away.

"You got your church suit for tomorrow?" asked Florence.

"Yeah, it's in the car," Mark answered.

Mark got into DELILAH as Florence followed him to the car, "Say good-bye to your daddy."

"Bye," said Freddie.

"Bring me something," said Malcolm.

"Malcolm! Stop begging," demanded Florence as Mark disappeared around the corner.

"If anyone is going to get anything, it's gonna be me in a chair getting a manicure and pedicure. Isn't that right, baby?" looking at Nadine,

"Mama needs some TLC." Then she studied her wrecked manicure.

Mark stood outside in an "AMT" security jacket with very bold white letters stitched in the jacket's front. A wild bunch of people walk in. Mark looks them over one by one. The wee hours of the morning pass smoothly.

At dawn, the light creeped into the horizon and the sun formed into a gigantic orange ball while Mark ushered the last people out of the strip club. Moments later, Mark changed into a dark blue pin-striped suit, light blue tie, and powder blue shirt, splashed water on his tired face, sprayed cologne on his neck and clothes, took a deep breath, and left.

In church later that morning, Mark struggled to keep his eyes open. All the guys were there with their families: Allen, Henry, Gene, and Travis. Grandma Pearl is there, too. While the preacher is in mid-sermon, Mark gave in and closed his eyes.

The preacher noticed Mark sleeping, "You let one sin creep in and the rest will follow. It's like a virus that takes over your whole life."

A snore escapes from Mark's nostrils and Florence nudges him. He wakes with a startle. He noticed the preacher looking directly at him, "Look at your neighbor and say 'prayer changes things,' now let us pray."

The young day had developed into a gem. Cloudless blue skies spun the silver sun into a magnificent jewel. Delilah never looked more beautiful as she sparkled from bumper to bumper sitting in the parking lot. Allen, Mark, Gene, Henry, and Travis are in mid-conversation next to her.

"Man, you need this more than any of us. You can't even stay awake—you working so much," explained Allen.

"But Allen, ain't none of us ever broke the law before," said Gene thinking it over twice times twice.

"We break the law every day, running a stop sign, crossing a double yellow—" reasoned Allen.

Gene broke in a little perturbed, "Man that's a little different than armed robbery."

"We ain't gonna take from nobody who can't afford it," said Allen.

"Just think of it as, we like Robinhood," said Henry.

"Long as I don't have to wear them tights, I'm game for whatever," said Travis.

"Let's focus in y'all. I like that you're getting excited. This is good, this is real good," said Allen.

Henry looked perplexed in the face, "How are we supposed to get past the alarms, surveillance cameras—I hear that place is like Fort Knox."

Allen eased a little closer, formed a little tighter circle, spoke a little slower and lower under the silvery sun. "I've been working at Dunbar for over two years now. I've got access to the whole goddamn facility. Here's how we do it." As he speaks, they all see the plan laid out.

The plan revealed six guys in black, but currently there were only five. How and why six, thought all five, especially Henry, "Why do we need six?!"

Allen explained, "That's my boy, Tyronne—you'll meet him later, besides, another body speeds time in the facility up. We gotta get back to make our alibi airtight."

Mark's family approached and Florence loaded the kids into the car, "Mark you ready?"

"I'm gonna catch a ride with Allen, babe," said Mark. "See you at home." He turned back to the guys despite a reluctant Florence, but she gets into Delilah and drives off.

"Now, can I get back to the plan?" said Allen a little disturbed.

"Please proceed," said Gene.

The group visualized the plan deeply in their minds while Allen narrated and addressed the rest of the queries:

"Alright," continued Allen. "So we approach the building at night on a Friday—because we get more access. First, we enter the locked facility—"

Henry interrupted sharply, "How we gonna do that? I ain't got no keys? Who got keys? Travis got keys—who—"

"I've got keys, motherfucka! Damn! Shut the fuck up!" roared Allen. The plan continues: Allen pulls keys out and unlocks the door. The guys enter. Moments later, the guys walk down the hallway, hugging the walls.

"Why we hugging the walls, like this?"

"Because you non-stop talking motherfucka, we need to avoid the cameras and security alarms. We just move as the camera pans. This gives up 30 seconds to move each time." The camera pans and the guys sneak by.

"Dope!" said Henry, "I love it."

Farther down the hallway, "Next, we're gonna meet some unwanted friends that we'll need to disarm." Allen and the boys take down the guards. They get the men on their bellies. Allen's eyes light up with power as he smashed a guard in the face. Blood flies out from a busted lip and cracked tooth—"

The deep vision snaps by Henry's strong voice, "Hold on—wait! wait! wait! wait!—we ain't gonna hurt nobody—you wanna hurt people?—Really?—Hit to the face?"

"I'm trying to say," said Allen, "We need to disarm them—and no—we ain't gonna hurt nobody."

"Seemed like a pretty hard hit there—you were so descriptive—I could feel it," Henry said.

Gene interrupted, "I ain't got no problem hittin' nobody."

Henry's frustration heightened, "Nigga please, we ain't talking about hitting women— we know you cool with that shit."

Gene responded, noticing the implication, "Fuck you!"

"Man calm down," said Travis, "We at church."

"You hit a bitch one time—ONE TIME and you branded for life," said Henry.

"I agree," said Mark. "We need to be like motherfuckin' King—not all pacifistic and shit."

Allen turns his attention to Mark, "What you think Mark?"

"A verbal threat can go a long way," answered Mark.

"Perfectly said," agreed Allen, as he wiped his brow.

"My Grandma used to threaten to flatten my ass with her high heel shoe if I acted up, but she never needed to cause—" said Henry.

Travis interceded, "'Cause you were scared of your Grandma."

The boys chuckled together.

"Please," said Henry, "I ain't the only one scared of my Grandma, Mark scared of his, too."

"Man, leave me out of this," said Mark.

"Alright," said Allen. As the group looks back at him, he continued," So then, after we disarm the guards—with words—"

Henry grins.

***

Still in the hallway, the group recaptured the vision as the guys disarmed the guards, gun to head and screaming, but no hits.

Allen continued, "We will need to gain control over the security command post so that we can get the truck inside."

While in the command post, Allen opens the gate and the truck pulls in. He smiles, watching the truck pull in and park. Of course, time seems to slow down. The other five guys enter, carrying bags of cash and loading up the truck.

***

"And the rest is easy," said Allen.

"What you mean the rest is easy?" asked Henry with little understanding and a distant look on his face.

The preacher steps up catching the tail end of the conversation, "Nothing worth attaining is easy boys." The boys stiffen from a seemingly sudden surprise.

"Did I interrupt something?" asked the preacher.

Allen was trying hard to regain his composure, "No, no."

"No Sir," said Gene quickly.

Gene thought fast. "We was just talking about how if you have a pure heart—a good heart then not sinning is easy."

The preacher smiled, "Amen to that." Everyone breathed a sigh of relief.

The preacher looked a bit unctuous and sweaty under the silver sunlight for it was getting hotter by the minute. He wiped his forehead with a hanky he carried in his top suit pocket. "By the way, are you still having that bar-be-cue at your place today, Mark?"

"Yes Sir," he said smiling. "We'd sure like to have you over."

"Okay gentlemen," said the preacher. "Then I'll see you there."

The preacher leaves and Henry picks back up the conversation, "What do you mean the rest is easy?"

"Let's get out of here and get that Q going," said Allen. "I'll fill it in later."

The late evening sun looked lazy and tired as if it had lost some of its strength for the weather was cool as a slow wind brewed up. The kids were running and jumping around and scurrying in and out of a rented jumper with the voices and screams of kids at play. The women were busy playing gin rummy and spades. The men had just completed a few chess games and dominoes when they decided to sit in a circle to drink beers and enjoy their surroundings. Bar-be-cue smoke wiggled and disappeared in the wind from two nearby pits. Florence attended to chef duties while talking to Clare, her sister-in-law, who was in her mid-twenties, pretty, shapely ass, light-skinned, D cups and heart-stopping cleavage. Monique is watching ribs on the other pit. Nadine is eating and throwing food in a highchair. The preacher and Grandma Pearl and other friends and participants eat, drink, and mingle in merry.

"Oh yeah," said Allen, "As I was saying earlier, the rest is easy and I mean it, too. All we'll have to do is lift and load."

"I like the sound of that man," said Travis. "Lift and load, you can count me in."

"Load," said Henry. "Load how much? How much are we lifting and loading?"

Allen paused purposely, "A half-a-ton of cash."

Monique with her shapely ass and gorgeous smile sauntered over to the table carrying buds and MGD's. Allen greeted her with a smile, "Thanks babe, how that food is looking?"

"What do you think," she said with a hip bump to Allen's shoulder. "The best chef west of the Mississippi is on it, and what y'all being so secretive for?"

"All babe, we're just fellow-shipping," said Allen.

"If I didn't know any better," said Monique, "I'd say you're part of the illuminati."

"How do you know we're not planning your birthday?" said Gene.

Monique eyed Gene surreptitiously, "Because this ain't no TV show." Then she continued after a slight silence, "This is a fine boys club." She placed the beers down, rolled her eyes, and then walked away.

Allen shouted after her, "I love ya babe."

"Anyway, what does a half-a-ton of cash calculate into, my man? I mean in plain English, how much is that?" asked Henry.

"Around 20 million or a little more or less," said Allen.

"That's a word up," said Henry.

"Yes, word up, saying 'word up' is like saying its 1986 and Cameo is singing and that shit means LISTEN!, now shut the fuck up and let me finish," said Allen.

"Sorry, sorry, my lips are sealed starting from right now," said Henry? "Damn, 20 million is delicious, but how we gonna get into the vault?"

Allen seemed anguished, "I thought you said you were done talking."

"That was my last question, I think," said Henry.

Allen continued eyeing Henry, "It's Friday night, so the vault will be open."

"Why?" asked Henry.

"That was actually a good question," said Allen. "Friday night and the weekend is when we transport all the cash for the weekend to different businesses, so we keep the vault unlocked for easier access."

Henry smiles, revealing a mouth full of fucked up teeth. "Damn you smart; you see that's why you're the boss."

Going way back to their childhood days when he promised himself he and Allen would be friends for life, and Allen always took the lead; but the word 'boss' made Mark noticeably cringe for those who were paying attention. As glamorous as it sounded, could he pull this caper off?

In good spirits of the moment, Gene took the opportunity to jest at Henry, "First thing you need to do is get those hideous teeth fixed."

Henry felt a bit threatened, "Man shut the fuck up!"

Travis jumped on the bandwagon, "Looks like your mouth got caught in a garbage disposal."

A burst of laughter ensues. From the pit, Florence turns her head towards the guys.

Clare and Florence were involved in a deeply personal conversation, "Did you hear anything I just said?" Clare asked. Deep in thought, Florence drifted and sensed a subtle change in Mark for Florence was an intuit woman and has always been since childhood. A football hit the pit she worked and brought her back to the present time.

"Barry, I told you about throwing that football around company!" shouted Florence as she dipped a dislodged rib into a pot of water to clean it.

"Sorry Sis, but Janine threw it too high," he said, grabbing the ball.

"Ah shit, Barry," said Florence. "You have to set an example for all these kids and people."

"Sorry again," said Barry, as he softly kisses Florence on the cheek and glides away. She turns her attentiveness towards Clare this time more acute.

Barry felt incompetent and returned, "You want me to get you something to drink?"

"It looks like you need it more than I do. Look how you're sweating," observed Florence.

"Maybe you right," reasoned Barry. Again, he kissed Florence on the cheek and hugs her around her waist, getting gobs of sweat on her clothes. She pushed him away with a wry face.

"Ewww!" said Clare. "How do you put up with that?" as Barry runs away laughing.

"You're so mean to him," said Florence.

"He likes to be pushed around by women, I know I'm his wife" said Clare. "Thanks to you and Janine." Then Clare takes a fat gulp of her MGD watching the kids play, and she continues, "You and Mark are a baby factory."

Florence stiffened, "Don't be jealous because you and my brother hadn't had none yet."

Clare shot back, "I don't want none no ways, get all fat and stretched out of shape for no reason."

Florence primps and shakes her hips, "Excuse Me?!"

"Oooo shit! Not you girl, you look good," said Clare, as Florence eyes her up and down with a smirk on her face.

Clare put her left high-heeled foot forward and wiggles her hips, "You look really good, but my people got hips for days and baby jus' goin' to accentuate that shit."

Florence still swiveling her hips, "You sure you don't want none of this?" Then Florence takes Nadine from her highchair, and holds her up to Clare as Clare shuns a bit.

"Damn she's cute," said Clare. "Nothing but curls. Can I hold her?" Clare kissed Nadine on her chubby cheeks and said, "You're pretty, just like your sexy ass mama." Then Florence slaps Clare playfully.

Meanwhile, the guys are still hatching over their plan drinking beers and smoking cigarettes and cigars. Again, they see the plan mentally unfolding as Allen speaks: "Like I was saying, we move approximately 20 million into the already parked U-Haul, and we do it all in less than thirty minutes." They envision the truck door shuts and the guys speed away covered and shrouded by the black of night.

The visions disappear as Allen stops delivering his plan and says: "There's a few details to work out still, but y'all leave that to me. I just wanna know if you were in or out before I do all kinds of crazy leg work."

Henry sat up straight with seriousness in his brown eyes, "Fuck the details, I'm in."

"How we gone split it?" asked Gene in great contemplation.

"Six players, six ways," answered Allen. "You don't have to decide now."

Henry slapped his right fist into an open left palm, "I'm decided, I'm in!"

"Can we get that guy a muzzle?" asked Travis unjokingly.

"Fuck you," said Henry. "I always express myself verbally."

Allen knew that the reality of his plan was like a slap in the face, "Listen, take some time for those of you who are undecided." Looking Mark straight in the eye, "But once you're in, you can't get out. I don't like you knowing, unless you got a stake in this."

Later, Mark pulls Allen to the side, and only then, he divulges his deeper feelings, "It's pretty risky, probably too risky."

"If its' worth having," said Allen. "There's always risks involved. No guts, no glory."

Mark scratched his head in the deepest contemplation, "Flo' ain't gonna like this."

"Flo' ain't gotta know."

"She gonna wonder how we got money all of a sudden," said Mark.

"Tell her AMT is taking off." Allen said in support of his plan.

Mark chuckles at the thought of AMT as he saw fragmented dreams begin to form from the boy who once saved his life with a plan.

Allen was adamant now, "What man? It's possible; we just need some seed money. We need money to make money."

Mark, still in deep contemplation, said, "I mean, if it was possible, why nobody ain't ever done it before?"

Allen was deliberate now, "Because most people are scared, but when you see opportunity you gotta grab it, 'member what you used to tell me? What yo' Jesus told you: 'I will seek opportunity, if not given opportunity, I shall create opportunity.'"

Mark's face smoothed over, "Yeah, Jesus, but what if we get caught?"

Allen leaned in with his most persuasive voice, "Listen, this can be done. I give you my word.

I've thought about ev'ry damn detail. We can't lose...."

Again, Mark was full of aporia and doubt, "What if we get caught?" he mulled over with conjecture.

With a strong sense of purpose, Allen countered, "What if we don't..."

That last statement shed the faintest liminal light on Mark's doubt while great possibilities linger in the deepest crevices of Mark's mind.

"You gonna be real mad when I'm swimming in millions and you in a kiddie pool filled with one dollar bills," hammered Allen.

Mark eased with a straight face, "I don't know, I gotta think about it."

"I even got somebody on the inside," said Allen. "I'm meeting up with them at work tonight."

# Chapter 10

It was a typical southern Californian mild and beautiful night as the Atlantic Ocean winds had long since subsided. The air seemed fresh enough considering the Los Angeles basin tended to trap polluted air by the nearby southeastern San Bernadino Mountains. The soft, glimmering starlight had recently appeared, although the city lights flooded the area. Intermittent ambulance and police sirens shrieked through the heavy air when Allen pulled up to the downtown Los Angeles Dunbar facility. As he walked in, the smell of microwave popcorn saturated the air, slight moans and groans were barely audible. The hallways were empty and shining clean. He could see cameras hanging from ceilings, walls, and corners, some panning, some stationary. Before he could make it to his office, located in the farthest west end of the building, he saw Molly sitting in the break room eating popcorn, watching pornography and Seinfeld, and nursing a coke up to her lips.

Molly is Caucasian, pretty at first sight with full red lips, a lumpy curvaceous ass, long curly blonde hair, a small waist, and light brown eyes. "I've been waiting for you, honey baby," she said as she flipped the set from porno to Seinfeld. "Don't you think that Kramer is the funniest character ever."

Allen smiled, "I'd rather watch the porno to get you more in the mood. I got a hard on just walking down the hallway."

"I've already got my hard on," she said. "My clit is as hard as a diamond."

"If I didn't know any better," Allen said, "I'd say you're as horny as a horny toad. Can't you see spikes sticking out all over my body, especially behind my zipper?"

"You're funny," said Molly, "But you've guessed right. I can feel myself cumming already."

Allen kissed her ruby red lips. She wiggled her hips as she dropped her panties with the fingertips of both hands. She quickly did an about face, lifted her skirt, and placed her size D titties on the break table, spreading her smooth tanned legs. Allen entered her as she gasped with a loud, "uh!" her hips finding that automatic gyrating movement as she groaned voluptuously and moaned deliciously. With her eyes squinted and her face squelched against the flat surface of the break table, she came with a loud scream muffled by Allen's hand.

"I think doggy-style is the best position. You get every inch of that dick, and all the power behind it," she said panting passionately. "Right now, I'll do anything you ask."

"Show me where you change the tapes in that secret video room," said Allen.

She looked back at him through sleepy eyes, "Later." She pulled her panties up where they rested on her red ten-inch stiletto shoes and fixed them in place with a wiggle of her hips.

Allen zipped up and pulled a whoopee cushion from his Bosca bag.

"What's that?" she asked.

He walked towards a certain office.

"He's not gonna think it's funny," said Molly. "Besides, he's on vacation for the next two weeks."

"Then he'll have a treat waiting for him upon his return," Allen said, grinning sheepishly as he squeezed it together producing a loud fart sound. He laughed heartily holding his belly like Santa Claus after delivering gifts.

Molly grinned, "You're a child with a big dick."

"It keeps me young and sexy," Allen said. "When I see an opportunity, I gotta take it. You know what I mean, jellybean?" He sensed the sexiness in her eyes and facial features.

She caught his eyes and smile, "You can't take every opportunity."

"Why not?"

She looks back down at her crotch and Allen focuses on what's in her mind. "Some opportunities will get you into trouble," she said.

In the corner of the room, TV cameras display the goings on around different sections of the entire facility. As Allen sits, Molly straddles him, deliberately positioning her crotch only inches from his face. His lips quiver, and his mouth naturally salivates. Allen smells the rare aromatic mixture of sex and perfume, and it arouses him like a sunflower that has recently caught the rays of intermittent sunlight.

Allen looks up at her sexy smiling face, "Some things are worth catching some trouble for."

She grabs his groin. She bends down rubbing her large breasts against his face. She moves her ruby red lips so close to his that he smells her naturally sweet breath; so alluring that they kiss long and hard. They finally separate.

"When you gonna give me a key to that room so that I can surprise you at night when you're all alone?" he asked with dreamy eyes.

"You won't need a key," responded Molly, "I'll be here if you want me here."

"Yeah, but what if I wanna drop something off?" Allen retorted mildly.

"Like what?"

"Gifts! Do you like Gifts?" Allen spoke softly, "I like to shower my women."

"Women!" Molly repeated loudly.

"I mean—"

She rose up in a steam, "No, you said women, that's what you meant. You still fucking around with her?"

"Baby, c'mon," Allen said in a convincing tone. "I meant to say in the past I shower women with gifts. And—"

"Fuck you Allen," she said in a vicious tone.

"You've already done that," said Allen trying to soothe with a jesting quip.

She slapped him, but he still managed to keep a straight face, "And you liked it." He approached her from behind, grabbed her around the waist, pulled her close, blew breath into her ear, and kissed her on the ear lobe. He softly whispered, "Don't be mad at me. I want us to take a trip to Catalina," he said as she turned away.

"Catalina!"

"You like that idea, baby?" he said, expecting a positive response.

"I don't know if I'd like Catalina," said Molly. "I don't like to swim, and I heard it's too expensive."

"You liked it when I was deep inside of you... Didn't you? Your pussy yielded to me."

She grinned in a mild heat as he kissed and tongued and monkey-bit her neck, "Do you still love her?" she asked.

She's my kids' mother. That's all. Nothing else," Allen replied as he spun her around towards him. "You know I love you, right? When we're young we make mistakes, but—"

Abruptly, she placed the key in his hand, "Make a copy and give it back to me." Then he answered with a kiss, "Make it tonight and follow me. It'll be our private place."

"Right away."

After the tour in the back offices, they came back in the break room. Allen softly stroked Molly's face and lips again and again and kissed her long and deep. He slid his hand along her curvaceous hips, unbuttoned her skirt, and slid his hand across her belly button. He found her sparsely hairy crotch and played there delicately, she yielded, cooing so passionately, and this time, he pulled her panties down.

She leaned closely to his ear, "If I find out you're fucking her or anybody, I'll make you pay."

"Sounds like a barrel of monkey's worth of fun," Allen said.

Again, they fucked like animals in heat.

# Chapter 11

Simultaneously, in Carson, Mark unlocked the front door to his house and walked into the living room where Janine is laid out on the sofa with her legs gapped open. There are several empty bottles of Night Train Express wine on the glass coffee table.

Janine sees Mark shake his head from side to side, "Fuck you!"

Florence attended West Coast University on Vermont Avenue in between two pregnancies and earned a CNA license. She was now working at Centinela Medical Center for several months. Mark walked to the bedroom and found Florence looking in the bathroom mirror getting ready for work. He sat on the king size bed as she primped her hair in the extra-wide bathroom mirror, donning a white nurse's cap and a white matching uniform. She is taking extra time with her cap and hair.

Mark noticed the special care and handling of the cap, "Baby, why you take so much time with that cap?"

Lightly rushing trying to pay attention to detail, Florence spoke a little louder than usual, "In training, the instructor emphasized the historical importance of the 'Nurse's Cap' and female nurse's uniform. The cap's original purpose was to keep the nurse's hair neatly in place and present a modest appearance. Male nurses don't wear caps. We had a 'capping ceremony' and we were presented with new nursing caps before beginning our clinical hospital training. Besides, the nursing cap was originally used by Florence Nightingale in the 1800's."

"Wow, baby. We've got another Florence Nightingale on our hands, but this time her name is Florence McCrary."

Florence smiled widely in the mirror as she finished up, "Baby, you're so sweet."

"I've noticed we've gotta a full house with Clare, Janine, and your brother," said Mark.

"And?" said Florence with some slight contempt.

"And," Mark responded noticing the dim disdain, "Why's your sister here? She's not gonna move in, is she?"

"Her and her man just had a fight," she said hurriedly.

"You know she can't keep a man," Mark said.

"Be nice," said Florence defensively.

Mark walked over to cool the exchange and kissed Florence on the neck from behind. "Baby, you look damn good in that uniform."

She giggled, "You silly."

He sexually slammed his body into hers, but she forcefully pulled away, "We can't afford for them to cut my hours if I'm late again."

He thoughtfully and sexually stopped her and pulled her close, "I'm proud of you. Doing what you set out to do."

She studied him intently, "Baby, you okay?"

Mark looked deep into her eyes, "Yeah baby, I just want you to know that I support you, whatever you do in life, I support you."

Florence noticed something different, something undetectably strange. "I know you do." She studied him more closely, "I support you, too, baby."

He tried again, kissed her neck, and rubbed her crotch. She broke away. "Baby, for real, I've gotta go."

As she left, Mark said behind her, "You gonna leave me like this?" He stood showing her an erotic erection.

Florence scurried out the front door.

Mark decided to watch some TV after he fried a double cheeseburger and some French fries. Football season was in full swing. Although the USC Trojans were having a dismal season, Mark was still a fan. He also liked ER and Jeopardy. Trying to catch a show, sitting in his Lazy Boy, he surfed channels for a moment while the TV light flashed across Janine's face in different colors. Janine just moved positions removing the blanket she had sprawled over her sensuous body. Her smooth sexy legs were on fire by the TV light. Mark could see the dark hairs dance on her pussy. Her body was delightfully well proportioned. Her breasts stuck up like miniature beach balls. Her thick thighs were the kind that invited the strongest-minded men to wanna jack off. Of Course, his panning eyes moved slowly up and down her sexy haven and fixed on her face. He noticed her watching him with the ferocity of a lioness in heat. He quickly looked away, but it was too late.

"I knew you wanted some more of this," said Janine with a soft and sexy voice.

"I'm minding my own business over here, Janine," he tried to say in his most masculine tone.

"When is it your business to look all over my body," she said condescendingly.

Mark slightly toughened, "You seeing shit, you need to go to a doctor. Get those hallucinations checked out."

"Okay," she said softly. "I'll pretend like it's all my idea if that's what you want."

She crawled to him like a stalking big cat, opened his legs and unfastened his belt.

"We shouldn't do this," warned an already beaten Mark. Defenseless, he closed his eyes while Janine went down on his already hard lump of flesh.

Clare watches from the hallway lightly panting, licking her lips trying to decide if she wants to engage or go tell it on the mountains.

# Chapter 12

In the meantime, over at the strip club in Hollywood, Gene is fucked up off cocaine, marijuana, and Old Taylor Bourbon with a sweet and sour chaser. He's getting a lap dance in a private room from Priscilla, a fine motherfucka by any stretch of the imagination. She has smooth dark skin, ruby red lips, big shapely ass, breasts that poke out to form the sexiest cleavage, eyes of fire light, and shapely legs that will overshadow a mannequin's. She was dressed in all red attire, the red V-back thongs situated around her crotch fit like a hand in a glove and the low waist band fit perfectly around her bare flat abdomen. Her halter top held up D breasts. Her ankle boots with six-inch stiletto heels revealed the acme of sexy. She was giving Gene a professional lap dance arousing his deepest desires, now, welling up from deep inside of him.

Gene opened his eyes, "You coming home tonight?"

His hands were around her waist with eyes closed when she answered, "Baby, you know I've gotta go to work."

Gene kept looking up at Priscilla, "You ain't gonna have to work here too much longer."

Priscilla's eyes widened, "Why's that?"

"I'm about to make a lot of money," Gene said with grave eyes and a broad smile.

She grinded hard on him for a moment before she stopped lap dancing and pulled her hair to the side. Enjoying it, Gene's smile disappeared. "Why the fuck you stop?"

"I've got to go make money," she said hurriedly.

"I told you I'm about to make a lot of money," he hastily repeated.

She pulled away and stood up, "That ain't tonight, so I gotta go." She kissed him on the lips, "I love you, don't be mad at me." With the sexiest switching walk, she walked out. Gene's eyes filled up with tears and he threw back another shot of bourbon as the open door unblocked. "I Believe I can Fly" was pumping loud.

Later that same night, Mark folded his hands to say a silent prayer by his bedroom window as the moonlight bounced off the silver crucifix around his neck. He opened his closed eyes and a vision of Allen appeared, "So you in?"

The next day, Mark stood at Allen's door after knocking and waiting for a response. When Allen saw Mark, a grin tickled the corners of his mouth. After knowing Mark since three years old, he knew the fireworks were about to begin.

The skyline of the Atlantic Ocean is the most beautiful in the world depending on the angle of the sun. The 72-story U.S. Bank Tower building glistened in the late evening sun as Officer Levine (in his thirties, Caucasian, blonde hair and blue eyes, six feet tall), just finished taking care of some banking business. He also decided to have lunch at the McCormick and Schmick's restaurant on the top floor. This time of day, he loved watching the setting sun from this venue. Orange reflections from the sun were sparkling everywhere bouncing off edifices and tiny cars traveling in a long line on the 5 and 110 freeways. The Palo Verdes Estates looked majestic as the would-be setting sun would momentarily kiss the mountain estates. A radio call interrupted this special time.

The 110 freeway south was studded with a maze of cars as he pulled over to inspect a blue Camaro sitting on the shoulder of the road. As Officer Levine approached the blue Camaro, he peeked inside and grinned. "Asshole," said Officer

Levine while motorcars zoomed past him. He banged on the window.

Officer Warren, who is now Detective Warren, was a Caucasian man with light-brown hair and streaks of gray around the temples, six feet one, with brown eyes. He's middle-aged now, still hungry for success and wore sunglasses and a cheap blue suit.

Officer Levine motioned, and Detective Warren rolled down the window, "What the fuck do you want?"

"Captain's been looking for you."

Detective Warren looked up through hazed eyes, "I'm working."

Officer Levine saw the empty vodka bottle on the passenger seat, "You get to run around playing detective and getting drunk while the rest of us do real police work and—"

Before Officer Levine could finish, Detective Warren rolled up the window and he lit a cigarette. The car filled up with smoke, as he sat there reflecting, Detective Warren heard and saw an image of the captain in his mind--*Are you fucking listening to me?*

The captain with white streaks running through a full head of hair, thick ear-length white-streaked sideburns, strong-looking cleft chin, high cheek bones, hawk-like nose, thin lips, blue eyes, and in his fifties met with Detective Warren in his office.

"I'm listening. How can I not, you've got a built-in blow horn," said Detective Warren.

The captain looked like he was getting ready to explode, "What? What did you say to me?"

Detective Briggs, sporting a round belly, in his forties, skin the color of walnuts, black hair, brown eyes, handsome facial features, wide nose, and full lips sat next to Detective Warren. Briggs has a look of compliance on his face.

"He's kidding, he's an asshole," screamed Detective Briggs. Detective Warren shot his partner a look of disgust.

"Warren," said the captain, "You can't Dirty Harry your ass all around L.A. harassing people who have already been acquitted of a crime."

"But she lied," said Detective Warren.

"Case is closed," said the captain in a voice just below loud.

"She lied," said Detective Warren. "She let her boyfriend take the fall. She's a heartless bitch."

"You're this close to meter-maiding," shouted the captain. "He held two fingers up with barely a centimeter of space between them.

"So, you're saying I still have some wiggle room?" quipped Detective Warren.

The captain nearly erupted, "Go fuck yourself Warren. Leave her alone, stop following her around to night clubs and being undercover as a fucking drunk, and get back to work before I fire your ass, both of you."

The captain slammed the door behind Warren and Briggs. "Wow man, way to have my back in there," said Warren as they walked to their desks.

"I do have your back, but I have kids and a wife and they like stuff like food and clothing, so gotta keep a job. Not all of us have the luxury of being obsessed with every case that comes our way," Detective Briggs said.

"I'm not obsessed," said Detective Warren.

A young cop scurried up, holding a pile of papers, "Detective Warren Sir, I have a record of all the phone calls made, to and from you know who for the past 15 months."

"I don't need them anymore," said Detective Warren.

"But I've been working on this for days," said the young cop.

Detective Warren looked at him hard, "I said fuck off." Detective Warren rose from his seat, "Sorry, I'm—"

"You're hungover," said Detective Briggs quickly.

"It's true," he agreed as Detective Warren pulled out a wrinkled $5 bill. "How about you get me a sandwich from the vending machine, kid, and you keep the change." The young cop left without taking the cash.

"You're an asshole," said Detective Briggs.

"What! I'm starving; can't a guy get a sandwich?" said Warren, as a tray of sandwiches was being carried by the young cop.

# Chapter 13

At the same time, at Allen's house, nearby in Compton, all participants were present. The southern California weather didn't disappoint as always for a songwriter, Albert Hammond, once wrote "it never rains in southern California."— But when it pours, man, it pours!

Inside the property, Monique was carrying a silver serving tray full of pastrami sandwiches, "Where do you want these, baby?"

Allen stood and grabbed the tray from her, "Thank you, baby."

She turned, stopped, looked over her shoulder, rolled her eyes on her way out. "I wonder what they're doing," she said out loud to the four winds.

"Dig in y'all! Monique makes the best pastrami sandwiches in the world," praised Allen.

The five guys gathered around the table and reached for the food. In the middle of the table, a makeshift model of the downtown Dunbar facility complete with employee Polaroids, camera positions, and a mini-getaway truck are displayed with magnificent colorful distinction.

Henry is the first to speak, "Is she cool with this?"

"She don't know," said Allen coolly. "She thinks y'all here for a security meeting."

Mark studied the model, "Man! This is impressive."

"Thank you! Thank you! My brother, it's all about the planning," he said pointing to a stack of pictures. "These are the employees. Oh, and another thing; a half-a-ton of cash takes up a lot of space. Gene is driving the U-Haul so Mark you and Tyronne take Gene's car to the job and drive it back when the job is over. We'll pick you up before the job. And Gene, you stay in the truck and neatly situate the bags so we can hop in that motherfucka and get the hell outta there."

At that moment, Allen reflected on how he acquired the photos:

*He carried a Minolta-35MM Polaroid Camera and stopped an employee; pointed the camera at their face, then snapped. He told them he was making safety inspection rounds and needed pictures for safety reasons. The camera flashed on many different faces.*

"You cooler than a motherfuckin' James Bond," said Henry.

"We need to have code names," added Gene.

"We should call each other no names," reasoned Mark.

"So, like I'm no. 1, you're no. 2, and—" said Gene.

Abruptly, Travis said, "Who says that you get to be no. 1?" The guys laughed.

Gene laughed, too, "It was just an example."

"Wow! That's a great idea," said Allen looking at Gene, then the model. "Good thinking, Mark. How'd you come up with that?"

Mark blushed, "Saw it in a movie once."

"Dope!" cried Henry.

"Alright fellas," said Allen. "Then it will be numbers, so let's assign them now."

Gene broke in, "All jokes aside, number 1 should be given to the master planner, the guy who has complete knowledge of the facility, Allen." Everybody agreed. "And he should also assign the numbers." Everybody except Allen nodded in agreement.

"Alright then, don't forget your number because your very life could depend on it. Mark you're number 2, Travis you're number 3, Gene you're number 4, and Henry you're number 5. It's not only important that you remember your personal number, but also you should remember your teammate's number. And when we're inside that facility, let's imagine that the audio can pick up the sound of a rat pissing on cotton in a hailstorm. We'll practice the number sequence daily until you know who's who like you know your own name."

"What about the security tapes? We don't want people to see us?" asked Travis.

Allen placed keys on the table.

"What the fuck is that?" asked Travis.

Allen developed a smile as large as the Grand Canyon, "The keys to the city, baby."

Gene caught the drift right away, "When do we do this?"

"Just got a few more details to work out and we'll be ready for Freddie," said Allen. "My homeboy Mario is in charge of watching the front entrance camera. He's like the Mexican Rambo. He's pretty damn serious about his shit job. The only thing he cares about more than his job is—"

"His woman?" interrupted Henry.

"Well," said Allen, "Not quite..."

A few days later, after the meeting at Travis's house, Allen and Mark went across the street to TGNY's and Newberry's looking for some special duct tape, pencils, styrofoam, toothpicks, Elmer's glue-all, and paper. They returned and Allen from memory made an advanced paradigm model of the building and drew up the final plans of the entire facility inside out.

Weeks later at a meeting at Allen's house, displaying a styrofoam model of the entire facility, he was more specific and serious. "This is the door we go through—these two doors we gone go through—this is the door that leads to the money—this is the door if they lock it, the deal is a bust cause there's no way to get in." They joked around for a few hours, and he went over it again and again and again. "Like I said earlier, we have to do it on a Friday because all of the vault doors will be open for ease of mobility and timing, and we may have to do it earlier because there's rumors floating around, they're gonna have to replace the cameras or the company might be moving to another location. So, from this point on, be ready for Freddie."

Mark cringed at the name "Freddie" because that was his real name, and nobody knew it but him. Could this be an omen of things to come? Allen meticulously planned everything, and he wanted everyone to be ready for something they'd never done or seen before. Mark envisioned if they were getting ready for Freddie, or if Freddie would be ready for them.

Early on a Sunday, Mark and Florence lie in bed. Feeling sexy, Florence straddled Mark with her naked pussy pressed up against his nose and lips. Mark sniffed and smelled cinnamon, Calvin Klein Eternity, and Gucci Guilty combined, a fragrance that he smelt so many times before. She wiggled and the orifice of her vagina slightly opened, glazing over with the silkiest salve and milky moisture. She moaned in anticipation, no doubt, preparing for an orgasm. No rhythm is created like she was used to.

With no response, she stopped, "What's wrong?"

"I've got lot of shit on my mind," he said.

She lifted herself and laid down on his chest, caressing him on the ears and nose, kissing him on the tip of the nose, and then the mouth. "I could help you get it off your mind," she said still caressing him up and down his body.

He stopped her, "Baby, not now."

Florence turned from him, humiliated. Mark got up and left the room. Florence's eyes filled with tears.

He fell asleep. Mark laid down in the living room on the sofa and watched the large octagonal wall clock with illuminating hands and numbers glow green in the dark. It read 1AM. Then, he decided to make an early morning call.

"Hey Grandma, I'm glad you're awake—I know, I know it's late, I'm sorry. I need you to pray for me—yeah everything's okay…I'm just going through something right now."

In the still of the night, his voice trailed off as Florence listened from the hallway.

When Allen made that statement weeks ago, it lingered in Mark's mind like an unforgettable statement of fact, or a lesson learned years ago. Mark cooled and cringed inside and took it as a good omen. A harbinger of healthy thoughts flooded his mind ever since. Nobody in the group knew his birth name was *Freddie*. As a result, Mark's fear dropped a notch from petrified to terrified. Now, it was too late to back out, but with the omen and greed, Mark conjured up the tiniest bit of courage. Growing up, Mark knew what his grandmother would say and what the preachers would say because by now, he had heard thousands of sermons—'Christians ain't supposed to do that stuff.' Instead, Mark negated the thought because he knew that no Christian would ever give him that kind of money—the kind that would set him and his family up for a lifetime.

# Chapter 14

Inside the Proud Bird restaurant, Allen looked at all five guys with fire in his eyes, "Here's our headset." They tested the headsets for operation. "I know what you're thinkin'—what if we get caught'—we won't get caught cause it won't be anybody there to catch us—and what if I bail out now and they get away with it and you'll be eating your heart out. I'll tell you right now, getting caught during the commission of this so-called crime is not our biggest problem. Our biggest problem will come after the so-called crime has been committed—handling the success and cash. It's only a crime if we get caught. Don't spend lavishly. Keep going to work. Keep doing what you're doing and spend your money slowly. Buy everything you can on credit. If somebody gets caught, keep your mouth shut and we'll take care of their family until they get out, forever, 'cause with this kind of money we gettin' ready to make, it can last for that long if we spend it right. We can turn our existing business into a multi-million dollar-a-year business and add on more businesses and beyond. Let's make a pact on that. If everybody agrees, let's form a circle and put our right hand in the middle and one by one say I agree."

They formed a circle and stacked their hands in the middle like spokes on a bicycle wheel and agreed.

Some days later, on one beautiful Southern California day, Allen arrived at work early. The eye in the sky moved farther west still throwing silver light down on all, and electronic eyes record, seemingly seeing everything the average eye could not see. The sun's warm tentacles tickled like a million miniature fingers that soothed all under it. Allen entered the front door and ambled down the hallowed hallways of shiny linoleum floors. People passed him with large, gorgeous smiles on their faces like everyone's in love with him. Everyone except for Murray, Allen's Boss; white, an obese unctuous looking soul in his early forties with a full crop of black hair neatly combed, brown eyes, thin lips, no cheeks and fat wide nose. He was the serious type. Murray was juggling some folders, coffee, and three jelly donuts.

Allen approached Murray, "Welcome back."

Murray shot back a very nasty look for Allen had pulled pranks on him before.

In his back-office, Murray wobbled in like a human drake as Molly rose and said, "Let me grab those."

"Shoo...get...I can manage," Murray said proudly.

He sat and then the sound of a loud fart echoed down the hallway. He spilled coffee all over himself, his desk, and the important papers he was holding. His face swelled with rage and contempt.

Close by, Allen grinned from ear to ear while Molly bit back a smile.

"Son-of-a-bitch!" Murray screamed in a hotbed of anger as he furiously wiped hot coffee off his freshly laundered white shirt and lightly colored trousers suffering burned skin and hands, wrists, and lower arms, thinking in advance of his huge laundry bill.

Minutes later in Mario's office, filled with pictures of his family and other episodes, Mario and Allen are in convulsing laughter engaging in a general conversation.

Mario wiped water from his brown eyes. He was of Mexican descent, four young handsome kids, a beautiful wife. Mario was a young-looking man in his mid-twenties, handsome bodily features, a smooth light-brown skinned face, a pointed nose, strong high cheek bones, a curly head of hair and sideburns, full pink lips, round chin, a cold black neat mustache, and a clean-shaven face.

"Who-sits-down-without-looking?" Mario stammered.

Allen stopped laughing in mid-conversation, trying to catch his breath, "That's what I was counting on."

"Brilliant bro, for real, for real, Molly said he dropped his coffee, and—"

"And his donuts," said Allen still laughing.

"Pendejo gordo!" said Mario as he laughed and stopped abruptly because something caught his eye on the camera. With laser focus, he watched the camera. On the camera, a group of teenagers skateboarded past.

"You're like a cat with those reflexes," said Allen.

"Gotta be bro, people do crazy shit. Gotta stay alert, know what I'm sayin'?"

"I agree," said Allen. "This is not the best neighborhood either."

"That's what I'm sayin'."

Thinking and planning, "Where's your baby?" asked Allen.

"Oooh yeeaahh," said Mario rubbing is hands together, "My truck?"

"What else would I be talking about," said Allen

"That's right," said Mario amorously. "My baby."

"That's right," Allen prodded. "Your baby girl."

"Ha, right, my baby girl," said Mario. "My Troka Loca, yeah, she's in employee parking, 'round the other side."

Allen fed into Mario's love for his wheels, "Those rims are sick."

"Better be, cost me half my paycheck," said Mario in a bittersweet baritone.

"It was worth it, I know," said Allen in the lead.

Mario imagined a series of camera shots as they talked about Mario pimping Troka Loca down the street and riding with his wife, Emily; a hot chola girl in her early twenties sitting close by his side showing off her mestiza beauty, making Troka Loca look even better.

"That's what I tried to tell my girl, Emily, but she's always bitching about something. She says I spend too much time on Troka Loca," said Mario in the depth of his feelings. "I told her the prettier the ride the prettier she is, too."

Allen spurred him on, "It's like osmosis."

"Yeah," said Mario, "Like transference, separation, mingling, and absorption. Like you put an ugly mofo in a Armani suit and he looks like Fabio and shit, and—"

"C'mon, Fabio, really?" said Allen.

"But my girl ain't ugly; you know what I'm sayin'," said Mario with a little contrition.

Allen nods in agreement, "The flames are sick, too."

"Bro, Bro," said Mario exuberantly. "She's fully fucking loaded with hydraulic suspension. I put 30' LCD TV in the ceiling, so we can fuck in the back, and we could look up and watch the shit in high fucking def—"

"Damn!" Allen shouted.

"I also put suicide doors on that bitch," raved Mario.

"Really!"

"Hell yeah," Said Mario in sheer souped up vociferousness, "She opens up with the touch of a button!"

"Wish my girl was that easy," Allen quipped quixotically.

Mario laughed hard from his belly, "Haaaa! Haaa! Haaa! Damn Bro, you funny for real, like stand-up comedian funny, you could give Paul Rodriguez a run for his money. You're like a black Paul Rodriguez, Paul Rodriguez but black, you know what I mean?"

"Maybe," said Allen as Mario got lost in talking about Troka Loca beyond a doubt.

"Yeah," Mario continued. "She's da' bomb though, for real; all purty and shiny and loyal and shit."

Allen sought his opportunity, "I'd be worried not having my eye on her at all times."

Mario had stopped laughing and praising Troka Loca, listening, "What do you mean?"

Allen straightened, "I mean, if it was me, I'd be putting her in sight right where I could keep an eye on her with one of the cameras."

Mario visually paused, he stirred, his eyes brightened, it sunk in, a smile formed, "Bro, I got a fucking brilliant idea."

Within an hour, Allen is on a ladder adjusting key cameras to face Troka Loca. The truck takes up the entire enter screen. As he made the final adjustments, he gave Mario a thumbs up in the camera.

Back inside Mario's office, Mario slapped his hands together like he was getting ready to have a threesome. "Yes, baby yes," he said as his fingers ran sensuously along the screen. His eyes watered in gratitude, "Sexy ass bitch."

Later that night, Miles sat in his office, the director of the facility, as Murray walked in. Miles is a mild-mannered man of big stature, 6'5"and 240lbs. He was Caucasian, a salt and pepper head of hair, clean shaven, brown eyes, aquiline nose, and well-dressed. He was doing paperwork as TV monitors blazed behind him. Pictures, certificates, and degrees are plastered all over the walls. The photos on his desk had a life-like resemblance, ostensibly, of family members. The black leather furniture, strategically situated, smelt like cowhide mingled with Renuzit, a gentle after-the-rain scent.

Miles looked up from intense thought, "What's on your mind Murray?"

"I can't take this shit anymore," said Murray. "That Pace fellow is going to give me a heart attack."

Miles looked at Murray's coffee-stained shirt and saw the discoloration on his badly burned hands and wrists. Miles leaned back in his chair getting ready to hear his story and explanation. Murray slammed the door still facing Miles and takes a seat.

# Chapter 15

At Allen's house the next day, the television screen read Sep. 12, 1997, a Friday. Rudy, Allen's six-year-old son, is watching Tom & Jerry, that could be heard from outside while Allen mows the front lawn. He puts away the lawnmower in the garage and hugs Monique as he enters through the kitchen door. Monique is busy preparing lunch.

Allen goes in the living room and sees Rudy's empty cup, "You want some more orange juice little man?"

"Yes Daddy, thanks."

With the empty cup in his hand, Allen stops and watches Monique bend and slide a pork roast into the oven, "Looks damn good."

"Me or the roast?" said Monique half-jokingly. He pauses an answer and she slaps him playfully.

"C'mere, I'm kidding, that roast can't hold a stick to you," Allen said, then he pulls her close and kisses her, "Baby, why you make a roast anyway? Mark is barbecuing."

"He told me he liked roast," she explained. "So, I figured it would be nice, you know, everyone else gonna bring chips and salsa and little stuff like that, but people gonna be hungry."

The phone rings like it has never has rung before, a voice with a message. Monique noticed the ring of urgency like an offbeat in an otherwise rhythmic percussion section.

"Okay baby," said Allen, "You're always thinking ahead anyway."

"I hate going to a party when there's no food around," she confirmed.

As the phone still rings almost to an annoying pitch, Allen says, "I got it, I got it, damn!" He picks it up.

"Well, you asked about the roast," said Monique, "Shit."

The phone still ringing beyond a normal length of time, Allen answers, "Hello, this is Allen!"

Then Rudy runs in. "More juice!" he said like his life depended on it.

"Calm down, Rudy," Monique demanded.

Amongst the cacophony Allen said, "I'm sorry Sir; I can't hear you—please hold on for one second." He covers the phone with his right hand, then says to Monique, "Baby, I'm gonna take it in the other room."

Monique pours Rudy's juice in order to soothe him as Allen picks up the phone in the other room and shouts from there, "Monique, hang up the phone, I got it." He continues and speaks into the other phone, "How can I help you on his fine day, Boss?"

As Miles speaks, Allen's facial expression changes from delighted to worried.

Being more intuitive than nosy, Monique walks over and quietly picks up the phone in the kitchen. She listens, "We're going to need you to turn in your keys today. You went too far this time; Murray's burns on both hands and wrists are extensive. He thinks your practical pranks are obsessive and you should be a clown in the circus." She gently places the phone back on the receiver and bewilderment and worry cross her face like a marching soldier marching to his death.

Allen listened and with melancholy and in a way trying to preserve his dignity and self-respect, and plans, he responds, "I can't turn them in today, we're having a family function. Can it wait until after the weekend?"

The voice on the other end of the line is solemn, "Okay."

Allen, with an indeterminable but sly smile on his face, said, "I appreciate it Sir. It's been nice working for you." A dial tone ensues.

Allen sits there for a moment, picks up the phone, and dials.

At the same time, nearby, Mark turns over meat on the barbecue while everyone else puts up decorations and lays up snacks. Janine walks out carrying a tray of raw, seasoned meat.

"I've got some fresh meat for you," said Janine.

Noticing the sarcasm and innuendo, Mark looks at Janine's sexy red miniskirt and gets immediately aroused, "Go ahead and sit it down, I'll get to it."

Janine looks down at her body and notices the bulge in Mark's crotch, "I know you will." She gives him a sexy look before she sets the meat down. She intentionally walks away in a sexy way, switching as he watches.

Then, Florence sticks her head out of the back door, so he quickly adjusts his gaze back to the meat on the grill. "Mark, the phone is for you."

In the bedroom, Mark is in full conversation with Allen, "We gotta do it tonight?"

"The word is out that they're putting in a bunch of new cameras next week, so tonight's the night."

Immediately after, Allen calls Gene.

Gene is at the U-Haul site on Crenshaw Blvd., near S. Western Ave., less than an hour later.

Allen told him to catch a cab. Before Gene left, he checked the newspaper for the weather report as a habit to dress accordingly. The day was predicted to be mild and sunny—81 degrees high and 58 degrees low with partly to mostly cloudy skies. Gene walks out with a U-Haul store employee, knowledgeable, fortyish, black, and sloth-looking and moved the same, "Sir, I sure hope you have a delightful move. I know how stressful a weekend move can be."

Gene says nothing, but he smiles graciously.

"Okie dokie," said the employee. "Have a nice move," quiet but strong, good qualities, then he handed Gene the keys.

Gene pulls out of the lot at breakneck speed, barrels down Crenshaw Boulevard as he blasts music and does a bump of cocaine. As the cocaine takes effect, he yowls with excitement and turns the music up full blast; Tupac's "Temptations" captures the moment.

Later that day at Mark's sister's house, around dusk when the sun reflected orange off everything that had reflective ability, the party is in its infancy stage—putting up last minute decorations, food and drinks. Mark is in the corner drinking a cold Corona with some E & J brandy chaser. He was nervous like a baseball player just before the first pitch of a World Series game seven. Uncontrollably, his forehead beads with sweat. Allen walks towards Mark with his Mexican friend, Tyronne, who is in his mid-twenties. Handsome, 6'0" tall, faded haircut, light brown skin, well-proportioned nose, full lips, and cold black hair. They both stood in front of Mark.

"Mark meet Tyronne—Tyronne meet Mark," said Allen as they met for the first time. Mark wipes the sweat off his brow, and then shakes hands with Tyronne.

"Don't worry," said Allen, "I filled Tyronne in on everything. He's down with the landscape of the city. He knows his way around this motherfucka. He can stomp with the best of 'em. If we had to go to war, he could carry his own weight. He knows he's number 6. He's a quick study. Once he meets the other guys, he'll flow like water."

"It's a little warm out here," states Tyronne, nicely trying to gain Mark's confidence in such short notice.

"I hate the heat," said Mark, feeling a bit more comfortable about Tyronne.

The party pumps loudly with a variety of hip-hop, R&B, and slow jams. Allen took Tyronne around to meet everybody. Dancing and drinking fill the atmosphere, and everybody is having a great time, almost oblivious to their natural surroundings. One of the sexiest women Travis had ever seen asks him to slow dance and grinds his genitals to liquid and a rock-hard mass.

"Hello, my name is April, you wanna go somewhere?"

Travis squirms with disgust, "I can't."

"Why not?" asked April, "I can feel you!"

"I got somewhere to be soon," Travis said with angst and anguish. "Maybe later."

"Where you gotta be?" she asked, wanting to change his mind.

Travis says nothing and melts into the crowd.

The six met at a table in the garage while the party was at its height. Without anybody noticing, they left one by one and piled into the U-Haul parked around the corner. They headed towards Gene's house where they changed into black clothes, black masks, and got their shot guns and pistols. After changing clothes, Mark and Henry rode in Gene's Hyundai, and then to Hill Street in the heart of downtown Los Angeles. As they traveled north on the 110 freeway, Mark kept hearing and seeing that episode with Jesus when he was eight years old: *I will seek opportunity, if not given opportunity, I will create opportunity.*

Now they were seeking an opportunity, after being presented with an opportunity, and they were going to create an opportunity. Although they carried guns and it was well-planned, Mark studied and watched the skid row dwellers who needed an opportunity, seemingly, more than anybody in the world. With grocery baskets carrying their worldly belongings, they slept on the ground, some with and without blankets. A flicker of lights flashed amongst a separated crowd as they leaned forward to light a pipe or cigarette. He thought that they would never get their opportunity before they disappeared from the face of the earth.

The downtown Dunbar facility resembled a plantation slave house in the middle of the city. Barbed wire lined the tops of fences and the obscure buildings resembled those on prison grounds. Some downtown L.A. hoes looked a little dirtier in isolated sections in this part of town. A short few blocks from the Dunbar facility, Mark and Henry parked the Hyundai and later rejoined the others in the U-Haul. Allen had instructed everybody where to park.

There were a few guards lolling around outside in front of the Dunbar depot when the U-Haul inconspicuously pulled up. They waited a few minutes in an alley until the coast was clear. Allen got out first and approached the front door of the depot. He knew that the cameras should be oblivious to him. He checked. They were exactly like he had left them. He stuck the key in the lock, the energy in his controlled, nervous fingers felt the tumblers weaken and give way like coins dropping in a vending machine. Allen motioned to the others. Only four filed out of the U-Haul like ninjas on a mission, dressed in all black from head to toe with only their eyes showing. They stayed tight in a single-file line. Of course, Allen, the lone lead, who had a key to open the first door with no cameras ever catching sight of them, was still nervous. Now, with Allen leading the fully intact group, they sidled in a close pack through the first door. Again, Allen inserted the key to the second door's lock. The lock clicked and ticked like a clock. They stayed close to the hallway walls moving in sync to the panning cameras. Each man waited his turn and moved one by one in sync to the eyes in the sky. The inside of the facility was well lit. Around a corner, Allen saw a security guard enter the bathroom. He motioned the others to disperse.

Once they were in past the two heavy doors, another security guard started coming down the hallway straight toward them. "Be still, motherfucka or I'll blow your head off!" said a menacing voice from behind from a black mask with three shot guns kissing the guard in the face.

"What door did you come out of," a heavy voice demanded.

The guard was scared shitless, "Man I don't want no part of this, I got kids. Y'all can take whatever y'all want. Just don't kill me."

"If you tell me which door you came out of, I won't kill you," said a husky voice.

He pointed, "I came out of that first door."

They duct-taped the guard's mouth and pinioned his arms and legs. Tyronne stayed behind with the guard and moved him into the break room. The rest went in that first door. When Mark saw all the cash in one place, chills ran up and down his spine like a dragster spitting fire to the finish line. Once the objective was in full view, the money bags looked like sacks of potatoes bulging at the sides stacked to the ceiling with brown tags attached to the ties in one section of the vault. In another section of the vault, bills were stacked neatly, eye-high from wall-to-wall. The smell inside the vault reminded Mark of the smell of the inside of his grandmother's purse.

There were three employees busying themselves, counting and wrapping money when the abhorrent assailants surprisingly entered the vault. Some employees froze in mortal fear for their lives and fell untouched helplessly to the floor. Money-counting machines still hummed as paper bills smacked loudly together mingled with the high-pitched screams of the two women working with the money.

"Be quick and shut the fuck up if you wanna live," cried a deafening masked voice.

The male security guard-employee nonchalantly moved like he was some sort of tough guy, noticed Mark. "Okay, motherfucka if you don't hustle, I'm gonna split your head open like a melon with this shot gun."

The male shook and shivered to every word, and then hurried his movements. Each employee was duct-taped in seconds and literally dragged across the linoleum floor to the break room.

Allen stealthily entered the bathroom after the security guard he first sighted, grabbed a chair from the cafeteria, and appeared over the toilet stall. "Time's up you stanky motherfucker."

"Fuck off," said the security guard without looking up. "Give me some peace."

A long shot gun appears overhead, catching his attention, "You drop one more piece of shit and I'm gonna blow your fuckin' head off."

Surprised, scared and trying to remain calm, the security guard said, "Can I at least wipe my ass?!"

Allen cocked the gun.

"Okay! Okay! Damn," The security guard said in defeat. "Can I just wipe?"

Allen athletically stretched and cold-cocked the security guard and left his pants down and dragged him into the break room.

Outside the facility, only moments later, Travis subdued two more security guards, "Look straight at the ground and not anywhere else or I'll blow your ass in half." He hog-tied them, got 'em and drug 'em towards the break room one by one.

Simultaneously, in the Dunbar facility break room, some employees are tied up with guns pointed at their heads. Among them are Molly, Mario, and Murray.

Allen comes in holding the security guard by the left upper arm; he pushes him to the ground. In a deeply disguised angry voice he said, "Found this one hiding in the shitter."

"Man, I wasn't hiding," said the security guard. "I was just taking a shit." Right away, the odious smell hit the breakroom, and everybody winced their face into a contorted mess. Allen kissed the shotgun to the guards' face one by one, "Shut up, motherfucka!" The guard he handled winced as large lumps of disgorged feces 'n shit fall to the floor.

Quickly, Allen grabbed every employee's keys and barked orders, "Number 3 and 4 watch them." Gene and Travis nodded while the employees whimpered and pled for their lives.

Molly cried like a baby, "Please don't kill us, please don't kill us."

Travis kneeled and whispered into Molly's ear, "If you don't shut the fuck up, I'm gonna rip your vocal cords out of your pretty fucking head and choke them back down your fucking throat." Molly grits her teeth as hard as she could to not make another sound, and then urine flowed from her crotch. Now, all employees are tied up with duct tape in the break room, including the four security guards.

Meanwhile, in the control room, only seconds later, Allen pressed a red button and the steel-latticed gate whined, lifted, and opened. Allen spoke into his headset. "Number 5; pull the truck up, now!" Minutes later, Henry reversed the U-Haul in the garage and nervous as hell, he mistakes the accelerator for the break and screeches to stop only inches from the loading entrance. At the same time, Allen, Mark, and Travis enter the vault and Travis reaches for a stack of money.

"Not those, they're in sequence," cautioned Allen. "Everything but those." Now, he pointed to the area of interest and safety, screaming in rapid succession to take all the good shit.

They made sure nobody flipped the alarm. Allen and Mark scurried through the facility and gathered the cameras and VCRs by ripping them from their foundation or snatching them out of the wall and putting them in the U-Haul.

The guys rapidly threw bag after bag after bag in baskets, and on drays in a pyramid until some of the bags fell loosely to the ground.

Allen screamed "2 and 6, I'm covering tracks—you two load it," said Allen in a frantic pace.

Mark, now in full and smooth rhythm, "Copy that."

Allen rushed to Mario's office and ripped the VCR from the wall.

Back in the vault, working at a stepped-up pace faster than comfortable, Travis picked up a bag from the wrong area and tosses it on the dray.

Allen hustled to Miles' office and ripped the VCR out of the wall with a crowbar he grabbed from a tool shed.

Allen rushed back to the garage and four guys are furiously loading heavy, semi-heavy, and light bags into the U-Haul. Under stress, Allen remembers, 'the secret place.' Gene is situating bags in the truck, his planned job. But Gene panics and jumps out of the truck and starts helping with the loading. "Let's hurry the fuck up."

"Get back so we ready," Mark screamed.

"Fuck that!" said Gene as he lifted and loaded twice as fast as anybody else.

"Number 1 said we need to play our position," said Mark in a stern voice.

Gene looked at Mark, as Gene was hustling, "I'm number 4 and I don't listen to everything that nigga says, like you do."

Thinking wisely, Mark ignored the comment. Oblivious to any chatter, while still in the compound, Allen hustled and unlocked the door with a copy of the key Molly gave him. Still hustling, Allen ripped the VCR from the back-office wall and ran out of the office past the breakroom carrying the VCR and screams, "Number 3 and 5, we've got enough, let's go! Let's go! Let's go!" Henry and Travis ran out, following Allen.

In the garage, U-Haul truck doors heavily shut after all six guys finish loading the last of the bags into an almost full trailer. Then, music blares, as they deposited all the firearms under bags of money.

"Man, Travis was like *Scarface* in there," said Tyronne climbing in the back of the van.

Gene, flustered and scared because he thought the pace was too slow, inadvertently throws the U-Haul in reverse and slams hard into a wall. A taillight cracks from the impact and lightly gongs to the pavement.

During the abduction sequence, Allen took Mario's car keys to Troka Loca, and gave them to Mark to drive back to the Hyundai. Allen knew that he possibly wouldn't see Mario again, besides, he never liked Mario's sated love for an automobile, and he probably wouldn't try to fuck Molly in it again. Mark and Henry took Mario's truck back to the Hyundai.

"What the fuck?!" cried Travis. "Ain't nobody chasing you, Gene."

Gene threw the van in drive-low and drove off into the downtown night. Dr. Dre's "California Luv" filled the van as the six guys tried to relax under the anxiety and excitement of the moments. With no one in pursuit and the downtown surface streets relatively clear, in unison, the guys howl and yowl with exaggerated enthusiasm, so loud and long that Dr. Dre's music was drowned out by the deep raucous cheers.

"Holy Shit!" cried Travis, "We actually pulled that shit off."

"We're not out of the woods, yet," said Tyronne. "We gotta get this shit to Long Beach."

"This shit is history," said Allen. "If we be cool and don't panic." Allen looked directly at Gene while he was talking in a fatherly tone.

Gene noticed the allusion, "Damn Allen, have you ever stolen $20 million before?"

"No!" he answered. "But I wanna be around to spend it."

"The worst part is over. Nobody got killed. It was so smooth, we didn't even fire a single shot," said Travis.

"If we just be cool and act normal and don't act nervous for nothing from here on out, we can fuck our wives and raise our children in peace and riches," reasoned Tyronne.

"We some bad motherfuckas," said Allen. "We're some niggas with money. If we handle this newfound success the right way, we can live like kings for the rest of our lives. Travis is right, just relax, Gene. In fact, everybody's right, don't start trippin' now."

Gene wasn't necessarily the best driver, but he was the most convenient. Being available to pick up the van with no mishaps worked well and now he was the appointed transporter.

"We just did that shit is all I know," remarked Tyronne.

"I told y'all," said Allen smiling. "Opportunity, baby, opportunity. And—"

Allen stopped talking in mid-sentence as he looked straight ahead transfixed by red and blue blinking lights. By now, the colored lights reflected off the cabin walls.

"Man, now what's wrong?" asked Tyronne, expecting an answer.

As the blinking patrol lights become brighter and more distinct, Gene slowed down calmly, especially, because of the guys' recent exchanges. "What the fuck, man, what the fuck?"

Allen sucked in a deep breath, "Relax!"

"I knew this shit would happen," said Gene trying to fight off the tension. "I knew this was way too easy."

"Damn! Damn! Damn!" moaned Travis.

"Chill man, chill!" said Tyronne as calmly as he could.

"You just sit back and be cool," said Tyronne as he pulled out a L.A. Dodger baseball cap and jersey and handed it to Gene. "Put this on pinche cabron and don't talk until spoken to."

"Where did you get this shit from? I ain't puttin' on these crip colors motherfucka," screamed Gene. "I live in blood hood; I'm from Center View, nigga, 169th and Avalon, blood."

"I know the score, bro," said Tyronne. "I ain't bangin' but I know how to get around this motherfucka. Why you think I'm still here between all this crazy shit? I always carry a change of clothes when robbin' rich motherfuckas," said Tyronne. "What difference does it make? A little blue birdie told me to bring'em. Now put this shit on, relax, and sing your favorite song."

"Put that shit on," Allen agreed, "And I'll play it by ear. Flow with it, baby, flow with it."

"Hold the wheel for a second then, motherfucka, while I change into these fuckin' crip colors," said Gene.

With his heart racing past his thoughts, the sight of the blue cooled Gene's mind down and the feel of the material calmed his nerves.

"Remember," said Tyronne, "Don't talk until they talk. Otherwise, you look guilty."

"Man, I got this," said Gene with some newfound confidence and less nervousness, "Relax!" He donned the cap and jersey as Tyronne shut the cabin-to-cargo window.

Gene pulled up to the officer as the lights reflected off his face and clothing. Allen is in the passenger seat playing off asleep.

"Good evening," greeted Gene as Tyronne shook his head in the rear.

"License and registration, please?" asked the officer.

Gene grabbed the license and registration and handed it to the officer. As the officer was viewing the documents, he continued, "Hideo Nomo, Ramon Martinez, Ishmael Valdez, and Chan Ho Park are having some fine seasons on the hill and Mike Piazza, Wilton Guerrero, Raul Mondesi are hitting the hell out of that ball and Greg Gagne and Eric Young, I think, are the best double play combination in the game," said the officer before Gene said a word after his greeting.

Gene was not an avid baseball fan, but he had seen some games, "I think Mike Piazza can kick Johnny Bench in the ass as a hitter."

The officer finished viewing the documents and averted his attention to the cab and roams a flashlight light around as if he was searching for something.

"What's the problem officer," asked Gene as calmly as he could.

"What's wrong with your friend," asked the officer.

Allen pretended to fully wake up after sleep. "We've been moving all day," he said in a groggy tone, wiping his eyes and holding his left hand up to shield the powerful light. "Is that light really necessary any longer?"

The officer shined the light away from Allen's face but searched it around the cab. "Moving is the third most stressful event they say, third only to losing a loved one and divorce."

"I agree," said Allen. "And I sincerely believe if we're not done with this last load, my wife is going to seriously think about divorcing me."

"You boys sober?" asked the officer in a perfunctory tone as he shined the light in Gene's eyes once again.

"What?! Yes! Man, we just trying to move before our wives have a hissy fit," said Gene.

The slits of the officer's eyes grew thinner, looking for the slightest hint of drunkenness, "We got a lot of assholes driving under the influence, especially on the weekends, in this neighborhood." Again, he shined the light in Gene's face and Gene covers his eyes and face.

"Damn! Man!" said Allen, "I haven't had a drink all day."

"Sorry," said the officer, "My job is routine and habitual. Where y'all headed?"

"Long Beach," answered Gene and "Boyle Heights," answered Allen in unison within timing constraints.

The officer cringed a little and raised his left eyebrow, "Which one is it fellas?"

Allen automatically snapped into a defensive posture of wits with the coolest disposition, "My girl and I are moving from Boyle Heights to Long Beach. My boy here was kind enough to help."

The officer pat Gene on the back, "Always the sinner, never the saint, huh."

"Sinner?" answered Gene, "Once you get to know him."

The joke seemed to be off beat but Allen followed his first mind as time seemed to stand still while in the back of the U-Haul, no breath escaped Tyronne's or Travis's lips.

"It's a saying, son," said the officer. "You should never read more than what you see." The officer was smiling as he handed Gene back his license and registration.

"Thank you, officer," said Gene as his Adam's apple slightly bulged.

"I'm just happy that you boys are moving to Long Beach and not the other way around," said the officer.

"Why's that?" asked Gene out of ecumenical curiosity in an attempt to furl a tighter bond.

"Boyle heights is swarming with dirty Mexicans," said the officer. "Mexicans, am I right, or am I damn right?" Then the officer laughed gutturally. Then, he answered his own question, "Right!"

In the back of the U-Haul, Travis points at Tyronne and fakes a laugh with his hands over his mouth.

Fully comfortable with his investigation and interrogation, the officer smiled and said, "You boys have a good night."

They slowly drove off, but Gene's damaged dander was decidedly raised, "Racist Fuck."

# Chapter 16

The drive back to Compton from the police check point was like traveling on Easy Street in Pasadena, CA. The 110 south was relatively without traffic. The few cars that were on the freeway were obviously searching for clubs and casual visits to friend's and family's homes. After a long work week, they had lived for the weekend.

After the jubilation period, the guys were not only tired but happy and sad, happy for the present and unsure about the formidable future. Gaining a record heist in less than an hour weighed heavy on their mind, but the feathery feeling of the thought of a half-ton of cash and the reality of 20 million of those pretty little green ones within their unlimited grasp was like the weight of the world on their shoulders. Cash, that almighty dollar; yes, it changes men from scum to saint in the bat of an eye. It is no doubt that a rising star gathers no moss and brings out the true personality of any person.

Mark and Henry waited for an eternity seemed like for the U-Haul to show its welcomed headlights in Gene's driveway. After they saw the U-Haul, they both cracked a smile, tensions eased, and they jumped out of the Hyundai like stalking panthers. Gene lived in Galaxy West, a tract that was built in the early sixties, a well-kept neighborhood of predominately two-story homes. He lived by Haskins Lane and Alondra Boulevard around the corner on Claude from the old Kytes mini market, a former popular landmark and micro shopping place for the southeast section of Compton.

The garage door to Gene's house quietly rose from the Genie Gene carried. The guys quietly greet with shoulder bumps and progressive handshakes. In the garage, Allen grabbed bags, flipped through a few, and tossed the guys a thousand dollars apiece. They changed clothes and hid the guns away in a locked cabinet. Four piled in the rear of the U-Haul lying on and surrounded by millions of dollars, and Gene drove the U-Haul back to the party in Long Beach with Allen in the front passenger seat enjoying the ride. They parked the U-Haul truck directly across the street from the party within direct view, and it became the star player of the evening. The music still bumped with bass-rumbling beats that could be heard from the garage. The cigarettes, weed pipes, cocaine spoons, and other paraphernalia that they left were untouched; so, they grabbed the stuff and melted back into the party. The most extravagant valuables untouched by other hands were the approximately $20 million left in the U-Haul. It was as if the money could speak and alert others of its whereabouts. The edges of the money were set in perfect stacks, but it had all the robbers on the edge of insanity just sitting there waiting to wreak havoc on every soul it could. But the robbers played it cool and drank and smoked and partied like they were there at the party all the time.

While sitting at a table listening to Mary J. Blige, "My Life," Henry asked Tyronne, "Why did your momma give you a black man's name?"

"Every woman has their secrets. My momma's thing was she liked to fuck black men when my dad was off working hard."

"You want a beer?" Henry asked Tyronne. Tyronne nodded his head up and down.

Now, rap music filled the air—"Rapper's Delight" by the Sugar Hill Gang as Mark walked into the kitchen. Everything was moving in slow motion as the music played on, Mark's favorite. Every song that played etched into Mark's twenty-seven-year-old brain like a poker brand that would stand the test of time. That's when Mark started drinking trying to calm down. He kept looking out the window while in the house. Since the party was in the backyard, the entire gang would take turns looking out at the U-Haul, like it had put a spell on the gang. Henry returned with two Coronas.

Allen saw Henry standing, "Why don't y'all have a celebratory drink with us. Henry handed Tyronne the Corona and rushed over to the table. Travis smoked bud, while Gene and Henry and Allen turned up shots and told bad jokes.

Allen, the successful mastermind of the fresh heist, laughed and joked until his heart's content, "Why was six afraid of seven?"

"I don't know, why?" asked Henry.

Filled with euphoria for many reasons, Allen said "Because seven eight nine." Gene laughed before anybody else. Then, a crowd of people began busting up.

"Hold on, hold on," said Henry. "I've got one: what has eighteen legs and catches flies?"

Gene still laughing jovially answered, "A damn spider, nigga, what else?"

Gene slapped the table once then twice almost toppling the bottles of beer and drinks on the table, "I've got one—I went to a psychiatrist, and he says, 'You're crazy.' I told him I wanted a second opinion. He says, 'Okay, you're ugly too!'"

Henry laughed before he answered, "A baseball team, fool." Henry laughed so hard that he showed all his rotten teeth, not giving a fuck because he was caught up, caught up in millions.

The laughter caught Tyronne's attention. He walked over to the table laughing and to twist a tighter bond with the guys, "You fools are crazy." After getting their attention, he said, "I've got one for y'all. After 12 years of therapy my psychiatrist said something that brought tears to my eyes". He said, "No hablo ingles."

Travis was sucked up into the moment like a hurricane, "Try this one on for size. Sincerity is everything if you fake that you've got it made."

Allen laughed along with everybody else, "Are you fakin' it, nigga?" Allen noticed Mark wasn't around engaged in the gaiety, so he shouted, "Mark!"

Mark appeared from the kitchen.

"Hey Mark," Allen said laughing. "Everybody's told their best jokes. You got one for us, buddy?"

Listening to the laughter kind of altered Mark's mood, so he obliged, "Yeah, I'll throw one in. "I was born a suspect. I can walk down any street in America and women will clutch their purses tighter, hold on to their mace, lock their car doors. If I look up into the windows I pass, I can see old ladies on the phone. They've already dialed 9-1-1 and just waiting for me to do something wrong."

Laughter erupted, but Allen caught the innuendo.

Loosened, the group kept partying and everyone and everything swayed to the music as Mark watched in his NWA gear. He looked past the swaying bodies and focused on the U- Haul truck parked across the street. In the distance, he heard police sirens. Living in the city, he detected the difference between ambulance and police sirens long ago. Mark looked around and nobody seemed to hear the police sirens but him. He could not take his eyes off the U- Haul and then red, blue, and white lights reflected off the U-Haul truck. Mark held his breath. Three sheriff cars sped by, then gone. Allen moved towards him, with a beer and a shot of cognac Courvoisier in hand, blocking Mark's view of the scene.

"Cheers," said Allen after handing Mark the beer and Yak and holding up his own. They clicked bottles and Mark tried to crack a smile with worry still etched on his face; then he snuck another look towards the U-Haul truck.

Allen listened to "Fuck wit Dre Day (And Everybody's Celebratin'), his favorite song as he is a bit more in solace for his life-long plans are falling into order. AMT, Extreme Entertainment, Real Estate, and whatever else money could buy. A man with a plan saturated his mind as he envisioned his queen checkmating his opponent's king. A large piece of the puzzle was put into place tonight. Part of the conundrum had been played and figured out. The riddles had dwindled down to a facile function, he thought. He, too, leered at the U-Haul parked across the street in sight to make sure nobody touches it without his permission. After all, it wouldn't be there without his master plan of epic proportions. For now, he would settle down and settle into the moment and enjoy the night, enjoy the party, enjoy the music, enjoy the rest of his life.

It could be said from his childhood that Allen was destined to be rich; not wealthy, but rich; for wealth comes from another place like deep springs bubbling deep from within the earth or high places existing far beyond the clouds. Allen grew up in a well-to-do middle-class family in a predominately black neighborhood, but his family wasn't wealthy, say, like the Hampton's, the Du Pont's, the Rockefeller's, or Howard Hughes's. His mother and father worked hard to provide for the needs for their family. Allen wanted to work hard, too; but he desired to be in the realm of the rich and famous, which was out of the reach of his familial culture and heritage, so he wanted to snap the sanguine strings of mediocrity. He wanted 'to have his cake and eat it, too' in a world of little understanding. But yes, he wanted to 'break the mold,' and create a new one in one desperate act—what will later be dubbed as the largest cash heist in America's two-hundred-twenty-one-year-old recorded history.

The party lingered on until the wee hours of the morning. The DJ purposely ended the night with a plethora of slow jams. April found Travis and they were hugged up most of the night in an isolated corner. The rest of the guys could have been nominated for acting awards by the Academy of Motion Picture Arts and Sciences or Golden Globe for they blended like chameleons revealing the least bit of outward tension. Considering, Allen thought the guys performed admirably as he watched and listened.

No doubt, the heaviest burden of responsibility rested on twenty-seven-year-old Mark's shoulders. The weight on his shoulders was only a small part of the avoirdupois he felt and carried in his heart. Half a ton in dry weight was heavy by any stretch of the wildest imagination, an amount that would strain a small crane—twenty of the world's strongest men combined couldn't even lift it with a snatch. But it sat in the front of the house in Long Beach and probably would be handled and counted at his house in an attempt to go from zero to hero. When the guests had bid their final good-byes and said 'we gone', the tight-knit group assembled in the empty house in the back of the party's house. To all concerned, the group told them that they were going to discuss AMT business in the backhouse. When everybody was gone, Gene carefully pulled the U-Haul around and they started bringing the money into the empty hostel. For a long moment, they just sat around marveling at their newfound wealth from their perspective. When the awestruck feeling waned, they started counting the money until the crack of dawn. Not even putting a dent in the count of the total amount after counting thousands, they decided to reload the overwhelming remainder in the U-Haul, which Gene took. They all took their trash and duffle bags and loaded it in their own cars. They all took equal stacks not beyond what was counted, as much as each person in the group could carry without counting it to the dollar. It was so much money until Mark never got around to counting it all. Allen, the mastermind, would count and recount and account for every dollar of the alleged $20 million in his everyday business dealings.

The next day, early in the morning about eight hours later, Mark had another scary episode since the alcohol checkpoint on the night of the robbery. Mark was taking some of his money into the house from his trunk early that Saturday morning after dropping the kids off at a friend's birthday party. He told his wife to go on in the house. Mark grabbed a bag of money that busted and wrapped bills had strewn all over the street. He had grabbed another bag that he luckily had available and feverishly started filling it, when his neighbor suddenly appeared.

"Would you like some help?" he asked as he walked with a brisk pace towards Mark.

Still with a large number of stacks lying in the street Mark unconsciously snapped, "No, no, no, I got it! I gotta surprise for my wife and kids I don't want them to see it. Please, I can handle it."

He bought the explanation and turned around. It scared Mark to the fullest because his neighbor was a Carson Sherriff. After frantically gathering the loose money, Mark sidled past Florence and put the money in the 'club' closet. The 'club' was the name of Mark's office. The three-bedroom apartment that they rented in

Compton had unusually large bedrooms and closets. For a rental, Florence loved it. One of the bedrooms was Mark's clubhouse where there was ample storage space in the bedroom's closet. With countless thousands of dollars in his office, Florence had to know about it. The group got together the next night and split a larger portion.

# Chapter 17

Early that Saturday morning, Miles walked into the downtown Dunbar facility and heard sounds of moaning and groaning coming from the break room, and as he got closer, he distinctly heard a woman's voice, "Help! Help! Help! Somebody help us!"

The break room door is wide open, and he's greeted by a personally unwelcomed sight that would fill his day with investigations and paperwork. The night shift of the facility is hog tied, sweating, and crying. Within minutes, cops, marked and unmarked police vehicles, and caution-cordoned tape create a maze for news trucks and federal agents to meander through to cover and investigate this unsuspected and enormous event. Cameras roll as a reporter, Gordon Tokumatsu NBC4, diligently covers the now known historic event as Detective Warren and Detective Briggs walk past the circus-like scene both wearing inconspicuous ray-bans.

"You must have had a late night," said Detective Briggs. "I'm willing to bet that those sunglasses are hiding something."

"Five to one, yours are hiding more than mine ever could," said Detective Warren in return. "Yesterday morning I made a 10AM promise that my 10PM self couldn't keep."

"And what was that?" asked Detective Briggs.

"Thou shalt not drink anymore vodka," he replied.

In tandem, they walk inside of the facility past the breakroom where the hysterically frantic Molly is recounting the incident to a police officer in his mid-thirties, tall, black, and handsome.

"They called each other by numbers, not names." Then she broke down in tears in the hallway.

This triggers a distant memory in Warren as Molly continued, "There were eighteen different hands groping my body," said Molly, sobbing.

"These guys were professionals," said Murray.

"We'll decide who was professional or not," said Warren.

Molly and Murray are stunned as Briggs and Warren walk past them. Molly is still perturbed and full of tears.

"Your bedside manner is improving," said Detective Briggs.

Briggs and Warren continue walking to the back offices and discover a hole in the wall where a VCR had been ripped out. Briggs and Warren exchange glances. The captain walks in with thin layers of sweat that formed on his brow. "I've been looking all over for you two. We got the Feds here and you're dicking around and making me look like a chump."

"The Feds," said Detective Warren. "We can handle this."

"Don't start fucking with me," screamed the captain. Then he exited with an attitude followed by Briggs and Warren.

With police and Federal agents hovering around the crime scene, a female FBI CSI agent in the garage is looking for and taking fingerprints as a perfunctory part of her job. She's a well-built brick house in her early thirties, Caucasian, blonde hair, green eyes, 5'5" tall standing in 3-inch stiletto heels, vermillion lips, and dressed in a light blue one-piece above-the-knee dress talking to FBI Agent Matthews, who is in his early forties, 6'0" tall, black, thick-chested, 15" biceps, high cheek bones, deep-brown eyes, and a strictly-by-the-book kind of guy who's taking notes when Briggs and Warren walk in.

Warren and Malone exchange a look and couple of glances, "Top of the Morning, don't you look stunning and lovely in that blue dress," as he uncontrollably winked at her figure.

Agent Matthews purposely stepped between Briggs and Warren with a bit of disdain in his voice. "It's surely nice that you two finally decided to wake up and join us after we've done all the work."

Warren extended a hand with a long straight arm. All four shake hands in an unsure respectable manner as Agent Matthews continued, "I'm Special Agent Matthews and this is Special Agent Malone."

"Nice to meet you two," said Briggs. Warren says nothing.

Already familiar with the formalities, the captain intervened, "Good, good, now that we have the introductions out of the way, let's get to work."

"I'm ready," assured Detective Warren.

Malone, 5 feet tall, Caucasian, blue eyes, red hair, looked down at her pad, "What we know is it took less than thirty minutes to pull this entire thing off and they left the place in mint condition."

"How'd they get in?" asked Warren.

"No sign of exaggerated forced entry," said Malone. "Someone had a key from my professional opinion." And then she held up a busted yellow taillight draped in a plastic bag, "We're thinking they hit the wall in all the commotion."

"If nothing else, nerves," said Briggs.

All four walked over to the vault. Pointing around as Agent Malone continued, "Some employees claim that there were ten guys while others said they heard an army of feet running throughout the building."

"We're going to have to interview everyone again," said Detective Warren.

There is a moment of tension between Warren and Malone, but she says nothing and leaves, "Where are you going?" Warren asked.

"You can take it from here," said Malone. "You don't need me," she said with a slight attitude. Before he answered, she was gone.

"Trouble in paradise?" Briggs said smiling peevishly having gotten there late in the first place.

Warrens runs after her, "Hey Malone, how much did they get away with?"

"$18.9 million," she said in a quivering voice.

After work on the following Saturday, Gene and Mark had taken off for Vegas. They had driven Delilah and she had purred and pulled the San Bernadino Mountains like a locomotive on rails, and she took the flatlands like they were standing still. They had started playing at 6:30PM and stopped at 4AM that morning and returned to Compton early Sunday morning. A few stars are still pinned in the sky when the sun threatened to rise. Mark found sleeping quarters on the living room couch, briefly, when Florence stood over him in her nurse's uniform. She nudged him, "Mark, wake up." Said she fervently, he still lies asleep. "Wake up!" she sprinkled some cognac on his face. He jumped up, "What the fuck, baby."

She held up the bottle of cognac when Mark responded, "What are you doing?"

"Where have you been all night?" she asked, her eyes demanding an answer.

Mark wiped his eyes as if they were full of sleep, "Working."

"Don't give me that shit," Florence fluttered, "I went by your job—"

Before she could speak another word, he said reluctantly, "Baby, I've got to tell you something."

He told her everything from its inception and, personally, lifted a heavy burden from his own shoulders. He knew that Florence was intuited in her approach to life and whatever he did, she would eventually find out. He had listened to Allen's advice when he said Florence couldn't testify against him, which made it much easier to say. He needed her confidence and support more than the scheming and conniving way, and he would tell her anyway at the appropriate time. He knew that many times in his life that control and the truth had collided to his temporary disadvantage. He couldn't lose Florence's trust.

They sit in the kitchen over coffee, bacon, eggs, grits, and toast. Florence's face is stricken in shock, "But baby, we didn't need this kind of money. We were fine."

Mark looked down at the steam lightly billowing up from his coffee cup and studied the light-brown color. He thought back to the first night he met Florence at the KFC, "I made a promise to you—"

When Florence shook her head, Mark stopped talking and took her face in both cupped hands, "I promised you if you stuck with me, I'd give you everything you've ever wanted."

Florence shuttered, "But—"

"Now I'm making good on that," Mark said passionately, as his hands dropped from her face and softly clutched her hands.

She defiantly pulled her hands away, "What happens if you get caught?!"

"We won't!"

"How do you know that?!"

Mark lightened, "Because Allen—"

Florence shook her head interrupting Mark's train of thought, "What!"

"Baby lis—"

"You always listening to Allen. He says jump you say how high, and this time you've jumped so high, you didn't even think about what would happen when you came back down to earth and real life sets in. Like what happens if you're caught? To our kids, to us?"

Mark listened, "Allen says—"

Florence steamed with anger, "If I hear that man's name one more time, I'm gonna scream!"

After a couple of days later, Florence was taking Mark to work, "I'm thinking about leaving you and taking the kids to the desert, maybe even Vegas, for a fresh start."

"That means we'll have to get a divorce," said Mark.

"Divorce is the dirtiest word in the English language," said Florence. "I'm scared you're gonna get caught and I don't wanna put the kids through that."

"Baby, I'm working two jobs," said Mark defensively. "We made a deal to protect one another."

"Mark, how can you be so naïve? If one of those niggas get caught before you do, they're going to sing like Whitney Houston," Florence started crying. "I'm afraid that you would sing, too. None of you have ever been locked up before or even faced that possibility. When danger is far off, everybody has courage, but when it's close, those big talkin' motherfuckas with hot words will start getting cold feet."

To Mark, everything she was saying made sense. "Okay baby, if you wanna take the kids, I won't stop you. But don't be hasty, plan your strategy and think ahead."

"Okay!"

Later that day, when Florence picked Mark up from work, she was in a mercurial mood, "We've been together nine years and married for four. I married you because I love you, not for your money. And now that you've got money, I'm not gonna divorce for that. I've noticed that that money didn't change you. I'm gonna ride this one out and see which way it goes."

# Chapter 18

A week had passed before the six decided to meet as a team again. They had closely followed the local news reports on all channels every day. Allen did as he promised and turned his keys in that following Monday, and Miles didn't bring up a word of the robbery in their exit interview, although the news outlets had carried it as the biggest and largest cash heist in United States history. There's no way that he could wrap his mind around the remotest potential of a young and simple guy from Carson pulling off a job of this magnitude. His mind was somewhere else thinking of a highly organized crime gang who had been casing the facility for years just waiting for the perfect opportunity to strike. There were too many variables to suspect him— the cameras, the several keys, the knowledge, the timing, the courage, the speed. It had to be a world-class caper. After all, nobody in American history had accomplished that feat before now. In fact, Miles rather admired Allen for his gregarious personality alone. He only fired him because he fucked Murray up while committing one of his pranks and practical jokes. That could have happened to anyone. So, in a fatherly manner, he advised Allen to cut down and saber his extracurricular activities in his future working life if he wanted to maintain long-term employment from anybody. So, he graciously accepted the keys and wantonly watched Allen leave.

The guys had stashed the money in three covert places before they convened at Allen's house. They brought all the cash together, except Mark's portion because it was already safe—Mark's garage and two separate self-storage locations for himself for smaller amounts. They did that reasonably quickly in case the investigations pointed towards Allen. Of course, they watched and moved when the heat had subsided a bit.

The busted yellow taillight was an unplanned red herring. The local police and FBI's only clue was a yellow piece of plastic so they investigated to the hilt but couldn't and didn't establish a heated connection. Like any law enforcement agency, they followed protocol to no avail until the next phase of their investigation took root. By this time, the guys had been counting the fruits of their theft for three days.

"We've been counting for days, how much we got?" asked Travis while in the confines of Allen's garage. Allen tied oversized rubber bands around six stacks of money.

"I don't know but we get $100K a piece to start with and the rest I'm taking to a secure place."

Abruptly, Gene stopped counting. "Where?"

"My grandma has a storage unit in Compton. We'll keep it there and access it when we need to."

Gene rises and gets in Allen's face, staring him down with balled fists. "Wait! Wait! Wait! So you gonna take the rest of the money and we're supposed to trust you?"

A look of resolve danced in Allen's eyes, "Yeah! You gonna trust me Gene because we split this six ways even though I've done more work than anyone else."

Travis saw that Allen's look was full of malice and that Gene waivered a bit, "He's right Gene, he has done more work and we're still equal partners, so—"

"So, stop being a dick, Gene," said Henry as he pulled Gene away.

"What's our next move?" asked Mark deliberately to slice the tension.

"We lay low," said Allen. "They're probably gonna pick me up pretty soon for questioning or to just shake the cage and—"

"Why?" said Henry. "We're like ninjas."

"I worked for the company. I knew everything about its operation. If they don't know it already, they will know that we are friends. Soon, they will probably question us all. Just don't panic because they have no evidence to prove anything. If we play the game smart, we can grow this opportunity and retire rich men."

Gene took a sniff of the money, "'bout to buy me a new suit and not those men's warehouse pieces of shit neither. I'm gone—"

"Hold off on that," said Allen with conviction. "No extravagant spending. Just live normal—have dinner, bills get paid—and keep going to work. We can't raise any suspicions."

The guys nod in agreement. Allen goes back to counting and stops when he comes across a bag of sequenced bills. "What the fuck is this?" He holds up the bills in plain sight.

"Looks like money to me," said Henry drawing some laughs.

Allen's gaze grows beyond serious. "These bills are in sequence; a schoolboy can track these in a windstorm." He eyed Mark, "Mark, do you have any money wrapped in these straps with these dates?"

"I don't know!"

"Here," said Allen handing them to Mark. "Take these straps and check."

"What should we do?" asked Henry out of ignorance.

Allen handed some more bills to Mark, "Get rid of'em, right away, burn'em!"

Counting the bills by hand developed blisters on most of the guy's hands and their hands got sore to the touch.

"Shit man," said Henry. "We need money counting machines."

"Stop being a pussy and count," said Travis.

"Maybe he's right," said Mark

"Good idea," said Allen, "We'll buy'em through the ATM business."

Although they were counting for days, they kept counting with a hamartia of judgment for they recycled the same straps the money came in.

Like the American flag, burning American legal currency is illegal, but it's also illegal to steal over $18 million by gunpoint. Counterfeit money burns green and smells like a pyre of raked burning leaves. Later that night, at Gene's place, Mark and Gene burned stacks of bills in bewilderment and disgust. "Now I understand what they mean when they say, 'we've got money to burn'," said Mark as he looked at Gene then at the burning bills.

"You ain't never lied," said Gene with tears almost in his eyes. "Seemed like the stupidest idea of all time. The things that money makes you do."

"Most black people ain't used to having money, and probably never will," said Mark with the most solemn look on his face. "We have to get used to being rich and get used to it fast. The Bible says that the root of all evil is money. We must realize the money isn't evil, but the love for it is. Burning this bad shit is like cleansing our soul."

Priscilla walked in the garage and sees a smoking tin trash can lightly billowing white smoke with a tinge of purple and brown. The fetid and sweet odor fills the garage and now Priscilla's curiosity is challenged, "What's burning?"

Gene stepped in front of her and blocked her path and view, "You weren't supposed to be home until 9."

"They had a fight at the club tonight; they sent us home early," she said.

"Would you mind your own damn business, please?"

Priscilla frowned, "I help pay rent in this bitch, too, so this is my business, too."

Gene gave her a hard look of superiority, she cowered and reluctantly left. The money is still burning. Gene needed help to recover from the confrontation. He took two sniffs of a bump of cocaine, "Ever since she's found out she's pregnant, she thinks she owns my ass."

"Hello," said Mark. "'Cause she do."

After burning countless thousands of dollars, Gene shrugged it off with a laugh and Mark turned his attention back to the money. "This shit is tragic. My soul is cleansed. There's got to be a better way than burning all this stinky money."

"I know how we can get rid of this faster and better," said Gene. "It's simple, doing what we like to do any way."

Mark's face glosses over with intrigue, "How?"

"Most of these bills are fresh off the printer, said Gene, "We could handle them better by spraying them with glass cleaner 'cause it keeps them from sticking. Let's take $10,000 in hundreds and spread and spray now. When they dry, we'll even be able to easily stick them in hundred-dollar-slot machines in Vegas".

The mantra, 'What happens here stays here' has never been truer in the mind and the case of Gene. Literally, Vegas is a world within a world and the Entertainment Capital of the World. It is true that the Flamingo in Vegas materialized in the mind of a gangster named Bugsy Sigel in 1946. Sigel was the brainchild and Meyer Lansky poured money through Mormon banks for cover of legitimacy that built the Flamingo in 1946. In 1931, gambling was legalized in Vegas fifteen years prior to Sigel's surge with the initial building of the Northern Club, now La Bayou, and Binion's Horseshoe, now Binion's Gambling Hall and Hotel. Historically, blacks were not allowed in Vegas, but The Lady Luck was the first casino and hotel to allow blacks, and Gene's father had told him the history many times when he was a kid. Gene and his father had gone to The Lady Luck on several occasions and played blackjack and craps together where Gene learned how to play these games well. Gene knew that they could launder the sequenced bills in Vegas with minimal suspicion at his favorite downtown casino, The lady Luck.

The lights, so many lights, bounced off moving cars like diamonds reflecting the most obscure light. Beautiful women and gamers poured out into the streets from casino after casino. Mark and Gene strolled into The Lady Luck and placed large sums of cash on the blackjack table and started playing without the stress of losing. The drinks kept coming and the cash was flying high. The casino lights bounced off Mark's face as his eyes closed.

"Wake up, man, it's your play," said Gene as Mark fought fatigue from many sleepless nights. To keep Mark awake, Gene started to casino hop. They went to the Excalibur, Monte Carlo, MGM Grand, New York New York, Caesar's Palace, Las Vegas Hilton, The Orleans, and many others. Gene and Mark were having the times of their life catching all the sights and sounds of the gambling city. The slots and video games gobbled up thousands of hundreds. They plopped down thousands in hundreds on the craps tables, played big for an hour in different parts of the same casinos, then left. They did the same in the Asian game section. Lost a few hundred in the games they didn't understand, then left. They bought souvenirs for their wives and kids in all the shops. It was perfect, not a single flaw, and they saw the bills transform from sequenced to an immense stack of bills that could not be traced.

# Chapter 19

Several weeks later, with nobody trippin', Gene rented another U-Haul and they met up at Mark's grandmother's house in Palmdale while she was out of town. They decided to finally separate all the money into six equal amounts. To cut down on a conglomeration of bodies and potential outbursts, they all agreed on just two dividing the final split. They agreed on Mark keeping Allen's and Tyronne's split and Gene keeping Travis's and Henry's split.

It was a rainy day in Southern California in early October of '97 and there were El Nino weather watches and flash flood warnings when Gene traveled the 77.7 miles to Palmdale from the storage bin in Compton. Only Allen and Gene had loaded the almost half a ton of cash in the heavy rainfall. They welcomed the cover of rain that took two hours to load. Mark was already there visiting in Palmdale when Gene made the call. They meticulously decided on their plans and Gene submitted in the cover of rain to make the transport. He took the 110 to the 405 to the 74. It was an inconspicuous three-bedroom house in a faraway rural setting. They both agreed it was the perfect place to conduct business.

A couple of thwacks on the front door slightly polarized Mark from his current duties, although he was expecting Gene. Dressed in heavy dark clothing and a black beanie cap, Gene was in good spirits. They gave each other a contrived handshake and a shoulder bump.

"Hey Bro, how's a brother doing after making history," commented Mark.

"To be truthful, nigga, I'm as nervous as a Bessie Bug on an electric blanket. Although I'm rich, I can't sleep," said Gene. "Every other second, I look over my shoulder to see if the law is coming."

"I know what you mean, Bro. Now I know how it feels to be a millionaire," said Mark, "and this pressure is a motherfucka."

"Allen planned the actual robbery well," said Gene. "But we really had no plan for storage and handling of the money afterwards. After we split the money on the robbery night, I took the money back to my place and parked it in the garage. I gave Allen the keys to the truck and to my garage and he told me to go pay for another month on the U-Haul."

"Didn't Priscilla get suspicious"?

"I told her it was AMT business," answered Gene. "And I went and rented another truck a couple of days ago. Allen helped me load the new truck. You know, Mark, I'm tired of handling and looking at all that money."

Mark shook a sympathetic head, "Let's get this shit split up to make the burden lighter."

"Allen and the guys agreed to have you keep his and Tyronne's portion and I'll keep Travis's and Henry's portion," said Gene.

"Okay, sounds like a plan," said Mark. "Let's unload this shit in the garage...get some foot lockers from Home Depot...divide it evenly... store it... give them a key and tell'em where it is."

"Soon as we get started, we can finish," said Gene.

Mark and Gene did not count the bills individually. They divided the bills by stacks and wrapper amounts, obviously, with the wrappers still attached for speed of the count.

They did not think of unwrapping or rewrapping the bills.

Since Mark was the only one who had the keys to his grandmother's storage unit in Gardena, he kept the stolen money there for him, Allen, and

Tyronne. Mark never found the time to count it all. And since his grandmother had a second house to Palmdale, he felt comfortable she wouldn't go there. And believe it or not, he never thought about the owner or one of the owners checking the unit for when someone has large sums of money on hand, they have to find somewhere to keep it. Besides, he had placed a large Schlage lock on the unit, his footlocker, Allen's and Tyronne's, too, and whenever someone from his family wanted something out of the unit, he would get it and bring it to Palmdale. Mark gave Allen and Tyronne a key to the storage unit and an individual key and directions to their personally named footlocker.

Back in L.A., Warren and Briggs mulled over the evidence finally coming to one conclusion after the yellow taillight grew cold.

"This had to be an inside job," said Detective Warren shuffling through some papers on his desk. "It was too clean. Although some locks were tampered with to give the illusion of a break in and an employees' truck was taken, this shit has insider knowledge stamped all over it. "

Briggs put on his jacket as Warren's eyes followed him closely, "Where are you going, we've got work to do?"

"It's my birthday," said Briggs.

"I didn't know," said Warren. "Your family planned something special?"

Briggs smiled widely, "Every year I get a blow job on my birthday, so I'm going home to collect."

Warren winked, shook his head, and grinned back, "She's a lucky woman."

"She sure is," he agreed. As he turned to leave, he stopped in his tracks as though he had a brainstorm. "We'll re-interview all of the employees tomorrow to see if we can get a hot lead."

The Proud Bird restaurant later that night lit up like a candle on a pedestal as Molly and Allen prepared to order dinner. The variety of WWI planes surrounding the property had always fascinated Allen, especially the Albatros D. III for he was a fan of Baron Manfred von Richthofen's movie, "The Red Baron." He had been a die-hard denizen of the restaurant ever since he was a teenager. The spectacular views through picture windows made him feel at home and he had snapped many pictures with his Minolta camera on the terrace of The Proud Bird.

Allen and Molly had been engaged in a lengthy conversation. From the swelling around her eyes, she had been clearly crying, "You said you loved me, "she said sobbing.

Trying with all his skill, he tried to assuage her tears and feelings, "Baby I do, but my girl and I are trying to work things out."

She sipped on a drink despite her melancholy mood, "I've been through one of the most traumatic things in my life and you're dumping me?"

Allen squirmed in his seat, "I'm sorry."

"You know what he said to me?" she said shaking her head from side to side with tears streaming from her eyes. Allen shook his head in ignorance. Molly leaned towards Allen. She recounted the cafeteria colors, the fetid smell of her surroundings, and Travis's demonic voice so vivid that she saw and heard Travis speak but her lips moved in a horrific flashback, "If you don't shut the fuck up, I'm gonna rip your vocal cords out of your pretty fucking head and choke them back down your fucking throat."

She heard Allen's voice invade the eerie scene, "Well, you do have a pretty fucking head."

Molly snapped out of the moment, "That's all you have to say?"

"Let's be real," said Allen surprised by all the drama, "You're still alive, aren't you—no harm no foul."

Molly cried harder, "This isn't a joke, Allen— this is my life."

"That's just my point," he said perplexed with a smirk. "You still have your life. Baby, I—I think you're overreacting."

"Overreacting," repeated Molly. She rose with rage written all over her face and threw a glass of wine all over Allen's suit. "One of these days, you won't be the one laughing," she said while trotting away crying hysterically. Allen played it cool, wiped his face, and finished his meal.

A few or so miles south in Carson, around the same time, Florence prepared dinner and tried to suppress some tears among a house full of playing and laughing kids. Clare was taking turns swinging the kids around in a clear place in the living room, "Guys, I can't—I'm about to pass out."

"Aw, c'mom!" shouted Malcolm.

"Yeah, one more time," agreed Freddie.

Clare fell to her knees gasping for air, "In a minute."

"Please!" shouted Malcolm.

"Yeah, please!" cried Freddie in succession.

"Ple—!" continued Malcolm.

"Stop whining," Florence interceded. "Let your auntie rest." The kids dispersed from their congregation and ran into another room.

Clare rose and approached Florence. "I didn't mind. Really, it was fun."

Florence looked down at Clare with tiny tears in her eyes as her voice cracked, "They need to know when to stop playing so much."

Clare grabbed Florence's hand, "Flo, what's wrong?"

Florence and Clare faced one another and then Florence collapsed in tears as Clare held her gently in her arms. Clare's intuition spoke, "Is this about Mark?"

Florence looked at Clare like an open book and Clare read her face, "We only cry like this over the men we love." Then Clare kissed Florence. Florence stopped it, but they stood very close to one another.

"I just want to make you feel better," she said.

Florence, flustered, went back to cooking in the kitchen.

Clare followed, "You deserve better than him."

Florence fought off the burden of the moment and summoned strength from far and near places. "He is loyal—that's the best thing about him. Once he believes in you and loves you, he is loyal to the end."

Clare listened with superior knowledge; she thought about how she'd seen him with Florence's sister.

Florence maintained her facial expression, "That shit's been going on for years."

Clare's face expressed shock, "And you're okay with it?"

"It's just sucking and fucking, Clare, it don't mean nothing, just like how this—"

Florence's eyes suddenly glossed over, and she kissed Clare passionately and hard, "You see, don't mean nothing." She turned from Clare and announced out loud, "C'mon kids, dinner's ready." The kids flooded in and Florence got lost in her thoughts as she watched the kids eat like hungry animals.

# Chapter 20

Two hundred and sixty-nine miles away, via the I-15 North, Mark and Gene are deeply involved in a blackjack game. Gene being the more experienced player constantly coached Mark on double downs, splits, hits, stands, and insurance. In a crash-course training session in a Lady Luck Hotel room, Gene cautioned Mark that blackjack is the toughest creative game in the casino to properly play. Gene said that you have to be a creative thinker by creating your own odds. The other games in the casino have their odds already set and it comes down to where you place your bets. For instance, in craps you place your money on numbers and let the dice dictate the action, whereas in blackjack you have to make a decision on every turn of the card, especially the up card, which is the controlling card for how you decide to play your hand. Surely, the up card decides how you play your hand.

He said that a stiff hand is between a hard 12 and 16 count because one more card could break or bust a stiff. Only then, there's a greater advantage to be creative and one should always double down with 11 and always split aces. Those hands are no brainers and when the house's up card is six or below, one should split all like kind, but never split faces or tens and double down eight counts and above and always insure a good hand of 20, two aces, or 11. He said that there is no guaranteed win except for Blackjack if the dealer doesn't flip blackjack over, too, and when the dealer has an Ace showing and the player has blackjack the player should always flip the cards face up if the dealer is dealing face-down out of hand and call out loud 'even money' or if the dealer is dealing face up also call out loud 'even money', the only audible call that has to be made in the game.

Let's go over insurance, mentioned Gene. Insurance is the most misunderstood play in a blackjack session. Most people say it's a sucker bet because of ignorance. But, as he mentioned earlier, basic strategy players should always insure 20, two aces, and 11. It's like protecting something of value—a home, car, boat, or even your life. Insurance in Blackjack is taken on the insurance line on the table. It's half of your original bet to cover the entire bet, but you can insure any portion of the bet because the insurance line will still pay 2 to 1 on a Blackjack. On the insurance line, the player is betting that the dealer has blackjack. Blackjack is with two cards only, 21 is with three cards or more. In actuality, the player insures a hand that's worth playing. Whenever there's an ace showing, the dealer will ask for insurance. Remember, only insure good hands. More times than not, the player will win more money over the long pull than if the player disregards insurance altogether. Moreover, when the player calls for 'even money,' the player is actually taking a short cut to insurance. If you bet a dollar in any of these table games, all you should want is to win is a dollar.

Mark grew up in a family that didn't play table games for learning to count, for fun, or to gamble. Primarily, because his grandmother was a religious-type person, and everybody knew she was the matriarch. Mark had a religious-based education that excluded many learning helpful techniques to uphold his general education. But Mark was naturally smart, and he saw things from a common-sense standpoint. This allowed him to have and maintain a steep learning curve. Therefore, he picked up concepts and fundamentals quickly and melted into situations quickly without notice until the time came to be noticed.

Although Gene and Mark had been playing for eight hours and both were winning by a 100 percent margin, Mark was getting tired, and fatigue was beginning to set in. "Man, how we gonna get rid of all this shit tonight?"

Gene watched his cards carefully, still wide awake, "What we don't dispose of, I'll get rid of." Gene and Mark played on for a while then traveled to the Flamingo to avert any suspicion.

In the downtown Metropolitan Detention Center (MDC) on 535 N Alameda Street adjacent to the Harbor and Pasadena Freeway North-South, the 5 freeway interchange sparkled in the noon sunlight. The high-tech 272,000 square-foot facility initially built as a prison looked like a downtown monstrosity of private ownership resembling a giant office building for the balconies, sunny atrium, and expansive plate-glass windows washed away that prison look. However, the MDC was still a prison housing pretrial inmates with no prison bars in sight and eloquent-looking hotel rooms.

Agent Malone and Detective Warren walked down the hallway, "So your captain tells me it's you and me today," said Agent Malone.

"And isn't this MDC the most beautiful prison in the world. A weekend in here is just like staying at the Mirage in Vegas. You Federal guys, oops, and ladies got it going on," observed Detective Warren.

"This job does have it perks among many mishaps," said Agent Malone.

"It's not like we're partners," said Detective Warren.

"I think the entire justice system should think of us as being one big team with interchangeable partners working towards the same goal," said Agent Malone.

"Are you done with your heart-warming speech, Pollyanna, because we got an interrogation to do?" said the detective like he was running things.

They turned the corner and walked into the interrogation room where Murray, Miles, Mario, and Molly sipped on their coffee before Detective Warren and Agent Malone interrogated them. They decided to interrogate all four together to let their real and deep emotions flow through interaction.

The interrogation room was large and spacious. A fresh fruit-filled centerpiece sparkled and spangled amidst an oaken walnut 20' by 10' table that was polished to a mirror shine. The same color high-back wicker chairs gave the room an outdoorsy atmosphere. The Carroll

Dunham and Louise Bourgeois paintings on the wall spiced up the atmosphere. The interior decorations were simply relaxing.

They sat down and proceeded as planned, "What kind of person was Allen Pace?" asked Detective Warren taking the investigation and interrogation personally because they struck in his backyard.

"Allen Pace was a total ass clown, fuck-up dickhole," said Murray looking down at the scars on his hands.

Detective Warren noticed strange twists, touches, bodily movements, and speech irregularities by Murray, "Do you have Tourettes?"

Murray swelled a little, "No, you fuckwad. This is how I talk."

They let him speak for a while, getting nowhere until he ran out of anger.

Miles began babbling away, "Allen Pace was terminated, but not disgruntled. He was a nice guy and very funny. We have very good people working for us, people with families doing honest work."

Before Mario spoke in the interrogation room, Murray and Warren looked him up and down as if they wondered how he got hired.

Determined to get some answers, Warren decided a straight-forward approach, "We've concluded that this had to be an inside job. How well did you know Allen Pace?" he asked looking directly at Mario.

"He always had my back," said Mario. "Even made sure my Troka Loca was safe."

Warren and Malone exchange obvious glances at one another, then Malone asked, "Who else had a key to the back office where the back-up security tapes were?"

Miles spoke out, "Me..." he paused and then said, "Molly."

Molly calmed herself before she spoke, "He was a jerk. I mean, poor Murray had third degree burns because of one of his stupid childish pranks."

Warren eyed Molly, "Did he ever play a prank on you?"

"No—no—no! We had a respectable working relationship," she answered. "Nowhere near smart enough to pull something like this off in my opinion."

"Molly," Detective Warren said seriously, "Did you ever give anyone a key to the back office?"

Detective Malone gave her a look as if I-got-you crossed Molly's face, and then she said, "No...just me."

The interrogation went better than Warren and Malone had anticipated. The strategy of a congregated interrogation gave them new possibilities. The money had to be somewhere, and somebody had to take it. It was so clean a caveman could have done it. Out of every procedure they ever learned in the academy, it pointed towards an inside job and they both knew that enough pressure could bust a pipe. They were convinced of everybody else but Allen Pace. Inferentially, all the smart fingers were pointing in his direction, so they called the only lukewarm lead, at best, they had, in for an immediate interrogation, even though he had been terminated on the night of the largest cash heist in American history.

A few days later, Allen walked into the MDC as calm as a cucumber, and although the facility was impressive, he knew that they had no hard evidence. He sat across from Warren and Malone.

Detective Malone began to the point, "Did Molly give you a key?"

Not knowing the answers to previous interrogations, Allen answered in truth, "Yeah, she gave me a key, so we could meet up and you know—"

"No, I don't know," said Detective Warren.

"I get it," said Agent Malone.

Detective Warren eyed agent Malone, "We get it, do we?"

"I mean, I worked long and hard hours and so did she, and sometimes, you accidentally fuck your co-workers."

"Side effect of the job," said Agent Malone.

"You know what I'm saying?" said Allen.

"Sure, a man's got needs," said Agent Malone.

They share an intimate moment then Detective Warren eyed Agent Malone.

"Hey Malone, I need a moment," said Detective Warren. They step out into the hallway.

"Side effect of the job?" said Detective Warren, "He's not your fucking friend."

"I'm gaining his trust, just relax," cautioned Agent Malone.

"No, you're not! You're not! You're being fucking played," said Detective Warren.

"By whom?!"

"By him!"

Agent Malone loosened and calmed down, "He's a nice guy, very charming. So he fucked a co-worker."

Reading the questioning, "He used her," said Detective Warren.

"If fucking a co-worker was a crime, I'm sure you and me and everyone else we know would be locked up and—"countered Malone.

Right then, Detective Warren in a dander hit the wall with a balled-fist and split his hand. Agent Malone jumped in surprise at the sudden outburst. He walked back in, she followed. Returning to the table, Detective Warren stood over Allen with a tiny fire in his eyes easily noticeable, so was the gash on the meaty part of his right hand as blood began oozing out.

"Where were you on the night of September 12?" asked Detective Warren

"At a party".

"You say you were at a party on the night of September 12".

"All night, sir," Allen said with total confidence.

Agent Malone espied Allen with a bit of skepticism, "Do you have people who can corroborate with this?"

Allen didn't blink, "Just everyone at the party." Acutely involved in the questioning, the two detectives didn't notice the trickle of blood oozing down Detective Warren's hand, but Allen did. "You know you should really get some ice on that hand before it swells up. What's the matter? Job getting to you?" Allen grinned in a heckling way and Detective Warren clinched his fist tighter and bit his bottom lip.

Detective Warren looked at Allen in bewilderment and disgust. "We've got a robber to catch. Don't leave town in the next few days. I'll need a guest list of that party, too."

"That was a black get-together party not a funeral. Where I come from, we don't make lists for get-togethers," said Allen.

"The way I see it, son," said Detective Warren, "Your only alibi is that party, and brother, I just don't take your word for it. You see, you're at the top of the list of suspects. If you don't give me a list of those participants, I'll just have to get it myself."

Allen felt the pressure, but he also knew he had control of the list, "Fine, I'll get it to you in a few days."

"Great," said Warren. "Here's my card."

Allen viewed the card for a few seconds and left the building.

When Allen left, there was silence that passed between Warren and Malone for several seconds and then...

"You didn't do a total shit job today," commented Detective Warren.

She packed her papers in total concentration, "Thank you."

"Yeah, it was a compliment," said Warren.

"You should work on giving more compliments," said Malone.

Somehow, for a moment, there was an attraction between them when Detective Briggs popped in, "Sorry, I had to take the kid to the doctor. Little fucker is always getting some foreign object stuck in his ear that the doc has to fish out." He noticed something between Warren and Malone, "Am I interrupting?"

"Of course not," said Malone.

"So, how'd it go?" asked Detective Briggs.

"Briggs, you and I will do some surveillance on Pace," said Warren.

"And I will continue to check every U-Haul company in the city to see if he rented a truck around September 12." Malone nodded and left while Warren followed her into the spacious hallway.

"So, it went well. Or?" asked Malone.

"Or, without a leg to stand on or a pot to piss in, I think he is as guilty as sin," said Warren.

The next day, Warren and Briggs began their surveillance campaign. As they staked out in front of Allen's house taking snapshots and motion pictures and gathering information about Allen's routine, they noticed no pattern of incrimination. Weeks had passed and nothing turned up. They began to wonder if they will ever catch a sign of guilt.

A few days later, Allen gave Detective Malone a list of the party. He kept incriminating names off the list. He knew that he would be questioned, so he played the game on his playground.

# Chapter 21

The AMT Security business was now in full swing after all business licenses, training, contracts, and the location offices were purchased and obtained. After a year, work was steady, and the twelve employees all worked fulltime, and the six friends had been hired on. Allen played a game of chess with himself as Warren and Briggs watched from an unmarked car. Allen saw them through his office window. He moved the queen and checkmated himself and grinned. A knock at the door broke his concentration.

"Hello Mark. What's going on in the world, buddy?" Allen asked.

"I'm still working two jobs as planned and I ain't splurging," said Mark.

"You cool, bro," said Allen. "If we all stick to the plan and keep our wives and girls happy, we'll get through this unscathed. By the way, how do you like the new office?"

Mark looked around, "This motherfucka is nice. When did you move on Vernon and Crenshaw?"

"Three months ago."

"I thought you were still on Florence."

"With all the shit we got going on we had to improve," said Allen. "This is the bowels of Extreme Entertainment. I'm the president, you're the vice president, and Travis is the accountant. Let me tell you what we've got. I've been consulting with that funny ass comedian Vince D. and we gone start a comedy tour called The Young Guns of Comedy at the Mark Taper Forum over on Grand Avenue starring and featuring Eddie Griffin. We also gone help Eddie as a silent partner finance his sitcom, 'Malcolm and Eddie.' We got a strip club, jumpers for kids, pager business, and a limousine service. I also met Norm Nixon and I hired him as a business advisor. Norm advised us to open up a club across the street. We already bought the property and the interior decorators said it'll be ready in a couple of months. Oh, did I mention Schruncho is a main act?"

"Daaamn! Schruncho is good. He sho' can identify with the hip-hoppers and our X-generation," said Mark "That motherfucka is funny."

Allen motioned to Mark with his head and shoulders, "You see that motherfucka over there, the blue Camero."

"Yeah!"

"He's watching us. Waiting for us to slip," said Allen. "If we keep doing what we're doing, we could run forever without getting hot."

"Will we ever cool off?" said Mark thinking way ahead.

"They say its $18.9 million," said Allen, "but we know it's more like $20 million is hotter than a kiln. Yeah, it'll cool off if we don't stoke the fire."

"When?"

"Give it another year and I think we'll be home free," said Allen smiling.

From that point on, Mark got deeply involved with AMT Entertainment. The strip club took off like a rocket where he was instrumental as the head of security and hired all security guards and took care of all the security arrangements and was the overseer for all the security contracts. They rented a townhouse across the street from the Carson Memorial where they ran an after-hours strip club on Friday nights. Allen, Mark, Travis, and Tyronne would recruit strippers from existing strip clubs. The strippers liked the idea of making extra money after hours and the idea blew off the chain.

Mark started working the bar and they started charging top dollar at the door and the results were astronomical. They added male strippers and they started making more money a night than Mark made on both his regular jobs. When the club opened across the street from the office on Vernon and Crenshaw, they rented it out to Orientals Monday through Friday and AMT would run it on Saturday nights where they would book Snoop Dogg, Eddie Griffin, Schruncho, Mike Epps, Jamie Foxx, John Amos, Morgan Freeman, Danny Devito, and others.

It's been a year-and-half now and Warren and Briggs still worked the unsolved case of the largest cash heist in American history. Inside the West Los Angeles Police Department on 1663 Butler Ave. in Santa Monica, Detective Briggs sat slumped in a chair while the TV blared in the distance.

Detective Warren stood studying the evidence board, "We got less than shit," he said as Agent Malone and Agent Matthews walked over.

"Nobody named Allen Pace ever rented a U-Haul truck," said Agent Malone.

Detective Briggs sat looking over some paperwork, "Big fucking surprise."

"This guy never paid a bill in his name; he doesn't even have a bank account. Aside from his social security number, he's practically a ghost," said Malone.

"All right, thanks," said Warren.

"You guys want to get some dinner later?" asked Malone.

"The wife waits," said Agent Matthews

"How about you, Warren?" asked Malone.

"Not tonight," he answered.

She shrugged and walked away and Detective Briggs prepared to go, too.

"You giving up too?" asked Warren.

"No harm, no foul, right?" said Detective Briggs.

"No harm?" said Warren.

"So, a few wise guys got off with some cash, we'll catch them sooner or later," said Briggs.

Detective Warren confronted Detective Briggs, "Doesn't it piss you off that some lowlifes think that they can get away with our hard-earned money?"

"These guys didn't steal from people like us Warren—so who cares, right?" said Briggs.

"Who cares?"

"Yeah, who fucking cares?" confirmed Briggs.

"If we just let this go," said Warren, "Every idiot out there will think they can just pull off a heist."

"Whoever did this—" said Briggs.

"Allen Pace," Warren said sharply.

Briggs sat up straight, "We don't know that. We don't know if it was him. But, what we do know is that whoever did this wasn't an idiot." He continued, "Never underestimate your opponent, Warren."

"We just need one slip-up then it will all come tumbling down like a house of cards, right?" said Warren.

"Go get some sleep," said Briggs. "And maybe get your dick wet tonight. You'd be less shitty to be around, I'm done." Briggs put on his hat and left.

Warren watched Briggs walk away. The TV seemed to come alive as the volume seemed to get louder as the news anchor delivered the news:

*"It's been a little over a year in what officials are calling the largest cash heist in American history. This group of armed mystery men got away with $18.9 million. The police have no match for this group of mastermind criminals."*

After hearing that, it was like a slap in the face, and Warren's anger blazed like a Matilja and Zaca wildfires. He slammed the office door behind him and walked hastily to the parking garage. Warren got into his blue Camero.

Malone knocked on the window. Warren rolled down the window, "I know, I know, a girl who can't take a hint." She held up a bag of Chinese food, "But I figured you'd be hungry while you and I run surveillance on Pace. I mean, I don't have anyone to go home to and I'd rather be working than sitting at home being crushed by the loneliness of my existence—you know?"

He motioned and she went around to the passenger's side. He unlocked the door. She sat down in the passenger seat, "Besides, I really want to catch these fuckers, I know you do."

"Where's your partner?" asked Warren.

"I'm looking at him," answered Malone.

Warren locked the doors automatically from the driver's side mechanism.

# Chapter 22

At the same time outside of the Proud Bird Restaurant, again, Allen admired the red-painted Albatros D. III, when James in his thirties, approached. For some reason, Allen could smell the fresh sea air and the stars glinted and glistened like jewels. Mark had given Allen three footlockers full of cash to include in their real estate investments a while back. This offering put a large dent in Mark's holdings. The rest of the guys, except Gene, negated Allen's request to invest. Allen got out of his red Range Rover, and they shook hands.

"How's my fine ass cousin doing these days?" said James.

"I'm sure Gene is taking good care of her by now," said Allen. As Allen and James walked to the front entrance of the Proud Bird, the planes resembled multi-colored pelicans standing in full plume with spread wings and James suited down in a dark blue Armani double-breasted tailor-made suit was used to dealing in upper-end real estate transactions for five successful years as the top producer for Fred Sands. Dark-skinned, tall, thin with handsome features, he walked with an elongated gait. As he politely opened the glass-door entrance, multi-colored lights bounced off the glass and filled Allen's eyes with dollar signs and financial security. California Real Estate, one of the best investments in the world, was the cleanest way to operate.

After being seated, James spoke first. "Merry Christmas to you and me because we're about to close escrow on three of the properties you liked. I just need you to sign some papers and we'll be on our way."

Allen looked straight-faced, "I won't be signing anything. I don't want houses in my name because they're gifts." He grinned large, "You don't own gifts, right? You give them to people."

James, being a polished professional, let Allen lead, "You're right? Of course, so where are these people?"

"They're on their way," answered Allen.

At Gene's house in the Galaxy West Estates in Compton, Christmas lights lit up his property. He and Priscilla just finished fucking for hours. After three or four rounds, Gene had fallen asleep and lost track of time when Priscilla had noticed a strange bag in the corner of the closet. When Gene awoke and lie in bed smoking a joint while Priscilla got dressed, he wanted to surprise her.

She pulled on her stockings. Gene approached her, "This ain't no respectable thing for mama to be doing."

"How else am I going to make money," she said in a hurried voice.

"I'll take care of it," Gene said assuredly. "I got a plan."

He moved quickly and grabbed a duffle bag and placed it in front of Priscilla.

"What's this?" she said.

Gene smiled, "Look inside."

She looked inside. Her eyes widened in disbelief. She pulled some wrapped bills from the bag.

"Gene, what did you do?"

"Got some startup money."

"From where?"

"ATM is doing great, don't worry about a thing," Gene said still smiling. "But, we about to take this money and invest."

"In what?"

"With your cousin, James," said Gene. "He still has the hook-ups in real estate."

"You want to invest all of this?"

"What else am I gonna do with it?"

"I can think of a lot of things."

"Don't be a smart-ass"

"Sorry, Deary," she said mockingly.

Priscilla caught the sarcasm on the run and went to the bathroom. Priscilla's face twisted in a bit of anger as she intimately stroked the cash straps with the sequenced numbers printed on them before she left. Gene switched bags when Priscilla went to the bathroom. They hopped in the car and headed for the Proud Bird.

The Christmas spirit was unfolding amongst the guys. They grew up believing in Santa Claus. But Santa Claus was a jolly roly-poly character with a long white beard to most. But to Mark, Santa brought back unwanted memories of the Nix Check Cashing robbery years ago when he was eight. Santa was supposed to be a giver not a taker. So, in the in the spirit of Christmas, he decided to be a good Santa. Blindfolded, he led Florence outside. Everyone watched anticipating the revelation, including Clare and Barry.

"Can I take this off yet?" asked Florence out of cataclysmic curiosity.

"Be patient, baby" said Mark guiding her carefully, "Merry Christmas!"

The blindfold was still on when he made that wish. Off came the blindfold, and before her eyes, she couldn't believe what she saw. "You did not!"

"I did!"

"Mark!" said Florence as she covered her mouth with both hands in pure delight. She ran over and kissed him with the tightest hug he ever felt.

"Do you like it?"

"I love it!" she said in tears. "You know, I could get used to this money."

They passionately kissed again, and she continued to check out the purple 1996 Plymouth Voyager with the kids, as Mark watched.

"Oh Mark, it's my favorite color, too, purple. How did you do it?" The kids were jumping and screaming while crawling in and out of the car.

"Nothing but the best, and it's fully equipped with leather seats and all the amenities they ever made," said Mark.

Florence viewed the keys in the ignition, "You kids wanna go for a ride?"

The whole family cheered and roared and jumped in the seats, including Mark. Florence exited the driveway and headed straight for the 105 freeway. While riding in luxury, it's as if he's dreaming. His kids are happy, his wife is happy. The world seemed to spin to his beat and rhythm, to his own inner song.

On the freeway, Mark was riding on a cloud, and he thought to himself: *And here I am living the dream. Happy wife, happy life they say—but this was more than happiness, this was destiny—I had made the right moves, set up the board just right, and got what I deserved. I only feel a little guilty—being a God-fearing man, but even Jesus, given the opportunity, would've preferred the finer things in life...Right?*

After that Christmas present, the heavy burden of just sitting on the money felt like a hen sitting on a golden egg had lifted a lot. Mark's family and friends began wondering how he was so free within his life and how these nice things started showing up out of nowhere. Although Mark worked two jobs, something was different, something was fishy. A security guard wasn't supposed to have the mentality of a superstar athlete, especially, in the lower and middle classes in black neighborhoods. Mark's uncles and aunties saw Mark grow from a baby, and they knew him—in some ways better than he knew himself, and Mark noticed that they could detect the changes. So, he devised an explanation for those who wondered about his seemingly subtle change. Change is change, no matter how much. He began telling everybody he recently collected on a settlement for ten thousand dollars from an automobile accident he had a while back. They all accepted the explanation and he lived in relative freedom from gold diggers, freeloaders, and free riders. To Mark, this life was so different than what he was used to—like beating a covey of killer ants on his clothes before they reached his bare skin.

Going to Vegas was complete solace for Mark, especially when he went with his family. Laundering the bills was a breeze and seeing Florence engage herself in the games and the kids watching kiddie videos gave Mark quality time to himself. Mark would spend time in the sports books, bars, souvenir shops, taxi rides, or just gazing out the empty suite's window, and he and his family would take these excursions three times a month after Gene introduced Mark to this newfound and welcomed sanctuary. Sanctuaries are supposed to be a sacred place free from any unwanted elements, but what you can't see can't hurt you, or can it?

In front of Molly's apartment in Hawthorne a few weeks later, Allen stood at the door. Knock! Knock! Knock!

Molly answered.

"Oh, hell no!" she said as she closed the door, but Allen blocked the move with his arms and feet.

Allen stood outside the door holding it open with minimal strength, "Molly, let me explain."

"Fuck you!" Molly screamed.

"I miss you," Allen admitted with total concern.

With those words, she submitted for a moment, "Why in the fuck do you lie?"

"Just give me a few minutes to tell you everything and you'll understand why," said Allen desperately.

"Why should I?"

"Because you're the only one I can trust."

She tried to speak, but Allen overshadowed her voice, "Besides, I never told them that you're the one who gave me the key..."

She realized that he had her. She opened the door a bit more.

Allen smiled, "That's more like it, baby." A grin crossed his lips. "Now," he said touching her face as he walked inside, "I have some business just off the coast of Catalina and I need you by my side."

She looked at him. Checkmate. "When do we leave?"

Some months later, spring sprouted multi-colored flowers and the air smelled like a can of air freshener had been sprayed across the southland. The mild easterly wind brewed up and ocean air mingled with the natural scent of spring and the dotted white clouds painted an idyllic scene across the blue sky as Allen and Molly sailed on a boat towards the Catalina Islands. The silvery sun still weaved through the clouds to find Molly in a bikini basking and tanning in the sun with Allen lying beside her and a towel wrapped over his torso and face.

# Chapter 23

Approximately one year later, outside of Allen's parent's house, he threw a birthday party and wedding anniversary for his mom in Carson. People partied and danced beside a figure-eight swimming pool. The pool was a gift from Allen. Mark attended the party and visited his people on the same day. From the street, among the various new cars, a long-lensed camera snapped a montage of shots: People coming and going carrying expensive gifts and large dishes of food. A camera from next door snapped a plethora of shots of the pool party where Mark was flirting with a woman as Florence watched with tears in her eyes.

Later that day, a flower truck pulled up outside of Mark's mother's house. The delivery man jumped out of the truck carrying a black bouquet of roses. He knocked on the door and Mark answered.

"I have a special delivery for this address, sir," announced the flower delivery man. He handed Mark the black roses.

"Sign here, please," directed the delivery flower man. Mark took the pen.

The same flower man hustled across the street, and at the front door cameras took snapshots as Allen was handed a black bouquet of roses as well. He took them and shut the door.

By now, in Mark's mother's house, he placed the roses on the counter and read the card and across the street, Allen does the same with his arrangement of flowers. In different places, they read the card simultaneously: *"I know what you did."* Allen laughed and lit the card on fire. And across the street, Mark stuffed the roses in the trash can and Florence walked out after she read the card.

Florence spoke from the bathroom, "Baby, you want me to pack you a suit in case we go see a show? Barry and Clare are going to follow us in their rental."

"Whatever you want," answered Mark.

Mark left the room and Florence espied the trash can with concern.

The Luxor on the Las Vegas Strip was the newest attraction in town. It was the talk of the entire southland empire of California and all its counties. Florence had made the reservations two months prior and now, the adjoining suites were available. The 30-story hotel, owned by

Vici Properties and operated by MGM Sports International, had a 120,000-square-foot casino with over 2,000 slot machines and 87 table games, and 2,256 rooms. Florence was dying to take this family vacation to spend some quality time and money with the family and to drive her brand-new Plymouth Voyager. She read about the Nile River Tour and wanted to revisit some ancient ancestral artwork on a boat. She'd read about King Tut's Tomb and Museum, a duplicate of King Tutankhamen's tomb as found in the Valley of the Kings near Luxor, Egypt.

She'd also read about the Le Ice Show, a Willy Bietak production, featuring National Champions Julie Brault and Norm Proft. With a company of 35, it was written that Le Ice added exciting special acts such as daredevil skater Steve Taylor who jumped through fire; Don Otto, the national diving champion (pyramid teams) who combined his talents with comic antics; Vladimir the flier; and singing sensation Paris Red. Florence also read about the 312- seat IMAX theatre, perfect for the kids, that projected a screen seven stories high with frames 10 times the size of the conventional 35mm film that resulted in awe-inspiring 2D and life-like 3D images with a 15,000-watt sound system, an eight channel multi-dimensional digital surround sound system, and a Personal Sound Environment head set with featured Liquid Crystal Display viewing technology. Both Florence and Mark loved 60s music. She read that Nefertiti's Lounge showcased Beehive, 60s musical Revue, and Coco & the G's.

After three hours of traveling north on the I-15 and through desert and around mountains, the Luxor Sky Beam came into view like a straight lightning bolt from heaven.

"Look everybody!" said Florence. "It's the Luxor Sky Beam. That's where we'll be staying. I've been doing some reading about it. It has a 42.3 billion candela luminosity. That's like 42 billion candles shining in the dark. That is the strongest beam of light in the world. On a clear night, they say that it can be seen by aircraft from 300 miles away."

The drama built the closer they came to the Luxor. The kids were squirming like excited mice in a cage. "Look mama, there's a statue of a dog-man," screamed Janine.

"Aww baby, you're so cute. That's not a dogman. That's a copy of the statue of the Great Sphinx in the Giza plateau in Egypt. That's a head of a man and the body of a lion. You see, in Egypt there's three great Pyramids built over 6,000 years ago. The Sphinx was a guardian of the great pyramids of Khufu, Khafre, and Menkaure. Many believe the head of Khafre is on the original Sphinx. Maybe one day we'll go visit the real Pyramids and Sphinx in Egypt. The real Sphinx in Egypt has no nose, because legend has it that Napoleon Bonaparte blew the nose off with a cannon."

"Ooohhh, mama," said Janine. "The Luxor sky beam is coming out of the Sphinx's head."

It was also Florence's first time seeing The Sky Beam from this angle. It was beautiful, she thought. She found parking in the structure. They took an elevator to the lobby. When they stepped inside the Luxor, Mark's eyes fell to his stomach. Florence had done the research and reservations to one of the most beautiful places on the planet. The Egyptian theme was magnificent, and it took him to another world. They had already seen the Sphinx and the obelisk outside, but the inside was breathtaking. Statues of Kemetic Kings, pillars with inscribed hieroglyphics, Egyptian paraphernalia situated behind glass displays, live palm trees, spiral staircases, mummy replicas, live-plant aquariums, automobile displays for contest winners, standing statues of scholars and Imhoteps, 20' by 5'replica of the Titanic, waterfalls, inside pools, ceiling paintings of the Last Supper, vaulted halls, an indoor obelisk, indoor city models, indoor shops, and much more.

Florence was writhing in excitement as she studied her watch, "We have one hour before 'Titanic' begins in the IMAX. We've got to hurry."

The massive lobby sucked them into a festive frame of mind, and check-in was speedy as 'speedy Gonzales' on a good day. The adjacent suites were immaculate at worst—indoor Jacuzzi's, walk-in closets, flat-screen T V's, cooled cold duck champagne in a bucket of ice, dining area, Egyptian pictures hanging in every room, and a king-sized bed caught Florence's sight at first glance for they were in a hurry now to make the IMAX on time. They all dropped their bags and saved the lounging for later.

Spectacular was an understatement for the beauty, and overstatements were not necessary for the experience. Giant Pharaohs standing with arms to their sides on either side of the IMAX entrance welcomed every one of all ages, religions, and colors with votive lights to enhance greetings of grandeur. A sphinx placed outside the entrance solicited a feeling of security and the Titanic Exhibition Artifact Distribution mural above the ticket counters seemed like they could be boarded and sailed imagined Mark. The 3D glasses that were handed out looked like a welder's shield absent the cap. Leonardo DiCaprio and Kate Winslet burned up the silver screen in their performance, and the family reclined to their suites.

"Didn't DiCaprio and Winslet do a fantastic job on that unsinkable ship?" said Florence.

"That white boy is a great actor, but I think the theme is, don't be in a hurry to go nowhere and the way some of those rich white men acted selfishly when they knew they were gonna die by dissing those women and children is the way people act in real life."

"Aww baby, you're such a powder puff, it's just a movie," said Florence.

"You'll be surprised how writers accurately portray the truth behind people and events," explained Mark. "Wasn't that a beautiful theatre with Egyptian theme in all?"

"You have never lied," replied Florence. "But in actuality that wasn't an Egyptian theme, it was a Kemetic theme. The people who built the original pyramids lived in Kemet, not Egypt. The Romans later changed the name when Scipio Africanus conquered the region."

"One reason I love you, baby, because you're so smart," said Mark.

"I can hear that casino calling my name," said Florence. "Let's situate the kids."

"Blackjack Attack is the best strategical game in the casino. If I can find some good teammates, we can make some money," said Mark.

"That's cool," said Florence. "But those bones are calling my name. I used to shoot on the street corner with my girlfriends—I seven eleven before you nine or five."

"That game scares me," said Mark. "I don't know where my money is going."

"Scared people can't win when it comes down to gambling and life," said Florence.

Such a profound statement, thought Mark, of how many things are related in the normal course of living life. The statement 'A scared man can't win' rattled Mark to his foundation because he was more scared than a motherfucka. Sometimes, it would show and sometimes it wouldn't; but he felt he could disguise it better in Vegas, behind the county line, within the city limits, in a hotel suite soaking in a Jacuzzi. If it was just him involved in the caper, he would be less scared, naturally; but he had accomplices, he had friends, he had a personality, and so did they.

The gambling pits were buzzing with action and Florence rolled the dice, "Seven baby, my baby needs a new pair of shoes."

Florence has a thousand dollars' worth of casino chips in her rack. An elegant black woman with salt-and-pepper hair and diamond rings on both hands stood beside her, "Baby, I've noticed how you've been betting and it's all wrong. Craps is the simplest game in the casino to learn how to play for maximum return on your hard-earned money. You can call me Crappie, what's your name, baby?"

"My friends call me, Flo," she said.

"You are true to your name, honey," said Crappie. "When you throw the dice, they hit the felt like putting a baby to bed, and I know that's a natural stroke. You have the ability to put these cubes on fire enough to burn down this building. One of the sweetest touches I've ever seen. Where did you learn how to play craps, Flo?"

"I learned to play on the streets of Los Angeles," said Florence.

"I dealt in Atlantic City on the Boardwalk for thirty years and I learned one thing: If you're not picking up money every time the dice come to a rest, except for seven, you're doing something wrong, unless you feel another objective."

Florence noticed that she wasn't picking up money consistently, so she asked, "How do you do that?"

"Just follow my lead, baby," said the woman. "And on a hot roll, you'll maximize your chips and dollars. I see you've got a bankroll of a thousand, you should play like it."

The elegant woman fingered a two-thousand bankroll after concentrating on her bets. "I have bets on the pass line, the five, eight, and nine, in the field, and all the hard ways, and ten times odds behind the pass line." Florence had never seen that betting scheme before. After all, she has said herself: 'A scared man can't win.' Florence had the dice, so she followed the elegant woman's bets. Her point was SIX so following the leader she made these bets: "80 inside, all the hard ways for five," she did not have to verbalize the bet in the field—a $5 field bet, a $5 pass line bet with ten times odds ($50) behind the pass line. Simple, Florence rolled for the thirty minutes without a seven and amassed four thousand in her rack after fluctuating her bets no more than $35 on a number.

In another part of the casino, Barry and Clare were playing blackjack and losing because of their lack of playing knowledge. Barry played third base and took a hit on a stiff with the dealer showing a 6.

"God damn, why didn't you stand brother," a bearded burly Caucasian man screamed across the table. "I had $200 dollars bet on that hand. Why do you people play this game if you don't understand it?" he kicked back his chair and left muttering.

"I had a count of 16," said Barry confused "That hand can't win shit."

"What he meant is that you should let the dealer bust. You shouldn't take the dealer's bust card," said Clare.

"Shit dude, I'm trying to win, too," said Barry.

Clare stood up, "Maybe we ought to go find Mark so he can teach you how to play or maybe we should just play slots, let's go."

The colorful Luxor bar was lively with people and the Green Bay Packers were playing the San Francisco 49ers for the best record in NFL football and the conference championship on Sunday and a crowd of fans were discussing the game. Mark decided to bet $1,000 on San Francisco. The cool blue theme of the sports bar and multi-colored overhead lamps eased Mark as much as he could be eased. He had already spent $2,000,000 on Vegas tables last year, and to him, the routine was getting old. He was getting a bit paranoid of being noticed and he was able to launder 75% of his heist money by gambling. To him, gambling was slow and hard, and it made him wonder how anybody could be a professional gambler. He had grown into a good Blackjack player only because it didn't hurt so bad losing all of the bets he made if he lost, he could still pay his bills. He knew that 75% of his double downs and splits, he wouldn't have taken if it was money he couldn't lose; otherwise, he wouldn't have placed those bets. Feeling a bit uneasy, Mark watched the room. He eyed security guards, undercover agents, and vacationers just having fun. His eyes were bloodshot, and he looked like he hadn't slept for days.

Later, Florence found Mark in the bar, and they retreated to their luxurious suite with three bedrooms, fireplace, fully equipped kitchen, and plush sofas. He locked a brown paper bag with 100K in bills in the safe. After, he sat in a comfortable sofa and listened to a homemade cassette on his personal boom box. Florence was tucking the kids into bed. The bed was so enormous that they fit comfortably. She kissed each of them on the forehead and tip-toed out of the room.

In another room, Clare kissed an inebriated Barry. "Baby, wait! wait! Let me just rest for a minute."

Clare looked at him with uselessness, "Baby."

She nudged him and loud snoring escaped from his lips.

"You're fucking kidding me," Clare said to herself, and then left.

Mark watched the flames in the fireplace that he started an hour ago and lifted a glass of complimentary champagne to his lips, but it was empty. He walked to the bar. He stopped in his tracks stunned to the hilt to see that Clare was going down on Florence.

Florence saw him from the corner of her eye moaning with pleasure, "Hi, Baby."

"What y'all doing?" Mark asked in sexy shock.

Florence's eyes roll back in her head, "You want to join us?"

He placed his empty glass down on the bar and enthusiastically joined them.

# Chapter 24

At the same time in Los Angeles, Gene strutted down the street donning new blue snake-skinned shoes and a blue silk suit, two diamond rings on both hands. He walked into AMT where they have built the business venue into an Extreme Entertainment Business also. They were booking big acts such as Luther Vandross, Diana Ross, Barry White, R. Kelly, Boys II Men, Heavy D., Seal, Brian McKnight, and Keith Sweat, and growing. Allen and Gene were the masterminds of the agency/venue/client relationship. In the beginning, they would contact existing stars and offer them more money to perform on Soul Train and other major venues in Los Angeles, such as The Greek theatre, The Hollywood Palladium, The Orpheum Theatre, The Avalon Hollywood, Concerts by the Sea, The Troubadour, and more. They met constantly with entertainment attorneys to write iron-clad contracts and let their newfound wealth roll over their competition. The business model for E E was elaborate. With the rise of extreme sports, AMT & E E took advantage of the opportunity to grow. Their store in Carson rented and sold everything from jet skis to parachutes of all makes and models. Their clients ranged from start-up singers, musicians, dancers, and stand-up comedians to Emmy winners. The posters on the wall advertised sports and entertainment personalities and equipment throughout the industries.

When Gene walked in the store, Allen was on the phone. Allen abruptly ended his conversation and confronted Gene, "You're gonna have to get your girl under control before she blows everything to hell."

"Allen, I'm sorry," he concurred. "She's greedy—you know how women can be."

Allen looked around the successful business environment, "Appease her."

"I tried," said Gene with complete understanding.

"I think you can try harder," said Allen with a series of serious looks in his eyes. "Unless you want me to handle it."

"I'll handle it, Allen," said Gene sensing what Allen was capable of. "I know how to take care of my woman."

Outside, sitting in his blue Camaro, Detective Warren like a hound dog is listening with Agent Malone in the passenger's seat.

"After almost two years, we're close to something, I can feel it," said Warren. Agent Malone looks hopeful with a nod of the head in agreement.

At Gene's house in Compton, later on that night, he can still see that sinister gaze in Allen's eyes as he surveyed his decked-out condo. Obviously, while he was putting a lot of time into E E, Priscilla was off spending a lot of money without his knowledge. They didn't mind her spending money, but she was taking it to whole new level, too conspicuous. Although the business was legit, her attitude changed from a hard-working stripper to a condescending, snobbish, pompous asshole and everybody knew it, even her. Her quixotic and peevish attitude made Allen sick, and he was willing to do whatever it took to douse her petulant and furious fire. Allen knew that this woman was the perfect exemplum of being unable to handle success.

Priscilla prepared a bottle while their baby cried, and Gene hovered over her. "I wouldn't be like this if you would've paid more attention to our little family and I didn't have to work at that damn strip club and had all those slimy motherfuckas looking at me like they wanted to fuck my eyeballs out, then chew me up, and then spit me out."

Gene clinched his fists like he wanted to bludgeon her to silence, "What'd you do with that money I gave you?"

"You didn't give me no money," she said whimpering through her teeth.

Out of pure emotion and reflex he grabbed her, "Don't touch me!" she screamed. "I'll call the police."

With his hands shaking her at the shoulders, close to rage, he said, "I gave you money."

Priscilla faced him, "No, you didn't give me money. You told me to invest it. You ain't never give me nothing and—"

Those words stabbed Gene in the heart like a sudden thrust of cold blue steel. Suddenly, red smeared before his eyes, and through a tunnel of hot and boiling rage, he grabbed her frantic-looking face with both hands and squeezed until she screamed and yowled like an annihilated animal.

He threw her to the floor, "What did you invest in, bitch?!"

With minimal control, he looked around the house and saw the new and expensive furniture.

He ran to the kitchen and grabbed a butcher knife. "Did you invest in this?" he sliced the leather furniture into slithers with each barreling blow.

"Gene don't," she helplessly cried.

He went through the living room smashing mirrors, breaking glass tabletops, slashing pictures on the walls, sweeping and smashing figurines off of end tables; he completely destroyed the room. When there's nothing more to fuck up, and he was mentally and physically satiated, he stood in the middle of the room blowing hard. Priscilla laid on the ground crying and sobbing uncontrollably.

Audible baby cries filtered into the room.

"We've got a daughter to raise," said Gene with water in his eyes. "Stop your bullshit threats, greedy ass, and start acting like you a struggling nigga. We ain't got time for that shit."

As Gene closed the door behind him, she reached for whatever she could and flung it after him, the butcher knife stuck in the door. Gene pulled up the U-Haul he rented the day before literally across the yard to the front door of the house and removed all the broken and fractured furniture and loaded it into the truck.

"If you want some more furniture, bitch, use the money I'll give you, now you have my permission."

# Chapter 25

At the same time, at the Luxor Las Vegas, Florence laid in bed. She leaned over to hold Mark, but he had gone to the window.

She stood behind him, "Come to bed?"

"I'm thinking."

Florence rested her head on Mark's shoulder and hugged him around his waist, "You're always thinking. What's the point in having all of this if you can't enjoy it?"

Mark faced her, "Do you enjoy it?"

"Yeah," answered Florence.

"That's what matters," said Mark happily because she was happy. He kissed her, "The other players might be a problem. Go to bed baby, this is me relaxing."

Mark continued to look out the window at the beautiful sights. At this hour in the wee hours of the morning, the Las Vegas Strip is still covered with people in the city that never sleeps. The people really look like they are dancing to the rhythm of the night, bouncing into one another as they pass, nodding and excusing in politeness. The powerful city lights bounce off Mark's face that makes his eyes flutter in dismal and happy thoughts. As his mind races in controlled thoughts, maybe just maybe, the thought crossed his mind, maybe exhaustion will kick in.

The next morning, surprisingly, Mark didn't feel fatigued. Through the skylights, the sunlight melted in as Mark and his family exited the elevator. A man in a black suit caught Mark's eye.

Mark and his family reached the concierge desk, "Pull my car up, please?"

The concierge nodded, bobbed, and weaved and got on his way.

Florence got Mark's attention with a smile, "Baby, me and Clare wanna play the penny slots before we go."

"We should head out."

"Why?"

"Flo," Mark said excitedly, "We need to go."

Mark took off towards the casino floor and the family followed suit. Florence carried Nadine while Malcolm and Freddie held their father's hand as Mark weaved through the crowd.

"Why we walking so fast?" asked Freddie as he half-ran holding on like a dangling garment in the wind.

"My feet hurt," Malcolm cried.

Mark spotted the back door as he pulled at his boys, "C'mon boys!"

Mark pushed on the back door only to be greeted by two Feds. They flashed their badges and ID.

"Come with us, please," demanded one of the Feds. Both were wearing sunglasses and dark suits. They stood out like a sore thumb, Caucasians, average height, and menacing looking.

Florence rushed up behind them, "What's wrong! Why are you detaining my husband?"

"We have a few questions for him," said one of the agents. "We'll call you the moment we know something."

Florence stood there with her mouth agape, eyes moistening, and body quivering slightly noticeable. At another part of the casino, another set of FBI agents took Barry for similar questioning.

In a private back room of the Luxor, Mark and Barry sat at a table in a gaudy lit room with the two federal agents breathing down their throats. "I'm Special Agent Lincoln and he's Special Agent Abraham," they said, flashing their ID. Mark and Barry eyed each other, then switched their gaze back to the agents. "We got word that you checked in with a stolen credit card. May I see each of your identification?" asked Agent Lincoln.

They both reluctantly reached into their back pocket fumbling at the same time for leather. They handed the laminated plastic to Agent Lincoln in the form of identification and credit cards. Lincoln leered at the documents like he already knew something. He studied and matched the information as his facial expressions remained unchanged. He handed the documents to agent Abraham.

"The card's not stolen," said Mark coolly. "It's my card."

"How about you?" asked Special Agent Abraham staring down Barry.

Barry looked like a deer caught in headlights while Mark fought to stay calm as beads of sweat formed on his brow. Barry cut the tension, "I've never stolen anything in my life. This is crazy. Is it hard to believe that a couple of black guys can afford all this?"

"Relax," said Agent Lincoln.

"Chill man," said Mark. "We didn't do anything wrong," he said, switching his gaze to both agents.

"I don't know about that," said Agent Lincoln as he scoured Mark up and down with his eyes with a looming look of disaster.

Agent Abraham sensed fear, "Both of you look guilty to me."

Mark and Barry jumped at a sharp knock at the door. A young local police officer, Caucasian with blonde hair and blue eyes, about 6'1" and some change, quickly relayed some information to Agent Lincoln who got the door. He left the door cracked as illegible voice undertones reached Mark's ears.

The voices ceased and Agent Lincoln reentered the room and sat, "Looks like two brothers fitting your description were the ones we're looking for. They just got picked up at another hotel."

Agent Abraham handed Mark and Barry back their documents, "Sorry for the inconvenience."

Barry felt his wild oats in a moment of triumph, "Y'all should be ashamed of yourselves, harassing some young black men for no reason."

Mark is visibly irritated at the comment, "Man, would you shut up!" He angrily pulled Barry out of the room.


Leaving the bright lights of Vegas far behind on the I-15 North, Florence squeezed Mark's upper leg by the crotch from the passenger's seat. "See baby, I told you, we don't got nothing to worry about."

Mark nodded unconvincingly, "I wish everything can turn out like that." He looked out the rearview mirror and then the back window by the turning of his head. The sky seemed endless but not with calmness in the dotted white clouds.

# Chapter 26

In the interior of the MDC the following day, Warren and Malone are at their desks when Priscilla approaches them carrying her baby.

"Thanks for calling," said Detective Warren, "You've been directed to us because the nature of your call. How can we help you?"

"I know who did that Dunbar Heist a couple of years ago," she said as she opens her purse and pulls out a handful of sequentially dated cash straps and places them on Detective Warren's desk. Of course, she had thought it over in her mind time and time again. When Gene squeezed her face, he looked like the devil himself. It didn't help that Gene carried both Priscilla and James to a remote location and roughed them up. She thought about their baby and if Gene killed her, the baby would be without a mother. At least the child should have a mother. She still had some of the money left Gene had given her. She also knew about the reward of $125,000 offered by Lloyd's of London for leads to the arrest of the robbers—

Detective Warren made sure of that. She'd use it to go to school, pay bills, and make a better life for herself without the devil and evil in her life.

When Gene got the call from Detective Warren on his private line at AMT, he knew that he had fucked up and landed himself in a pile of shit. But after two years, he would try to come up smelling like a rose. Besides EE and AMT were going strong and all six partners in crime were growing with the business.

In the interrogation interview at the MDC, Gene sat with the confidence of a King. He wasn't poor and despicable, but rich and on the verge of infamy.

"Where were you on the night of September 12, 1997?" asked Detective Warren.

Bells started ringing and then a continuous peal of bells went off in Gene's head. Before that question, he had been hearing beautiful chimes, but now, his ears screeched and blipped with worry. "I don't recollect that night, should I?"

"Maybe or maybe not," said Detective Warren. "Let me tell you what happened that night: the Dunbar facility was robbed of $18.9 million, and you must know that it was the largest cash heist in American history year-to-date. Now, does that date ring any bells?"

Gene was flushed inside, but tried to keep a straight face, "Yeah, that was in the news, some real hot shit. Everybody who is somebody, I guess, heard about that."

"You know, according to the law, whoever was involved can get as much as twenty-five years, unless a deal is offered," said Agent Malone.

Gene felt a slight shiver run up and down his spine, "Whoever did that shit is probably long gone by now and moved out of the country."

"I beg to differ, son," said Detective Warren. "You see, I've always maintained that it was an inside job. In fact, over time we deduced the suspects to one suspect, Allen Pace III. Does that name ring a bell?"

Gene exploded inside. Both law preservers noticed a slight twinge in Gene's demeanor. Gene gathered as much of himself as he could, "I never heard of that name in my circle of friends."

Detective Warren opened a manila folder full of incriminating evidence that was on the table when Gene walked in, "Have you ever seen this guy before, or better yet, do you know him?" The pieces of paper he was clutching, he showed it to Gene.

*A picture of Allen and the wire transfers.*

A feeling of defeat choked in Gene's throat and his face darkened a-half-a-shade. The detective removed more pictures from the file folder and showed them to Gene. He was now at a dozen and counting. Those previous pictures were just jabs when he showed him the picture of himself with the other five guys that was the knockout blow.

Gene fought back tears and could see everything crumbling right before his eyes, "I didn't take no money from no Dunbar heist," he screamed like everything on his body was tasered but his mouth.

The trained law officers were dismantling a financial monstrosity brick by brick. Then, Detective Warren removed some money wrappers from a sable pouch lying in the file, "Do you recognize these?"

Gene felt the vice tighten around his life to the point of suffocation. His breaths were now sporadic and off-beat like a first grader in a Yale University classroom. He thought about requesting a lawyer, "I'm not saying another word without my attorney present."

Warren smiled, "An attorney sure would be a present for you right now, but Christmas just passed, and besides, it's tied up with lace ribbon and a chiffon-lace bow but I don't think you're gonna like what's in it. If you make a deal with me right now, I swear you'll be out of a federal prison in five to eight years or even immunity from prosecution. I want two things right now: Allen Pace III and whatever's left of the money. And if you don't go for the deal, I'll do all I can to help every judge in the county shoot for the entire time the law allows for aggravated strong-arm robbery—25 years."

Caught between a runaway train and a stone wall, Gene's emotional and angry side began to flourish. He felt it like a hot spring geyser rising from his feet, slowly crawling upward. Every agreement that he ever agreed to with the guys flew out the window and flew away to another world. A lawyer would cost money, but he had money. Besides, the money he had, he would always have until the day he died.

With anger diluting rationality, he finally looked up with red fire and tears in his eyes, "I want that shit in writing about the five-year deal or immunity. Hell, I'll move to Mexico when this shit is over. I always wanted some real Mexican pussy."

"We're going to need a list of names," said Malone, who was present and part of the tag team from way back.

"Hold on just one god damn minute," said Gene, "I need my affidavit first."

***

It has been said and everybody knows, or they should know, that a chain is only as strong as its weakest link. And where does strength come from? Some say you're born with it. Some say it can be learned or gained. It's also said that we're all selfish by nature, but some believe we learn this widespread attribute. I tend to agree with the former, and we learn how not to be the latter. A noble man or woman just as the captain of a ship at sea will go down with the ship if anyone alive is still on it.

But Gene was not the captain of the Dunbar Heist, just a link in a chain.

***

Gene started scribbling for more than an hour, listening to the clock tick away his freedom. When he finished reeling, he stretched his arms out across the table.

# Chapter 27

The next day at AMT and E E, Allen, Mark, and Travis talked strategy, shop, and generalities in the back room while other employees worked with customers and established clients.

"It turned out we just looked like two other brothers they were looking for," said Mark jocularly.

"That's crazy man. Fate can be a motherfucker," said Travis.

Mark still holding his gut and laughing, "The Fed even apologized for the inconvenience." The guys continued to laugh and down beer after beer.

Later that night and a little buzzed from the beers and juiced and geeked up from the conversation, Mark unwarily jumped in the Plymouth Voyager and slowly drove off with a blue Camaro on his tail. Minutes later, he pulled into his driveway in Compton. He turned off the engine, sat there, and breathed a sigh of relief for his recent encounter with the FBI and getting home tonight without incident. Suddenly, without usual notice, some flashing bright red, white, and blue lights reflected in his rear-view mirror, hitting mark in the eyes so hard that he shaded his face with his right hand. The lights stop flashing. The blue Camaro was in plain sight now and revved its engine, making an ominous and menacing sound as if to say 'I gotcha.' With tinted windows and engine screaming, the sound seemed to echo and reverberate throughout the entire neighborhood.

The sound drew Mark out of his car. The car backed up into the tip of Mark's driveway, stopped, and peeled rubber for twenty feet as it sped down the street. Mark ran out into the street and watched the dark mass turn the corner as the foreboding sound reached back and seemed to handcuff him by the soul.

Detective Warren looked in his rearview mirror and grinned as Mark stood in the middle of the street. Mark grabbed his cell and immediately made a call. Allen answered; Mark spoke eerily and quickly while standing under the streetlamps, "Yo Allen, this Mark. We gotta talk," he waivered. "We gotta talk. Things are heating up." Mark hung up, took a deep, deep breath and looked towards the starry sky. He seemed to be searching for something up there in the stars.

Florence noticed him and quickly ran out to the street, "I heard all that noise, are you okay, what's going on?"

He walked towards her, "Nothing, go back inside."

The following night in the back room of the strip club in Carson, Mark is having an orgy. His phone rings at the same time he's having a paralyzing nut. After the phone had rung several times, he let it go to voice mail. His partner's simultaneous orgasm burst with screams and now she was kissing and licking his dick with her teeth and tongue, desperately trying to keep the flesh hard for another round. Occasional screams of pleasure sporadically rang across the tiny dressing room that stuffed twelve people on the shag-carpeted floor and sheet-covered couches. To Mark, this orgy was like a present to himself, spending time with his partners in crime before something else happened.

The following day, Allen and Travis closed big, important deals with major clients as Mark drifted and daydreamed into another world. He was devoutly distracted. Allen noticed his peculiar behavior and pulled him aside, "What is going on with you?"

"I'm seeing shit," said Mark in a quandary.

"Blue Camaro," resounded Allen.

Fear covered Marks face, "You know it?"

"He's trying to rattle you," said Allen. "Just be cool. Go party and take your mind off of things."

"I don't buy this. Something is brewing and it's not beer," said Mark.

"Man, you know I always got your back, right?" Mark acceded with a nod. Allen continued, "I mean it. I always got that bag of marbles on me just waiting for the right moment."

Mark drove home later that day with the bag of marbles on his mind. Marbles are one thing but stealing somebody else's money was another. He walked in the room of his house and changed his clothes.

Florence saw him come in and dress to leave without a word, "Where are you going?"

Before Mark exited the living room door, Florence blocked his path, "Move Flo."

"Mark, we can deal with this together, whatever the hell is going on," encouraged Florence.

Mark looked away, out the front living room door, "I need some space."

"Your grandmother called earlier," said Florence. "I fixed her a plate of food. She wants to see you."

Grandma Pearl's house was always the acme of comfort for Mark, ever since he could remember. All through school, he did his best thinking there. There was no better protection in the world because the walls seemed to calmly talk to him and the floors seemed to hold him up when he was falling and the rooms relieved the pain and strain of everyday life.

Grandma Pearl unwrapped the plate of food, "Ooohhh, she didn't have to do all this."

"She was cooking anyway, it ain't nothin'," said Mark as if he was standing beside himself.

"Mark, c'mon now, anytime a woman does anything, you need to show her a little bit of gratitude, otherwise she may claw your eyes out when you least expect it."

"Where's mama at?" asked Mark lookin around.

"On some date with a man I ain't fond of," she said taking a bite of food. "This is gooood."

"The way of the world," philosophizes Mark.

She notices Mark lost in thought, "What's going on, baby?"

"I wish it was Marvin Gaye's song right now. But it's true that mothers are crying and far too many brothers are dying. We've got to find a way to bring some lovin' here today. Fathers, we don't need to escalate. War is not the answer, only love can conquer hate." He said in a more alluring tone than Grandma Pearl had ever heard, "I gotta tell you something, but I don't want you to be disappointed in me."

"Baby, whatever you got to say, I'm always gonna be yo' grandma, no matter what."

That same night, Mark was a bit relieved from his talk with Grandma Pearl for she really lived up to her name, Pearl!, because out of all the precious gems to be found on earth, it's not the refraction but the infraction of the substance for the understanding of life. She said that success is like riding in an airplane because from afar, looking at the ground, it looks like you're crawling but in reality, you're traveling 300mph.

The next morning, while in their bedroom, Florence was getting ready for work, "Baby, can you take me to work? Clare needs to use the Plymouth Voyager today."

"Can you find a ride home?"

"Sure," she said as she grabbed her coat.

On the way to work, Florence and Mark sat in silence. She looked in the backseat and noticed a box of chocolates, a stuffed animal, and a large duffle bag as Mark sees her face cover over with happiness and excitement, "I was s'pose to give that to you yesterday, but—"

She leaned over and kissed him. "It's okay," she said as she smiles at the chocolates and teddy bear.

"You're the best, baby," said Mark already realizing her deep understanding.

"I was thinking, maybe we could go away somewhere together; just me and you. My sister-in-law can watch the kids and we could get to know one another again."

Mark saw something in the rearview mirror—a blue car—false alarm. Florence said concerned, "Baby, did you hear me?"

"Yeah, baby, yeah, that sounds nice," Mark answered through the distraction.

They pulled up in front of her job; Florence felt that Mark was distant. She got out, "Baby, I need you here with me," she said before she slammed the car door. Florence felt the slam of the door echo through her body and her mind reflected something sinister as if she'd never see Mark again. Mark drove off while she hugged the Valentine's gifts in a loathsome clutch.

While driving down Crenshaw Boulevard, Mark turned the music dial up to an ear-splitting volume as he listened to 'I believe I can Fly' by R. Kelly. Those all too familiar red, white, and blue flashing lights glowed behind him. Behind the glare, he saw three Crown Victoria's following him. He heard the whining sound of a helicopter above, but he can't see it; it's so close that he could hear the whirling blades whistle through the air. Scared, he punched the pedal to the metal and ran a series of red lights on an uncrowded street, but two Crown Victoria's are nailed by oncoming traffic, but still, one Crown Victoria is coming hard in earnest pursuit. Mark grinned as the fear had worn off and turned into sheer survival and he made a quick turn down a narrow alley.

The helicopter pilot spoke into the helicopter's loudspeaker, "Changing route with my eye on the prize, over." The helicopter's powerful beam of light stretched straight like a long mighty arm of inescapable power in the early morning, as it stuck to the Plymouth Voyager's every move. The helicopter changed direction and followed the chase as Detective Warren kept the helicopter in sight. The helicopter pilot spoke into the radio again, "The driver of the Plymouth Voyager with license plate number FLO 4EVR, pull your vehicle over immediately." Through the cracked driver's side window, Mark heard every word as if it was a death sentence. He didn't panic, but he was scared as hell. Detective Warren stayed with the chase as Agent Malone sat in the passenger seat jabbering into the radio bouncing from side to side.

"He's a slippery motherfucker," said Detective Warren with a little worry in his voice.

Mark reached behind the driver's seat and retrieved the duffle bag that he named "FUBU"— For Us By Us—and put it in his lap. A thought flashed in his mind, then he turned east towards the original neighborhood—Compton/Carson. Flying down Alondra, he crossed Main and turned right on Avalon and right on 169th street and began throwing handfuls of paper bills from the driver's seat. As the police helicopter filmed the chase, other networks picked up the action news. Local news stations scrambled helicopters and the chase broke on all the major news stations. People stopped in the neighborhood, picking up one hundred and twenty dollar bills. Mark rolled through familiar streets of old friends, childhood crushes, and partying holes, flicking out legal tender form fender to fence. They saw him coming on the TV and they lined the streets fighting over and picking up bills. The police were discouraged by the onlooking recipients of all ages—old ladies and men and children. It rained money for more than twenty minutes.

Still speaking in the radio, Agent Malone's volume eked, "This is Agent Malone requesting back-up."

The chase was on and in full swing. Tires screeched and rubber burned as they hit hair-pin turns, jumped curbs, sideswiped parked vehicles, and sirens blasted as other cop cars joined in the chase. In the excitement, Mark didn't think freeway, just driving as long as he could until he was caught. He turned down a side street into a cul-de-sac and thought about running, but he exited with his hands high in the air as an automatic response. Warren ran up with gun in hand, spun Mark around, and handcuffed him while Malone read him his Miranda Rights.

Warren held Mark's head and shoved him into the backseat, but not before he said one thing, "Didn't think we'd catch you, did you?"

Mark looked up with something else other than fear in his eyes, "Everybody gets caught."

That line triggered something in Detective Warren of something that happened a long time ago at a bank robbery in Compton when Warren said that same thing to a child; it was the eyes that brought the memory back, those mirrors to the soul, those mirrors to life, those mirrors to the truth. They locked eyes for a long moment. The truth passed between both of them and then

Mark's thoughts took him away: *I read somewhere once that there are no such things as coincidences; that we were born with our souls intertwined with one another—and one day, this connection will be illuminated. So me and Warren, we were always connected.*

Then Warren tamped Mark down into the back seat of the car. The city lights burned like a furnace as they bounced off Mark's face. Like the millet in bread and life's teamwork in relationships is a basic ingredient in living and prospering. Mark knew that his goose was cooked in the light from the city lights and zooming car headlights that bounced off glass that all danced in Mark's face. His look seemed to soften. His stress seemed to dissipate. He finally breathed.

At Brigg's and Malone's personal offices on Sepulveda and Wilshire, Mark sat in the interrogation room ready to deny everything they threw at him. Detective Warren entered the room with impudence written all over his face, but a subtle reverence creeped across his brow that Mark noticed. Warren pulled back a chair, sat, and flopped a collage of pictures on the table, "If you fight us, we're going to fuck you up. We don't pick up nobody until we know we can win a case. There's nothing you've done in the past two years that we don't know about. We knew what color your shit was on Thursday and every day of the week and, son, you need to eat more veggies. I actually could have stuck my finger up your punk ass and gave you a woody, that's how attached I am to you motherfucker. If you fight us, you'll be a very old man, before you get out of jail."

Mark was taken aback by this lawman. While he was trying to sidle and handle millions, this lawman was accumulating scores of evidential pictures against him and his cronies. The demeanor of the FBI quickly grew on Mark before he saw the pictures. Right then, the thought of the old maxim flashed across his mind, 'The long arm of the law' had never been truer. Then he saw the pictures reaching back as far as two years ago—the clubs, the parties, the Vegas trips, all six guys of the robbery, all their kids, wives, girlfriends, and associates; he laughed and cried when he saw clear, glossy-colored pictures of Grandma Pearl. At that moment, common sense gobbled up Mark's pride like a famished wolf on a sheep. There was no need to fight any more in a losing battle. Plans are steppingstones to a higher place to a finer zone. Out of all the plans they'd ever planned, they seemed to be exploding in Mark's face. "Don't I get a fuckin' phone call?"

Detective Warren looked at Mark with angst, "Calling a lawyer is a waste of time. Johnny Cochran wouldn't have a snowball's chance in hell to get your punkass off." He paused looking down at his stack of pictures, "We have this motherfucker in custody," growled Detective Warren, pointing at Gene's picture. "And he sang like a bird in front of the Stellenbosch University Choir."

At the mention of Johnny Cochran, Mark's mind began to see possibilities of hope. The O. J. Simpson trial was one of the biggest, widely covered trials of the decade and O.J. was acquitted when most of the populace thought he did it, especially the white populace. Since Detective Warren was white, Mark sensed that Warren felt the same way. The case was so popular that Mark himself had done some personal research on Johnny Cochran just in case the team needed him. In his research, he found that Johnny represented Tupac Shakur, Todd Bridges, Jim Brown, Snoop Dogg, Riddick Bowe, Reginald Oliver Denny, Geronimo Pratt, and Marion Jones.

Most of his clients were black athletes or entertainers who were underprivileged in terms of the law. Johnny Cochran, known as the man with the 'Magic Touch,' for getting Tupac released from New York's Riker Island prison for allegedly sexually assaulting a Manhattan, New York woman on $1.4 million bail. Todd Bridges was acquitted for cocaine abuse. Jim Brown was acquitted for rape charges. Snoop Dogg was acquitted of murder charges. Riddick Bowe was acquitted for kidnapping charges. Mark thought his representation of Reginald Oliver Denny was brilliant because everybody thought he was a black man's lawyer, but he was taking a white man's case. He sued the police department for not protecting a white man's civil rights in a black man's neighborhood because they intentionally vacated and deserted the neighborhood and wouldn't return. He won a $450 million settlement for Geronimo Pratt for false imprisonment. He successfully defended Marion Jones for being accused of doping during her high school career. Mark's research was extensive, but on second thought, he didn't call Johnny, he called Phillip, "Hello Uncle Phillip."

"Is this you, Mark?"

"Yeah, they got me uncle. I was thinking about calling Johnny, but I called you instead."

"Calling Johnny just gone cost you mo' money," said Uncle Phillip in cracked words. "If you did it, you did it. I know you brothers had a plan on if you got caught. Now, the shit done hit the fan. If the other guys haven't squealed like a pig, they probably will. Now, you gotta watch yo' own ass. Now, you mentally free but physically locked up. That will give you enough time to think about yo' future. You still young, you can get through it."

"Thanks, Unc, I'll see you later."

When Mark hung up the phone, he felt as free as the times when he was in Vegas. Although he saw pictures that they took of him in Vegas at the slot machines, bars, and gaming tables; he at no time felt threatened because he thought within the city limits of Vegas was his only escape from a $20 million weight on his shoulders. It was a home away from home. With tears in his eyes, Mark reviewed the pictures and he remembered somebody saying, 'a picture is worth a thousand words,' but as he perused over these pictures, they were speaking more like a million words. The memories were distinct and dominating, his friend's smiling faces and their girlfriends' and wives' happy faces. His wife's smiling face and his kid's joyful faces. Grandma Pearl's smiling face. All the places where he had hung out, the probing cameras had been. How could he have known? They discussed the possibility of being investigated, but they were like ghosts in his life—they were there but they weren't there. When Mark finished viewing over 100 photos, he leered at Detective Warren, "What the fuck do we do now?"

"The way I see it, son, you give us the rest of the money; tell us everything you know, and only then we can make a deal," said Warren.

Mark sucked in a large swath of air, "What kind of deal?"

"Five years instead of twenty-five, son."

Mark's throat fell to his stomach. His best friend wasn't around with a bag of marbles. The detective was throwing mental punches hard and straight enough to knock him out. He knew that he had a right to have an attorney present, but what the fuck was that gone do? Prolong the inevitable, patch up an unpatchable hole, try to put a ban-aid on a neck of a decapitated head, and try to save the world from its sins.

"I ain't got no money, I gave it all away," said Mark with a strong undertone.

"Who were the other guys involved?"

"I ain't gone tell you shit that you already know," said Mark with tears in his eyes.

"That's not the way it works," said Detective Warren with a clam voice. "That's not the way the game is played. You played ball on your own turf two years ago when you robbed the federal government, hard-working people, and honest taxpayers of their money. You also terrorized the shit out of innocent people. Now, the game is being played on my turf and you have the last inning to score. It's up to you; you can make contact or strike out. You're going to do time, but it's a question of how much time."

Mark reluctantly listened, "I didn't rob the taxpayers; I robbed the Federal Government and I like football better than baseball."

Detective Warren cringed and a silent thought ran across his mind—*this motherfucker is slippery. I knew I knew him*—Detective Warren pushed a pad and pen within Mark's reach, "You either write or roll the dice."

"I'd rather do 100 years than to tell on my friends," said Mark sniffling.

Detective Warren smiled with remorse, "I've got news for you, son. I truly admire your nobleness, but that dignity may not be worth twenty years or twenty cents because I already told you those very guys you are trying to protect have thrown you to the wolves, under the bus. You are exposed as a drunken and drugged-out whore in an army barracks. Either you sing your own song, or you may never get the chance to sing again."

Mark had watched the Godfather movies, all three parts, and he knew the meaning of the words "snitch" and "fink" and "rat," besides, he remembered their agreement and was willing to stand beside and honor it, "I don't believe a word you say. You have pictures, but I don't believe my friends would tell on me, and if they did, I won't tell on them."

"I can believe how naïve you are, son. You're young and uninformed with your whole life ahead of you," said Detective Warren.

"And my life wouldn't be shit being a snitch," bellowed Mark.

"Did you burn money in Gene's garage?"

Mark caught the drift before his mind could accept the anger, and he gave Warren the most pitiful look he couldn't have known. Nobody in the world could have known that but him and Gene. Reality took precedence over the metaphysical management of faith. Mark felt the pressure taking over his body like a disease, "Yeah, I did it on September 12, 1997."

"Did you have keys?"

"No."

"Who had keys?"

"If Gene told you about the burnt money, he told you who had keys," sniveled Mark. "I ain't no snitch."

"How many were involved?" asked Warren.

"I was involved," said Mark. "Let those other motherfuckas give you the details you want. You got us all on film. What more do you want?"

"I'll tell you what I want," said Detective Warren in a rage. "I want the rest of the money and I wanna know where it is right now."

"I told you," said Mark with cleared eyes now. "What I didn't spend I gave it all away."

Detective Warren wanted Mark to turn over like a sleeping cat, "You're going to cook for this. I'm gonna throw you under the jail where the boilers are flaming hot. You'll probably never get out."

"I'm sorry detective," said Mark. "That's not your decision to make."

Handcuffed and bewildered, they took Mark to MDC on Alameda and the 101 freeway where he was locked up till the arraignment.

# Chapter 28

In light of the evidence gathered against Gene Upshaw and his formal written confession, Detective Warren attempted to convince the DA while making a surprise visit at his personal residence to unleash the wolves.

"You want me to play judge, jury, and executioner based on your current evidence is like putting a noose around my own neck," said the DA.

"But sir," said Detective Warren with fire in his eyes, "I've got written confession from Gene Upshaw and the new compelling evidence that the broken taillight from the U-Haul rented by Gene Upshaw is a match. Gene Upshaw is loaded with cash. Through our research we know that he has multiple visas. The rest of his gang can disappear tomorrow, and they could literally transform into some ghosts. I mean, disappear into thin air. Once they find out about Upshaw, they'll have the means and the motive to lam out. We're both on the same team. We put criminals away. I realize that the judge can kick your ass over an arrest if we don't get a conviction, but this guy is guilty as sin and I got original money wrappers, eyewitnesses, and the lab just gave me word on that busted taillight is a match, and we know that Gene Upshaw rented the truck the day before and took it back in a reasonable time after the robbery. If we don't get them now, I'm afraid we're going to lose the opportunity to get all of them. We've been following this case for over two years, and I don't wanna lose one motherfucker."

The DA listened with scrutiny and weighed the legal ramifications against the new-found evidence, and he said, "Go get their asses."

In a well-coordinated effort of well-informed manpower and intelligence, law enforcement officers of L.A. County unleashed their powerful arms to grab their number one suspect and other suspects in the largest and smoothest cash heist robbery in American history. A bevy of radio calls rang out over police communications networks, and the law quickly scrambled towards their objective.

Simultaneously, outside Mann's Chinese Theatre located on 6925 Hollywood Boulevard in Hollywood, California, and a Los Angeles Historic-Cultural Monument, Henry is seated with popcorn and soda in hand getting ready to watch The Godfather, II, III, a limited release and marathon. Henry loved going to the movies alone and The Godfather was his favorite movie. He had planned on being there for the duration. A patrol car rolled up and the giant awesome awning on the theatre reads: 'The Godfather Marathon' and magnificent mural displays Marlon Brando dressed in black tuxedo with a red posy on his left notch lapel and a black puppeteer's hand holding a rood lever with pendulous rods.

Two armed men jump out of the unmarked patrol car and enter the theatre. Henry, by now is enjoying the movie as his focus is superimposed on the images of the movie. A funny scene rolls, a bloody horse head in the bed, he grinned, revealing a whole mouthful of shiny and straight teeth. He felt something strange and cold against his right temple and neck. He turned and looked slightly upward. Shiny gold and silver badges fill his eyes. He knows. He closed his eyes in defeat. Henry walked down a theatre aisle in handcuffs and outside, he's shoved into the unmarked police car as a parade of people watch in shame.

Tyronne is lying in bed in the Snooty Fox motel in West L.A. with a smile painted on his face as a sweet tenderoni rides him like a rodeo star. Her firm D's bouncing to the rhythm of "Rapper's Delight" and her hips thrusting and swiveling with the power of a jackhammer while Tyronne's face twists and contorts with poignant pleasure. Three SWAT members burst through the door and the sweet young thang jumps up and screams, and Tyronne is paralyzed with fear and ignorance in his birthday suit. Being overpowered, he said nothing with a knee in his back squirming under the pinion of the handcuffs and assault rifles pointed at his head and emotionally distraught because he was naked and didn't have time to catch a nut. His woody petered faster than a DeLorean.

At the same time, Travis sat in the AMT office examining the day's books when SWAT officers leveled the door with a hand-held, piston-loaded, steel barge batter ram without any prior notice followed by Detective Warren and Agent Malone with revolvers in hand carrying large sacks on their backs from which wooden handles could be seen.

"What the fuck," screamed Travis as a bevy of assault rifles kissed his face.

"Get on the ground!" screamed a SWAT officer. They quickly stormed the shop with itchy trigger fingers searching every inch of the room and found the back-office door and immediately broke it open with the battering ram in one motion. Seconds prior, Allen had caught his nut from a blow job and laid relaxed on a couch breathing hard when he first noticed the assault rifles through dreamy eyes. The SWAT is yelling vulgar instructions as the woman who delivered the blow job is reduced to mortal fear, "Please don't shoot! Don't shoot! Don't shoot!"

Allen said nothing, trying to figure out what the fuck is going on, while Detective Warren rushed in his face, "You're under arrest motherfucker for the Dunbar heist. You have the right to remain silent. If you say anything, motherfucker, it can and will be used against you in a court of law. You have the right to an attorney. If you cannot afford an attorney, one would be provided for you. However, in your case, affording an attorney shouldn't be a problem. Do you understand these rights, nigga?" Now, motherfucker, do you have anything to say to me? The language alone told the whole story. Now, he was a nigga like he always was. As long as they had the upper hand, he'd always be a nigga to certain ones, anyway.

"You-can't-do-this," stammered Allen. "I'm innocent!"

"The judge or jury will make that decision and we'll make sure you get your day in court, motherfucker," spoke Detective Warren.

Allen thought of Mark and the bag of marbles. Somebody took his marbles while he wasn't looking. He instinctively reached for his pocket; his pants were still down.

"Freeze, motherfucker," said Detective Warren.

Allen couldn't move a muscle, not even bat an eye, in a reversal of disgusting irony. They wanted a reason to kill a nigga and a motherfucka. Who? He thought of Gene and Priscilla—God damn! *I should have killed that bitch like I wanted to. Gene was always the weakest motherfucka in the group. He let that bitch fuck us all, instead of getting fucked.* They dragged out Allen and Travis together. They looked at each other in total defeat, but in the back of the mastermind's mind, he always carried an extra bag of marbles somewhere.

"Alright guys," bellowed Detective Warren handing out huge bags. "Let's dig, that money is here somewhere."

A well-decorated shop was being torn to bits at the walls with shiny-tipped axes. Particle board chips, drywall dust, and wood fragments were flying everywhere and whizzing past Allen's ears. A thick fog of Drywall dust began to settle heavily on Travis's and Allen's head and clothes. Expensive inventory was being chopped up like firewood. Priceless memorabilia was being smashed and ripped like yesterday's trash. If they kept it up, thought Allen, it would cost thousands of dollars and invaluable memories to repair and replace. Each swing of the ax cost money, big money.

They were getting tired now. "Why are you stopping?" screamed Warren.

Four officers demolished an entire fifty-foot wall before Detective Malone ordered them to stop.

Then Agent Malone stepped to the forefront, "Warren, there's nothing here."

Warren grabbed an ax and went to the walls himself, and with every thrust, he spoke, "We. Just. Have. To. Look. A. Little. Harder." He stopped and took some breaths, "I won't have some petty, uneducated street thugs outsmart me." He lifted the axe and delivered one powerful final blow to the wall.

# Chapter 29

Detective Warren wanted this one on his own. He was like a vicious attack dog given the order to attack. He had been chained up and tethered by the law that he had sworn to protect and serve for over two years now because he didn't have the evidence, he needed to do what he liked best— putting criminals behind steel bars.

Allen sat in a room at the MDC with pinioned hands and feet like he had done to his coworkers just two years ago.

This situational irony never crossed Allen's mind, but detective Warren salivated at the mouth to remind Allen, "How does it feel to be the one tied up like you did to hard-working people in the break room of the Dunbar facility."

Allen felt the sting, "I never tied anybody up."

Detective Warren pulled out his dossier full of pictures and flung them on the table so hard that Allen felt the whiff of wind tickle the hairs on his face, "We know everything you've done since the robbery. It's only common sense it had to be an inside job. Smooth as silk is an understatement as to how you pulled this shit off, and needless to say, you're smooth as silk yourself, but that smoothness is about to get as jagged, jaded, and as rough as a motherfucker. You're about to go down, son."

Allen viewed the pictures with a grain of salt, "So you've got a bunch of pictures, photos, or whatever you wanna call'em. But the last time I checked, in order to have a murder, you need a corpus delicti and in order to have a robbery, you don't necessarily need the money, but you need evidence to prove anything."

"Why do you think you're here, son?" said Detective Warren.

"Because I wanna be is not the answer. I'm here because your ass dragged me down here," snapped Allen.

"Why do you think you're handcuffed, and your feet are bound?" Detective Warren said with contempt.

"Accusations!"

"There's overwhelming evidence against you, son," said Detective Warren. "And any jury in the land will probably find you guilty."

Detective Warren smiled a victory smile. He thought, "Those guys who you thought were your friends have sung the prettiest song ever sang. In fact, we have the musical notes written in four-four time with the treble clef symbol neatly printed at the beginning on the staff complete with five lines and four spaces."

"Yeah, right!" Allen snapped. "I'm innocent til proven guilty, and you got nothin' but a bunch of circumstantial evidence and their words against mine."

Detective Warren let Allen talk, then he reached into his bag of tricks and pulled out a yellow sequenced money wrapper, "Does this ring a bell?"

When Allen saw that all-familiar cash wrapper, he gulped. He slightly breathed offbeat, his eyes darkened a tad, his hands shook and shimmied ever so slightly, "We can call my lawyer in now. This is bullshit."

In their formal agreement, it was stated that if Sharpio had to join the interrogation, it would cost Allen, substantially more money. The ace in the hole had been played and Allen wanted to trump it. Now, he was willing to spend every dollar he was worth to stay out of jail—a sudden switch from arrogance to defensive.

Detective Warren rose and trudged out of the room. He returned momentarily with Attorney Sharpio.

"What's the problem?" asked Sharpio.

Before anyone said a word, Attorney Sharpio noticed a melancholy look on Allen's face, but a flicker of light danced in Warren's eyes.

"Your client is guilty of robbing the downtown Dunbar facility, and I'm going to lock his ass up until he's an old man," said Warren with the ferocity of a famished mountain lion searching for food.

"Hold on now," said Sharpio. "You can't take the law into your own hands and make verbal threats without evidence. My client is an American born citizen, and he has certain inalienable rights. Watch what you say detective. It can be used against you in a court of law."

"Very well said by a high-priced attorney, but I have indisputable proof that your client is as guilty as hell in the firelight of sin, and the law will dice and fry him like a big fish. Zorro is my favorite movie and Zorro always gets his man," said Warren with the arrogance of an Aragon Knight.

"The knights of Aragon were a secret and proud group, detective, and the law prevails in this country. Unless you have what you say is indisputable proof, my client walks out of here a free man, right now," said Sharpio with equal fierceness. "Now, we would like to see that indisputable proof that you claim you have."

"Fuck FRCP rules, I have overwhelming evidence against your client as the mastermind of the Dunbar Heist. He had the opportunity and the motive as a trusted employee to subdue, threaten, and take corporeal advantage of innocent-minded people. This motherfucker had esoteric knowledge of the facility and five motherfuckers who he trained, schooled, and procured to commit the heist, and I have at least one accomplice who will testify in court against this smart-ass Allen Pace III. There is no way you, Sharpio, can emotionally or legally or rhetorically wiggle your way out of this shutdown case," Warren said while placing a brown money wrapper on the table dated and initialed.

When Allen saw the wrapper, his heart jumped a beat and froze over like the Arctic Ocean in the wintertime. When Sharpio saw the wrapper, he mentally calculated several defense maneuvers. Sharpio also thought if this were a boxing match, since he'd been a fight fan for years, he just took a sharp, paralyzing blow to the gut. "You could have found that on the street. That piece of paper has no connection to my client."

"The court will establish the connections. I've done my job and earned my money, and the Lord knows I didn't have to take it by gunpoint from innocent people," said Warren."

With the production of the wrapper, Allen thought back to Mark and Gene on the very day he told them to get rid of the money. Bills that should have never been taken and bills he should have taken care of himself. In fact, there are a lot of things he should've taken care of himself. But, he's only one man with a weak link in the band.

"This is more than a piece of paper," said Warren. "This is a twenty-five-year sentence."

Sharpio saw which way this case was going. He had defended guilty clients before, and this case was pointed in the same direction. But his job was to make the best out of a bad situation. If his client was guilty, his job was to make him less guilty. After discovery, he would know everything they had, and they wouldn't be here unless they had something. "Okay detective, you've made your point. We'll see you in court."

Allen had not been granted bail.

Like the pressure in a paper pipe, Allen poured over material for weeks getting ready for the other shoe to fall. He wanted Johnny Cochran as a lawyer, but he was out of town on another case, Allen was told. Yes, he knew in his heart that he was the kingpin of the largest cash heist in American history that only two years ago saturated every media outlet known to man. He found another lawyer through family and friends.

No matter what, he wanted legal representation for an already convicted man—himself. He wanted to make the best out of a bad situation, choose between the lesser of two or more evils. With his ducks in a row from his perspective he'd fight this case forever. Now, within the MDC on a turn of events, Allen reflected on his initial interrogation in the same room in the same seat and by the same detective. He knew that he had come full circle and this time he was the caught culprit, but he would deny every accusation in the book despite what anybody said. He would never confess to this capital crime of epic monetary proportions.

# Chapter 30

On the day of the arraignment, Allen and Henry saw each other for the first time, since their arrest. Gene was MIA. They all knew that Gene had been the first to be locked up, and logically, he was the reason why they all were there. So, Gene had ratted everybody out and, honestly, Allen was the only guy who had an idea of what really happened. And Allen knew that Gene and only Gene was the reason why everybody was held responsible for the Dunbar Heist, the biggest cash heist in American history—bigger than the 1997 Loomis Armored Car Robbery of $18.8 million, the 1997 Loomis Fargo Bank Robbery of $17.3 million, and the 1983 White Eagle Robbery of $7.1 million—was going straight to jail.

Two years had covered the Dunbar Heist Case with some decadent dross that seeped through the cracks and crevices of the finest friendships and relationships and moral fibers that bind friend and foe together. On the one hand, the six perpetrators of the heist were split asunder by greed and selfishness and the other hand, the arrestors oversimplified a perfunctory investigation into a personal vendetta. For a fact, the case was left to no allusion save for one big factor, there was $10 million of the $18.9 million reported stolen still missing, and without it, the case is still not completely solved to future infamous date.

The trial's dates were to be set by the popular Judge Judy Schnider. She was chosen to preside over adjudication of the arraignment. CBS wanted to suck every bit of juice out of the peach to promote their fledgling television program. Judge Judy would preside over the arraignment and read the charges to each defendant. On the day of the arraignment, events had taken place so fast until no one had heard from Gene or Priscilla, especially Gene. Once an integral part but minor player of the plan, he had dropped out of sight. With so much taking place presently, he was the least on anybody's mind. The press was actively involved in the biggest cash heist in American history without the smallest bit of accurate knowledge.

The popular Judge Judy elegantly sat on the bench in a black robe, white-laced collar, and petite white earrings with her alluring brown eyes and captivating smile. She placed her bifocal spectacles on and peered down at Mark from above the lenses' rims with a tilted head. Her familiar concerned look with brown curled eyebrows and same color pixie cut hairstyle caught Mark's attention.

"Freddie Lynn McCrary, Jr., please stand," said Judge Judy. "You are charged with conspiracy to commit a robbery, using a gun during a crime of violence and interfering with interstate commerce, and 24 counts of money laundering, and income tax evasion. You have been eye witnessed by at least one codefendant at the Dunbar facility on the night of September 12, 1997. How do you plead?

"Not guilty."

Faces turned and some small grumbling could be heard. All four defendants' eyebrows furrowed. They thought they knew Mark's real name, his legal name, but the only name they knew was Mark. There were more mysteries to unfold.

"Henry Jones, Jr., please stand. You are being charged with conspiracy to commit robbery, using a gun during a crime of violence, and interfering with interstate commerce, and 24 counts of money laundering, and income tax evasion. You have been eye witnessed by at least one codefendant at the Dunbar facility on the night of September 12, 1997. There's also evidence against you for having large sums of cash on hand over $10,000, that you electronically wired $100,000 to your codefendant Gene Upshaw Hill on multiple occasions. How do you plead?" How do you plead?"

"Not guilty."

"Allen Pace III, please stand. You've been charged with conspiracy to commit robbery, using a gun during a crime of violence and interfering with interstate commerce, and 24 counts of money laundering, and income tax evasion. As a former employee of Dunbar, you were entrusted to protect and serve on the highest standard known to man. You have been eye witnessed by at least one codefendant at the Dunbar facility on September 12, 1997. How do you plead?"

"Not guilty."

"Travis Tollson, please stand. You've been charged with conspiracy to commit a robbery, using a gun to commit a robbery during a crime of violence and interfering with interstate commerce, and 24 counts of money laundering, and income tax evasion. You have been eye witnessed by at least one codefendant at the

Dunbar facility on the night of September 12, 1997. How do you plead?"

"Not guilty."

"Tyronne Jonson, please stand. You've been charged with conspiracy to commit a robbery, using a gun to commit a robbery during a crime of violence and interfering with interstate commerce, and 24 counts of money laundering, and income tax evasion. You have been eye witnessed by at least one codefendant at the Dunbar facility on the night of September 12, 1997. How do you plead?"

"Not guilty."

"Very well," said Judge Judy. "Bail will not be granted. And let me inform you as a group, if you guys have decided to tell on each other, that is a little more powerful than circumstantial evidence, but let me inform you, there is more compelling evidence against you—the broken tail light has been linked to the renter of the U-Haul, Gene Upshaw Hill, and some money wrappers have been linked to Gene Upshaw Hill, some of the money that was taken from the Dunbar Heist on September 12, 1997 have been linked to Gene Upshaw Hill. It is of grave importance that you make your decisions wisely because your jail time will directly reflect on what course of action you decide to take. Unless otherwise indicated, the trial is scheduled in 90 days from this date on March 18, 1999. Good luck to you all. Court is adjourned."

After hearing the evidence, Florence gasped and held the children. The whole family was there: Grandma Pearl, Lady Sue, Lady Lucy, his sisters, Janine, Clare, Barry, and all of his uncles. Mark looked over the courtroom and looked at his family in their eyes one at a time. His eyes glossed over and filled with tears, but he held his head high and walked slowly towards the entrance/exit door to the cells and before he reached the door, he passed Allen. Allen had a glint of humor in his eyes, whereas Mark's eyes cried.

"It was an opportunity," Mark whispered.

Allen looked sorrowfully at Mark. "Somebody stole my marbles," he said as he took his place in front of the bailiff.

Before the door slammed, Mark got one last look at Allen and turned around to the gallery and hung his head low. Mark looked into space and mumbled: *That was the last time I saw my brother, my friend...* Through the doors, all of the Mastermind Gang are carried away until the day of justice.

Judge Judy handled the arraignment in her usually responsible, honest, straight-forward style by putting all the cards on the table. Frankly,

Mark liked her personality, and now he could make the best decision for himself. He watched her as she left the bench thinking to himself of how he wanted to thank her.

Thus, the arraignment was over for five of the primary suspects of the 1997 Dunbar Heist. All codefendants pleaded not guilty, except Gene Upshaw Hill who was not present. Each defendant was assigned a court-appointed attorney even though they had money, except Allen. They were playing a ruse trying with all their might to manipulate the formidable U.S. legal system. The defendants heard the evidence against them, and of course, it was circumstantial at best, but fallaciously powerful. Bail was denied because of the magnitude of the case—too much money and a fear to flee. The defendants' right to a speedy trial was granted of course, and the trial date had been set.

After hearing the charges against them, and with the advice from each guy's attorney, they all made a trip to the Attorney General's Office over on Spring Street. All of the defendants conversed with attorneys and everybody, except Allen Pace III and Henry Jones, changed their plea of not guilty to guilty. Of course, the pros were at work and even the defense attorneys, professionally, were trying to save the guys' time from prison;

so, most of them yielded to the overwhelming evidence.

After the visit to the Attorney General's office, three of the Dunbar Heist gang decided to give up the ghost and plea bargain at the behest of their attorney's advice. Judge Bird was selected to preside over the hearing. A separate small and quick juryless hearing took place where three were sentenced after confessing their guilt. Allen kept thinking the judicial tactics of the law were all so powerful because all five of the gang was present even though he and Henry, without waiver, pleaded not guilty. The gavel reined in Allen's attention. The first words he heard was like a friend getting knocked out cold in a bar brawl.

"Tyronne Johnson," announced Judge Bird. "Please stand. On the night of September 12, 1997, you willfully entered the Dunbar facility in downtown Los Angeles and subdued several employees under gunpoint and restricted their movements against their will and with accomplices took over $18 million in cash. All other charges are dropped. I sentence you to ten years in a federal detention facility. Do you have anything to say?"

"No."

One man down, and from the mood of the court, more men would bite the dust, the dry dust of incarceration, the dry dust of separation from society, the dry dust of loneliness. But mentally, Allen was trying to blow the dust away to settle on something else far, far away. He wanted to nullify his acute senses, but to no avail. The next sentencing stung his ears like a hard-hit snare drum at 3AM in the morning after an early recline.

Freddie Lynn McCrary, Jr., please stand; for the robbery of the Dunbar facility that you confessed to being a part of under the same circumstances of your accomplices aforementioned. I sentence you to 10 years in a federal detention center. Do you have anything to say?"

"No."

After those words, Allen cried a river of tears inside because it was no way on earth he could help or change the situation. Yes, he could fight the good or bad fight. There wasn't a single marble left in his bag. He watched Mark and Tyronne with Travis to follow and waited for his turn. Somewhere down the near line.

Allen watched Mark at the podium with natural remorse and his heart was full of contrition because Mark was like a brother to him no matter what. Reaching way back when he was four years old, he reminisced to playing cowboys and Indians and watching Conjunction

Function and he could hear Mark reciting every word of the song. He reflected back to their job at Kentucky Fried Chicken. He thought back to the time when they played their first chess game. He also reflected on the orgies they engaged in. He thought he could be hard, but then again, nobody could be that hard. He wasn't raised that way. His family had always showed him love. His father was strict, but he never abused him. His mother was sweet, and she always consoled him. He couldn't stop thinking that he was built to care. So, a tear trickled down his cheek and he didn't care who saw it. His friend had confessed, and Allen was hurt. Not the kind of hurt like a physical blow, but the kind of hurt that wells up in the human heart. An abstract hurt that nobody could see in blood, only in tears, and who really knows how deep that hurt goes?

"Travis Tollson, please stand. For the robbery of the Dunbar facility that you confessed to being a part of under the same circumstances of your accomplices aforementioned. You also have a pending case of money laundering that we have not yet decided. We will deal with that later. I sentence you to 10 years in a federal detention facility that is subject to change upon further investigation and knowledge. Do you have anything to say?"

"No."

"I see that we have some family members and interested parties in the gallery. Would anyone like to speak before we adjourn?", asked Judge Bird.

There were mumbles, groans, and a stir when Ben stood up in the back of the courtroom. All 6-foot 2 inches of him dressed in a blue suit and red tie. With a long gait, he approached the podium.

"My name is Ben Johnson. I'm a retired city worker of thirty years. I've been knowing Allen and Mark since they was kids. They was some of the best kids morality can buy. I know what I got to say won't change things much. But I couldn't live with myself if I didn't say what's on my heart. I loved those boys. I was a mechanic for the city, and I'd fix neighborhood cars, and Allen and Mark would help me on the weekends and after school. Together, we repaired over 500 cars. I kept records. We did engines, transmissions, body work, and all sorts of other repairs. They were hardworking kids. I don't know why Mark got involved in this Dunbar Heist stuff, but I just heard you give him 10 years. He may have stole some money, but Mark wouldn't hurt a fly. His mother and grandmother raised him well and both those boys respect people and Allen's parents were model parents. Why'd Mark do it? Maybe he was takin' advantage of an opportunity. Maybe he wanted to be rich. Maybe he thought it was the perfect crime. But I ask you, the court, to be not so hard on these boys. They ain't hardened criminals. Besides the mistake Mark made, I know the world is a better place with them in it."

As Allen and Mark listened, they both openly cried.

"Thank you, Mr. Johnson, for your comments, thoughts, and feelings. It's people like you that make this country great." Judge Bird paused, "Is there anyone else who'd like to speak?"

There wasn't a stir.

"Allen Pace III and Henry Jones, Jr., you are here by my request. If at any time you feel like you've got something to tell me. We can save precious time and resources, if not, the precious feelings of our friends and loved ones. You two will be tried later for a crime that your associates admit that you were involved in, too, and may God be with you. You're all excused."

# Chapter 31

Travis, Mark, and Tyronne had already heard their sentences. Henry and Allen were left because Gene was separated from the group. Obviously, Gene was the ringmaster of information and the entire case hinged upon an insider informer. And again, situational irony reared its formidable head of justice for the whole operation succeeded up until this point because of inside knowledge. On a concurrent case connected with the Dunbar Heist, the FBI uncovered a money laundering and income tax evasion scheme that took place in Las Vegas concerning Gene Upshaw Hill and Travis Tollson that took on the tiniest profile. At this point, over two years after the Dunbar Heist had been successfully engineered, huge amounts of the $18.9 million was spreading like a virus throughout the economy's financial bloodstream that was being detected by one of the smartest criminal detection forces in the world, the FBI. Big money has a way of leaving a trail that can be easily followed by the bloodhounds of the law.

***

Two lawyers by the names of Frank Sumoto and Iglesias Ibn Sheik were being investigated for money laundering and income tax evasion for structuring financial transactions and subscribing to false income tax returns. Sheik, a Santa Ynez Arabian horse-farm farmer owner, would plead guilty to 7 counts of money laundering and was sentenced to 30 months in a Federal Prison. Sumoto admitted he received $1 million from Tyronne Tollson and Gene Upshaw Hill, who helped steal millions from the Dunbar Heist. Sheik and Sumoto, bagmen, who conspired depositing the million into Sumoto's trust account to buy houses in Las Vegas and pay large salaries through the dummy company called Combustion Processing Manufacturing Corporation, a Houston-based company that developed machinery to clean contaminated soil after oil spills. Sumoto had issued a W-2 tax form to Gene Upshaw, implying that he earned large sums for legitimate work through the dummy company. Finally, the broken taillight that first presented itself as a red herring transformed into one of the hottest pieces of evidence in the entire Dunbar Heist case linking Gene Upshaw Hill to the largest cash heist in American history.

***

# Chapter 31

On the day of the trial, cameras buzzed, cameras shot and snapped, reporters reported, but since it was a federal case to be decided by a Federal petit jury, the authorities involved kept it on a low profile. The two defendants, Allen Pace III and Henry Jones, were represented by their own attorneys from the same firm on an agreement that Shapiro would be the lead attorney. If Allen Pace III was acquitted, Henry Jones, Jr. would be dealt with later. In any case, the judge would give the sentencing according to the outcome of the jury's decision.

"All rise," commanded the bailiff.

Judge Bird was a happy-go-lucky sort of person, white, with white hair and blue eyes. Her many distinguished honors gave her a cryptic air of confidence and control. She was elected as a Southern California Super Lawyer in the field of Alternative Dispute Resolution, ranked as one of the top 50 lawyers in California, received the UCLA achievement and YMCA silver achievement Award.

She took control immediately, "Please be seated. Members of the jury, I am happy to see that you made it all here in one piece this morning and I hope that the early morning L A traffic did not present a problem to any of you. We're happy to have you. In a just a minute, I'm going to ask for announcements in this particular case and would ask if you would listen attentively to the clerk and the announcements by the court and the attorneys who will speak to you in just a few minutes. However, this case is unique on two accounts. One, it is the largest cash heist in American history. Two, because the nature of this case both codefendants will be represented by two different attorneys from the same office. Mr. Sharpio will take the lead of first chair. Mr. Clerk, if you would, please, call this next case for announcements."

The clerk stood up next to the bench in a blue suit and red tie with a smileless face, "The United States of America vs. Allen Pace III and Henry Jones, jr."

Judge Bird continued, "The prosecution is ready."

"Yes, Your Honor."

Judge Bird continued, "Defendants ready."

"Defendants ready," answered Sharpio.

Judge Bird continued, "Let me explain a little bit about how we will proceed during the course of this proceeding. First, we'll have opening statements; first, by the State since the burden is on the State to prove guilt beyond a reasonable doubt since they have that burden, they have the opportunity to go first with an opening statement; then an opening statement will be made by Mr. Sharpio. These opening statements are not evidence. Evidence you're gonna get from the witness stand or from exhibits that will come in during the course of the trial are often stipulations. That's where the attorneys agree that something is a fact. That's the evidence and it's from those facts and that evidence, that you will determine whether the defendants are guilty or not guilty. Ms. Sugar, you may proceed."

"Thank you, Your Honor," said Ms. Sugar. "I'll need a few minutes to receive my final instructions."

"Very well," said the judge.

Allen sat with his attorney with a solemn look on his face. He had grown a thick black beard and at first glance, he looked like Teddy Pendergrass. But Allen wasn't concerned with looks. Actually, at this moment, he was more concerned with humanity. His time in detention had altered and ramped up his thinking. He looked around the courtroom and his eyes attached to The Great Seal of The State of California. He studied each figure and ruminated on the symbolic drawings etched on its face. For just the other day, while sitting in his room cell, an evocative writer caught his attention with some unknown details about the seal—the writer noted that "The Great Seal" was adopted at the California State Constitutional Convention of 1849 and had undergone only minor design changes. Since then, the seal was standardized in 1937. Allen could remember while reading that ART is a motherfucka. ART is deeper than he had previously realized because ART speaks a million words if one knows how to listen. The seal featured the Roman goddess Minerva Athena in Greek mythology which was goddess of wisdom and war, a Grizzly Bear, the official state animal, feeding on grapes representing California's wine production, a miner representing California's gold rush and mining industry, a sheaf of grain representing agriculture, and sailing ships representing the state's economic power, the phrase or word "Eureka", meaning "I have found it" and Allen focused on the shovel, toolbox, mining pan, and the mountains in the background. Then he compared "The Great Seal" to his conscripted group's situation, his people's situation, his own personal situation—OPPORTUNITY. He thought how many opportunities are floating around unnoticed in the ordinary course of events. Work to make money. Punch a clock after you get to work, and one can't punch it too soon or too late because there's only a twenty-minute window of opportunity. Go to school to get a good job—preschool, grade school, middle school, high school, college in all its phases. How many opportunities does one get to go to college? Back in the day, black people had no opportunities. Good jobs—few and far between for most. There were so many discriminatory practices until good jobs were almost nonexistent creating less opportunity for people like him. He was like a ship representing economic power to all he encountered. Yeah, he stole, but how many have stolen from people like him, he thought. The gold rush—how many had stolen someone else's claim on gold minds. Strength—he was like the grizzly bear standing upright on hind legs protecting and taking food to feed their young. The Miner—he dug up millions. And then the interjection—"Eureka"—"I have found it"—he thought, I have found it in the form of $20 million of those evil pretty little green ones. And finally, there was Minerva Athena the Greek goddess of wisdom and war and commerce and the arts. He thought that he himself was wise and had been wise. He built EE and AMT from a tiny seed of thought to a monstrosity. And now they were getting ready to accuse and try him of being the mastermind who stole the show of $20 million. He thought silently and murmured inaudibly— "I sought the opportunity, I was given the opportunity, I created the opportunity."

And then there is the business about the money itself, besides its only money, but is it? It has been said by some that money is a medium of exchange and, philosophically, that the love of money is the root of all evil, not some evil, but all evil. Lloyd's of London is the biggest underwriting insurance company of insurance companies in the world. No doubt, they had a hand insuring the reported and recorded $18.9 million that was stolen from the Dunbar depot. After doing his homework on Lloyd's of London in Lime Street of London's primary financial district in the city of London, Allen wasn't surprised. It was founded by Edward Lloyd at his coffee house on Tower Street. Allen found that it was not a company, but instead a corporate body governed by the Lloyd's act of 1871 and subsequent acts of Parliament. Lloyd's serves as a partially mutualized marketplace within which multiple financial backers come together to pool and spread risks. The underwriters or members are both corporations and individuals, and traditionally, Lloyd's shared risks as individuals, and even during stressful times in the midst of natural disasters, Lloyd's made billions in profits—a drop in the bucket to what the prosecutors claim what was taken. It was fascinating to find out that Edward Lloyd got started by selling reliable shipping news during the slave trade. Lloyd would insure the loss of ships and the death of slaves. Allen thought what sweet irony of revenge for all those dead slaves in the form of money. But Allen knew that Lloyd's would want their money back in the general scheme of things. Furthermore, the Lloyd's Act of 1982 redefined the structure of the business to separate ownership of the managing agents of the Lloyd's underwriting syndicates from the ownership of the insurance broking firms which wasn't doing the real work—underwriting. A powerful and relentless foe if they wanted to be. Big in America but small in Europe was this squabble over $18.9 million. However, he sat in court awaiting its mercy or its mercilessness.

The courtroom was full of interested spectators that consisted of pros and family. Allen's head wasn't on a swivel, but he had seen his father, mother, sister, and a multitude of associates in business and otherwise. Sharpio was the consummate professional working with the tools he had available to him. Allen paid him in cash, and Sharpio knew that the cash had Dunbar Heist written all over it; but it wasn't the first time he had defended a guilty client. Sharpio felt in his professional and pure heart that he was fighting a losing battle, but he was paid to go down fighting. He would be a protective shield as long as he could to defend a mastermind.

# Chapter 32

The gist of the case revolved around Allen Pace and everybody who was somebody knew it. His so-called accomplices were only minor players in the bittersweet case of two centuries because the fact spoke for itself—the largest cash heist in American history. Bitter, because the entire case was downplayed by the government, primarily, because of its embarrassment to the US government. Sweet, because average guys from the Compton/Carson area of Southern California in the minds of many eluded capture during and after the robbery, for two years of an unprecedented amount of money that nobody had engineered in the history of America.

The prosecutors wanted Allen Pace III so bad that they could taste it, including the supposedly impartial judge, but the law had to take its course toward the unknown but suspected end. At another end of the courtroom, Allen espied "Lady Justice" situated so elegantly in plain sight—a symbol of judgment, he thought, not to take lightly but misunderstood by far too many. Years ago, when Allen was in high school, he took a criminal justice class, and with the help of his instructor, Mr. Justice, a black man, and his own inferential understanding, he surmised: Lady Justice held a scale in her right hand, sported a blindfold over her eyes, held a downward-pointed sword in her left hand, wore a long dress, and stood barefoot—all symbolic. The first thought that came to his mind was that the personification of justice in balancing the scales dates back to the goddess Maat, and later changed to Isis. He knew that the goddess Maat was of the Kemetic black people, but this picture portrayed her as white. And he also knew that the Greeks changed her name to Isis. He knew that the entire concept of the scales derived from 'the weighing of the heart against the feather' in an effort for his ancient ancestors to be accepted into the spiritual realm in the afterlife. If the heart was heavier than the feather, there was no entrance. Allen continued to ruminate, and he was taught and believed that the scale symbolized: duty and luck, the blindfold symbolized: fate and destiny, the sword symbolized: retribution and payback. Payback weighed heavy on his mind, and he didn't want that sword to slice and dice him to tiny pieces. He did his duty and now he needed luck, because, honestly, he didn't know his fate.

"How do you feel?" asked Sharpio as he shuffled through a stack of papers on his counsel table.

"I feel like shit because retribution is a motherfucka. I think you already know what I know, what I've done. But I've got to deny this shit to the bitter end. I've got to maintain my moral integrity, however decadent."

Sharpio squared his eyes to Allen's eyes, "I've defended people from all walks of life, and many of them guilty. I am a professional counselor and culpability does not pay the bills, especially if the charged crime is not heinous like serial cold-blooded murders, child molestation, mayhem, rape, or murdering for selfish gain. I have turned many cases concerning on defying logic or moral turpitude and I knew the client was or wasn't crazy. Your case is different; in fact, I actually admire its brilliance. You were Robinhood."

With that made statement, Allen knew, "All I can ask counselor is to give them a good fight."

"You've got it, big guy."

The sound of the gavel rang through the courtroom like the peal of the Liberty Bell rang on the day of the reading of the Declaration of Independence because a few in the gallery mumbled in conversation. "Quiet in the court, please," shouted Judge Bird striking the bench with the gavel.

To Counselor Sharpio the Liberty Bell had historical and personal significance because of the crack it developed while ringing just after the death of Chief Justice John Marshall. The historical significance was after an aged bell-ringer rang the bell on July 4, 1776, upon hearing The Second Continental Congress's vote for independence; the bell became famous after an 1847 short story after the celebration of George Washington's birthday. The personal significance was the courage of the men that caused us all to be free from tyranny under the control of a monarchy. Thus, both sides were poised and ready with enough paperwork on the counselor's tables to clog up an industrial toilet.

"Ms. Sugar," said Judge Bird in a silky suave voice, "Are you ready for opening statements?"

"I am Your Honor," she replied.

Draped in a blue skirt suit that finished just above the knees, she walked around the counselor's table to the podium to meet the Grand Jury that was composed of four women and eight men, and only one black female and male. The selection of the jury was a tedious and arduous process because out of the one hundred summoned only twelve would serve and honestly either side psychologically and emotionally wanted the jurors they could get. Ms. Sugar was happier with the selection.

"Your Honor," she said looking in the judge's direction, then facing the jury. "Ladies and gentlemen of the jury, we have probably the most important case in the history of this country before us. In our illustrious history of America, there has not been more than $18.9 million stolen in a robbery before. I am going to present evidence that the Allen Pace III," she points at him, "Who we believe was the mastermind behind the robbery, and Henry Jones, Jr. his accomplice," she points at him, "Who aided in carrying out this historical, yet heinous crime. Our evidence will put these two men at the scene of the crime and between and inside the doors of the Dunbar facility in Downtown Los Angeles on Mateo Street in the early morning darkness of September 13, 1997. The prosecution will probably present mirrors, pulling rabbits out of hats, and magical hallucinations but evidence not stipulation must prevail and deem these two men guilty beyond a reasonable doubt. We will prove that Allen Pace III did not have enough money to finance a popcorn stand on the corner of Wilshire and Vermont, let alone to finance a multi-million-dollar business without ever opening a bank account, unless he took that money from Dunbar. We will systematically prove that these two men by deductive reasoning alone held the so-called smoking gun that cost you the taxpayer millions of dollars to painstakingly investigate for over two years before we gathered the damaging evidence to put them behind retributive and correctional bars. After presenting all the facts and evidence, I'm sure that you will find Allen Pace III and Henry Jones, Jr. guilty of Robbery in the first degree. Thank you for your time."

"Mr. Sharpio, you may proceed," said Judge Bird from the bench.

Through experience, Sharpio fully understood the 'the similarity effect' of psychology. Sharpio was simply sharp but not sharp wearing a neatly pressed men's warehouse navy blue suit, matching navy-blue tie, white shirt, and black inexpensive Florsheim shoes. His brief case was of simple black leather with a black-gilded latch to avert attention to himself. Although he was not married yet, he wore a wedding band and a wristwatch that didn't sparkle under the courtroom light. He walked with head up, shoulders high, and flashed an occasional alluring smile that charmed more than it fascinated. He was an actor on a Shakespearean stage and the jury connected to him before he spoke with powerless power.

Before he spoke, he espied the jury like a trained animal. Sharpio looked at the eyes of the jury, a practice so focused that he could monitor the pupils from dilation to normal. He turned towards the bench, "Your Honor, clerk, prosecution," then turned square to the jurors, "Ladies and gentlemen of the jury. Thank you for your service to humanity. It was John Donne, the great poet, who said, "Any man's death diminishes me, because I am involved in mankind, and therefore never send to know for whom the bell tolls; it tolls for thee." I had to quote one of the greatest thinking minds in our history because we are getting ready to try the largest cash heist in American history. And you, the jurors, as a part of mankind, have been called to answer the bell to find my client not guilty for a crime that he could have not possibly committed because he simply was not there. I will bring forth witnesses to corroborate my client's claim that he was at a party in Long Beach when this crime took place. I will bring forth witnesses and psychologists to substantiate my client simply was not smart enough to commit a crime of this magnitude that boggled the mind of Harvard-graduated criminologist for two years because he was too dumb to pull it off. I will present information to prove that my client never owned property or a bank account in his life. Let me ask you—how can a poor, despicable, abject dummy rob $18.9 million from a Fort Knox-protected facility and put the smartest criminal minds in the recorded history of the world in an embarrassing quandary? I'm sure that you'll come to answer—he can't; therefore, you must and I'm confident that you will find my client irrevocably and unequivocally not guilty. I thank every soul in this courtroom for their time and patience, especially you the jurors."

# Chapter 33

The prosecution built the best case they could on circumstantial evidence that tied a formidable knot, a nodule of twisted lisle twine that was hard to untangle. As the case progressed, the accomplices were turning like a doggy-style sexual act. Everybody except Mark had turned state's evidence. Gene was never in court to be seen and Allen knew that he may have received immunity from prosecution due to his position on the board, the board of the entire ordeal from arrest until now.

The state in conjunction with the federal government tried their best to keep all defendants separate and scared as the trial progressed. But the law itself states in Article 10 of the Universal Declaration of Human Rights, the Sixth Amendment to the United States Constitution in a clause that all have the right to a fair and speedy trial, presumed innocent until proven guilty, and to be tried and heard by a jury of your peers dating back to Magna Carta. All five defendants participated in these rights, and all pled not guilty at the arraignment. The power of the state began to loosen a once tight-knit group and family members like Tide lifts soil and dirt out of clothes and dishware.

During the trial, Henry Jones, Jr. did not take the stand but Henry Jones's father, Mr. Jones, testified in court that his son robbed the downtown Dunbar facility on September 12-13, 1997. No Doubt, scared, the elder Jones felt guilty for laundering $177,000 through his laundry business. He testified that his son initially told him that he had earned the money in a drug deal, but later admitted once the heat lay dormant, they took it from the Dunbar facility. Of course, Henry was shocked that his own father told on him and that his father was protecting his own ass, but later, he rationalized that use of cocaine and money doesn't mix well, much like gasoline and fire.

The prosecution presented the broken taillight, which within time, a FBI metallurgical expert matched the broken taillight to the U-Haul Truck rented by Gene Upshaw Hill the day before the robbery and returned some time after. The prosecution presented several $100,000 electronic money transfers from Gene Upshaw Hill to Henry Jones and mentioned the Sumoto and Sheik case, tying it into Henry Jones and Gene Upshaw Hill. The prosecution also presented the original money straps dated and signed by an official Dunbar employee, Mr. Murray. The prosecution showed pictures to the jury of all six defendants hanging out conversing with one another in their hang-out circles from the south bay area of southern California to the Las Vegas casinos. Somehow, they had even managed to get pictures of Gene and Mark with piles of chips in front of them on gambling tables. They presented pictures of the brand-new Plymouth Voyager after the heist. They had pictures of Delilah, Florence's 1964 Chevy classic, before and after it ran the fancy chromed-out wheels.

With the instincts of an Afghan hunting dog, the law had suspected Allen Pace III from the case's inception. Like a white-hot iron spoon to a hungry man the law couldn't touch it to feed but the law could see it and watch it from a demure distance away. For two years, that spoon had been white hot until it took a scoop of money wrappers and a busted yellow tail light to cool it off. The prosecution skillfully tied the six accomplices together and painted a picture of friendship in the jurors' minds. Ms. Sugar constantly went to the courtroom easel with different color highlighters, mostly red, green, and blue, tying lifelong friendships together between the defendants. She called on Travis Tollson and Tyronne Johnson to testify against Allen and Henry. She presented evidence that at an early age Allen and Mark lived across the street from each other as early as three years old until middle school. She showed evidence of when Allen and Mark worked together at KFC; she produced paperwork and presented how all six defendants worked together for Haze as security guards and gained experience with guns. She showed pictures of parties in front of the strip club in Carson, in front of the club on Florence and Crenshaw. She had the jurors leave their seats and view the pictures up close while she explained every detail of what she thought they were doing. Many times, the jury would react to the evidence presented against the prosecution with subtle head shakes, faint facial movements, and restrained body movements.

One the other hand, the defense called state-accredited psychologist, several participants of the September 12-13-1997 Long Beach Party alibi, business associates, and family members. Sharpio worked hard at casting doubt on the timing of the robbery, saying that anyone who could drive from Long Beach to downtown Los

Angeles and load half a ton of cash into a U-Haul within an hour is impossible by any stretch of the imagination, and he also said that the smartest criminal mind in the world couldn't do it and the odds of that happening is $18.9 million to 1 on the worst day in the history of the world. On the easel he drew up a schematic. He called cartographers and drew upon their spatial knowledge to emphasize the timing of the robbery. He called "Deal Experts" from Travelzoo to outline travel time to and from Long Beach to downtown Los Angeles on a Friday night in an effort to quash the prosecution's theory of the possibility of timing. He developed algebraic equations of time and distance and fully explained to the jurors it was next to impossible for his client along with his suspected accomplices to be anywhere near the downtown Dunbar facility in time to successfully complete the robbery of such huge and heavy amount of cash. Sharpio subpoenaed school records and vigorously amplified the fact that none of the accused was college material and also amplified what he called 'the jealousy factor' of all humans and how Napoleon Hill featured In his book "Think and Grow Rich" that there are seven major negative emotions: Fear, Jealousy, Hatred, Revenge, Greed, Superstition, and Anger. Sharpio displayed this material on a power-point presentation.

Although there was no evidence of the two suspected robbers sitting in the courtroom ever setting foot inside the Dunbar facility on September 12, 1997, the circumstantial evidence piled up so high against them that ATLAS couldn't wrap his arms around it and lift with a heave-ho.

Of course, both defendants were represented by attorneys: court appointed from Sharpio's office for Henry Jones and a private attorney Sharpio for Allen Pace.

"Put me on the stand, I'm tired of this shit. This place is flowing with blood up to our knees," said Allen in disgust.

He had Sharpio to call him to the stand, "Why do you think your alleged accomplices are saying you were the mastermind of the Dunbar Heist and present there on the night of September 12-13, 1997?"

"I know these guys. They are my associates in business. But I don't have the foggiest idea of what they're talking about. On the night in question, I was at a party all night. I think they're motives for doing this is jealously. You see, I had passionate sex with each and every one of their wives or girlfriends, and each and every one of them knew it."

"I have no more questions Your Honor," said Sharpio.

"Would you like to cross examine?" the Judge blared from the bench eyeing the prosecution.

They hesitated a little from the prosecution's table, "No, Your Honor."

With the penultimate blow thrown, Allen returned to his seat at the counselor's table. In a rare state of mind, he lost all contact with his surroundings and deeply thought to himself:

*To have or to have not? That is a question to be answered by all of us. An opportunity appears then leaves in an instant, gone forever lost in the vice-grip of time. Time could be sweet or sluttish, but opportunities appear every so often, maybe once in a lifetime, and then again, never. We learn, we grow, we sleep, we die; and in learning and growth do we put ourselves above others or share the fruits of our talents and build nests and teds for the weary. Dreams, they came and went of friends, foe, and all people; plans for the future, or no plans for an insolent-minded drub. Yeah, there is the stew, for in that lifetime dreams have come and gone. And when dreams are no more, the proud will devour the dreamless; for who would consider time to waste or to use. Time is forever to the dreamless and time gives way to the dreamer. So, the dreamer spurns not and accepts the fate of his actions. Patience is the stuff that the unworthy know not of and his actions may take a quietus by his own words, by his own actions. To grunt under a heavy burden and not give life a chance to prosper, to flourish, is the sin of sins. So, the burdens must be withstood until the opportunity arises again. That uncharted country where no man has gone before can be charted through the dreams of opportunity.*

Like sentry Doberman pinschers, the FBI kept a low profile and a tight leash on presumably their most embarrassing case in their relatively young history. It is a fact that the FBI was established on July 26, 1908, under the name of Bureau of Investigation (BOI) by Attorney General Bonaparte by using Department of Justice (DOJ) expense funds. He hired thirty-four people that included some veterans from the Secret Service to work for the new investigative agency. It was designed to be an autonomous investigative agency reporting directly to the Attorney General for which Bonaparte hired Stanley Finch to be its first Director. In 1932, it was renamed the United States Bureau of Investigation. In 1935, it was again renamed the FBI and functioned as an independent service within the Department of Justice that same year.

Despite its infancy of numbers, the FBI employs some of the smartest minds and undertakes some of the brightest tactics and crime-solving strategies in the world to protect its citizens, and to protect the country from foreign invaders and domestic disturbances. Allen and both legal sides understood this function of power of the FBI, considered by many as the best crime fighting force in the world. Offense and defense was the name of the game for the attorneys and the name of the game for Allen and Henry was to stay out jail and not to be reduced to less-than second class citizens and payback money that would take several lifetimes to payback on an average job such as a security guard.

"Ms. Sugar," said Judge Bird, "Would you like to submit your closing argument to the jury?"

"Yes, Your Honor."

Sugar approached the jurors, looked all twelve square in the eye before she spoke. "Your Honor and the people of The Great State of California, ladies and gentlemen of the jury. We live in a country that if you work hard and sacrifice your trivial passions to make a good living, it can be made free from extortion, larceny, or armed robbery. Armed robbery is a felony in the State of California. Robbing is described as taking or attempting to take anything of value by force or threat of force or by putting the victim or victims in fear, or in common law robbery is defined as taking the property of another, with the intent to permanently deprive the person of that property. This case is about six men who on the night of September 12-13, 1997, subdued and terrorized nine employees at the Downtown Dunbar Depot in Los Angeles with the intent to deprive them of money that they were entrusted to handle, guard, protect, and distribute to the public. Aggravated robbery involves the use of a deadly weapon or something that appears to be a deadly weapon. We have heard testimony under oath that the robbers on the night in question appeared to have shot guns and hand guns to consummate their objective. According to Article 13 of the Universal Declaration of Human Rights, a citizen, which is International Law, has the liberty to travel, and work in any part of the state where one pleases within the limits of respect for the liberty and rights of others. I think we have proven beyond a reason of a doubt that Allen Pace III planned, conspired, and conscripted six of his close friends to take $18.9 million by gunpoint from the vault of the Dunbar facility. And during the commission of this horrible crime, under the leadership of Allen Pace III, whom you see in this courtroom today, and a member of his cadre, Henry Jones Jr.," Ms. Sugar paused and pointed directly at Allen Pace III and Henry Jones, Jr. "As a trusted employee, Allen Pace III, he and his accomplices willfully entered the facility of Dunbar with keys entrusted to Allen Pace III and took the guards by surprise and with inside, esoteric, and specialized knowledge of the facility removed all the recording devices so that this heinous act couldn't be traced. They took blatant advantage of each and every employee working on that shift by pinioning their arms and legs in order to restrict their movements, thereby depriving the victims of their freedom to do their job, to work, that night. These two men," again she pointed deliberately holding the finger for a long while at the two defendants, "were placed at the scene of the crime by their own accomplices, the money wrappers, $100,000 in money transfers, the broken taillight. And I reiterate all this evidence places Allen Pace III and Henry Jones, Jr. inside the doors of the downtown Dunbar facility on September 12-13, 1997. Although there was no physical damage done, the mental damage that they did that night was immeasurable and you should find both of these men guilty of armed aggravated robbery to the full extent of the law."

When the prosecution finished their closing argument, the federal petit jury looked like deer with headlights in their eyes. Not stoic but compassionate are conjunctive terms that fully expressed the way the petit jury looked to the trained eye of Sharpio. His total focus was to connect with each and every juror in that jury on this day.

The judge peered at Sharpio, "Counselor, you may close now."

This was a criminal court case fought in a modern court room in Los Angeles not on an ancient battlefield in Asia Minor or in a boxing ring in Manila. To all those concerned, Sharpio's love for sports and battle significantly played a part in his everyday life. As a hobby, he studied the Trojan War and as a kid, he was a fan of Cassius Clay, who later became a Muslim and changed his name to Muhammad Ali. He tried to adopt traits of Achilles and Ali because he thought they were some of the finest warriors of all time whether they are myth or real. He didn't have a sword or boxing gloves, but he knew the rules of law and he had a firm background in logic. He knew words were his arsenal and how to use and apply them to ultimately win bloody battles in the court room.

Sharpio paused purposely to throw what he hoped was the last blow. He turned to the jury and smiled softly, looked at Lady Justice and The Great Seal of California attached to the wall behind the jury box, and looked at the American flag, then with a beautiful smile looked at each twelve jurors with an 'I've got something to say' attitude. He turned slightly towards the bench, "Your Honor," he slightly bowed, and then turned square to the jurors. "Ladies and gentlemen, mothers, fathers, grandmothers, and grandfathers of the jury. The prosecution states that this case is about six men who engineered a robbery of the downtown Dunbar facility on the night and early morning of September 12-13, 1997. Ms. Sugar is right that is what this case is about because my client was not there that night. He was at home enjoying his family attending a birthday party over at a good friend's house. You have heard testimony that put the real robbers in the facility for the less than an hour timeline. That sounds to me like, and I hope it sounds the same way to you, that some highly professional bank robbers who cased the location for months or maybe longer with some sophisticated equipment took that money. Please bear in mind that my client's mother is an elementary schoolteacher. Homework and test scores can get you an A in the classroom, but in the real world, that A is reduced to common sense, God-given talent. My client barely finished high school and any psychologist in the world would tell you that he is not college material. I produced evidence by a trained psychologist that my client's IQ is 75 which is just 5 points above the low average and in the lower median. If my client would have gone in that facility the night of September 12-13, 1997, he would have been in there so long that he would have never come out alive and with the responsibility of five other people that would have made the task much more difficult to successfully complete. In light of this knowledge, it was impossible for my client to enter and exit the facility in question without getting his head blown off. We have here the prime of life of a man's life in our hands today. We can either squeeze the life out of that man or open our palms and do the right thing and let the innocent sparrow go and enjoy the challenges of life. We know that his father is an engineer for Northrop and his mother is an elementary school teacher for the L.A. Unified School District and that my client was brought up in a middle-class family of hard-working parents. My client saw his parents work towards retirement all of his life. He knows what it is to work hard. He is a cut from the mold. My client knows the difference between right and wrong, hard work and laziness, taking and receiving, robbing and working; and the circumstantial evidence that the prosecution has garnered is simply not enough to prove beyond a reasonable doubt that a reasonable man or woman could truly say in their heart that it is convincing enough to convict a man with below average intelligence of a master plan that stumped the brightest criminal minds in the world for two years. I beseech, I implore, I beg you, I ask you to let an innocent man go free from the palms of your hand and do the right thing by returning to this court room with not guilty verdict." Sharpio paused and took a deep breath, looked each juror in the eye, and said "Thank you for your time jurors and Your Honor, and prosecution. Thank you for your cooperation. Thank You for your willingness to do the right thing and thank you for your precious time and sacrifice for your family, something that I know my client would love to do—get back to, his family."

# Chapter 34

"Would you like reclose, Ms. Sugar?" asked Judge Bird.

"Yes, Your Honor."

Sharpio was not surprised for the court to allow the prosecution to deliver the very last blow. Ms. Sugar stood before the jury like a towering green citadel.

"First of all, I'd like to remind the jury to read and stay close to the admonitions—your instructions given to you by the court and the facts of this case. The prosecution has presented indisputable facts in this case during the three weeks that we have been together. A man can't be two places at one time and the facts state that Allen Pace III and his cohorts were inside the downtown Dunbar facility robbing it on September 12 through September 13, 1997. Anybody can have a lapse of judgment. The participants at the party may have had a lapse of judgment, but those six perpetrators and violators of the law did not have a lapse of judgment because they were actively, methodically, judiciously, intentionally, recklessly, and blatantly robbing the Dunbar facility. Thank You."

The trial, in a figurative sense, was a slugfest in every sense of the word. After three weeks, both sides had presented their best case and put their best foot forward. Judge Bird scanned the courtroom and noticed the empty and tired faces of the jurors, "Alright ladies and gentlemen, we were here late last evening so we're going to adjourn for the evening now. Please be back tomorrow morning. We'll start promptly at nine o'clock. Please read and remember the admonitions of direction and procedure. Are there any questions? You are excused. Have a nice evening."

There it was, thought Sharpio. The last six words the jury heard were "robbing the Dunbar facility, thank you" and they had to sleep on those words with them unconsciously ringing in their ears all night long.

The federal petit jury had heard all the facts and saw all the figures and now it was time to choose a foreman, convene, deliberate, and decide the fate of two young men who were accused of gang-stealing $18.9 million by gunpoint. Again, although there was no evidence of someone actually setting foot in the facility, someone did, and Allen and Henry and the others were the only suspects who had made any sense of being there in the first place, however asinine, of committing this historic class robbery; so the prosecution hung on like a hungry pit bull on a poodle to the only food in sight—Allen Pace III. But Allen Pace III and his attorney were like a rare breed of the poodle family—a bull terrier. Weakened during the trial, the Pace camp was licking their wounds because the facts are like a video tape and the evidence is like audio, and combined audio-visual, is like being there live in Memorex or panoramic living color. The trial was over and handed to the federal petit jury that reclined to their chambers to begin deliberations.

# Chapter 35

A guy named Demetrius Devereaux assigned juror number twelve of Mexican French descent, black hair, brown eyes, and in his early fifties, was elected as foreman after an 8-4 vote.

"Jurors, thank you for your appointment and choosing a foreperson. I will diligently and honestly perform and try to perform these duties to the best of my ability. First of all, I'll take roll. I realize that of this moment, we are strangers; so, when I call your number, stating your name is optional but tell us a little about yourself, please. All jurors number 1 through juror 12. Let me remind you, most of the time, we'll refer to each other by number. I know it's a bit ironic because it was testified in court that's the same system the robbers used. In my experience, numbers are a bit impersonal, and impartiality will help us to decide the fate of these gentlemen more fairly in the long run."

"Juror number one," said Demetrius, he took roll systematically.

"Present," said juror number one, Caucasian, blue eyes, thin lips. "I have nothing to hide or protect but my country. My name is Lucas, George Lucas. I am a retired soldier and sergeant in the marines. I had several tours of duty in Viet Nam. I am 68 years old. I am married with three kids, two boys and a girl, and I have five grandkids."

"Juror number two."

"Thank you, sir, I'm present," said juror number two, Caucasian, blonde hair, brown eyes, full lips, aquiline nose, high cheek bones, and full bust. My name is July Jones. I'm thirty years old. I've never been married but I have a boyfriend. No kids. I graduated from UC Berkley with honors. I work for the federal government in the DOJ as legal secretary."

"Juror number three,"

"Present, this is my maiden voyage. My name is Terrence Bradley—Caucasian, 6'-2"tall, brown hair, blue eyes, thin muscular build—I'm thirty-five, not days old, but years old. I'm an electrician. I work for Brigg's Brothers construction company here in L.A. I am not married with a girlfriend. I love all sports and skiing in the winter on Mammoth Mountain. I graduated from Loyola with a B.A. in Psychology."

"Juror number four,"

"Present," said a dark black woman with salt and pepper natural hair cut low, brown eyes, and a gorgeous smile, pug nose, pursed lips, round face, and dewlap chin—I've served on juries before. I'm sixty-eight years young. I have five kids and ten grandkids. I am a retired elementary school teacher. I like playing bid whist and spades. I walk for exercise."

"Juror number five,"

"I'm here in the flesh," said a light, brown-skinned male with light brown eyes, neat black curly hair, well-proportioned nose and cheekbones, full lips, and a strong character presence. "I work at Walmart, sometimes seven days a week, to feed my family of two kids. I have thirty-six years on this earth. My wife works, too. I like playing soccer and videos games."

"Juror number six."

"Present, foreperson," said a white male with blonde hair, blue eyes, and a handsome and well-proportioned face. "I am forty-five years old, and I'm fit as a fiddle. I work for LPL a CPA firm in Los Angeles as a senior accountant. I'm a pencil pusher and a numbers cruncher. I handle millions of dollars' worth of accounts and advise clients on their money. I like fast cars and hot women. I'm a scratch golfer as a hobby and I like soul music."

"Juror number seven."

"Present," said a dark black man with a head of white neatly combed hair and a matching in color trig goatee that also matched the sclera of his eyes. His high cheek bones pronounced his semi-flat nose and the inside of his lower lip glistened with a pink sheen. "I'm 68 years old. I'm a retired rubbish collector for the City of Los Angeles, that's a euphemism for a trash man." Demetrius smiled. "I like going to Vegas to play table games. I've been married to the same woman for forty-six years. My wife and I had five kids and I out survived two sons. Currently, I have two lovely daughters and a son and 10 grandchildren, and soon I'll have great grandchildren."

"Juror number eight,"

"Present," said a white female with curly brunette-colored hair that flowed past her shoulders halfway down her back. Her hazel eyes highlighted her couture-designed eyebrows that started at a ring-shaped brown pearl and ended with awl-shaped point. Her ruby-red lips stood out like a pretty picture painted on soft ecru-tanned canvas. "My name is Cheryl Livingston. I'm forty-eight years old. I'm a homemaker with three children—three boys, 10, 8, and 6. My husband is a pilot who flies for American Airlines. I like figure skating, gymnastics, and swimming. I like playing word games—text twist, Sudoku puzzles, crossword puzzles, rebus, and completing jigsaw puzzles."

"Juror number nine."

"Yo como presentan," he said laughing. "Present! I'm an American-born Mexican. I grew up in Compton. My grandparents owned a house in Taco Flats back in 60's and 70's. I am thirty-three years old. My mom and dad stayed in the house with my grandparents while they both worked for the City of Compton. I graduated from Compton High in '95. Yeah! Go Tarbabes. Just like my parents, I work for the City of Compton as one of the best janitors in the world. I like soccer, video games, and computers."

"Juror number ten."

"Present," said an American-born middle eastern male of average height, brown eyes, puce-colored skin with brown overtones, a long, bony nose, lips like brown rose petals, round cheeks with a natural slightly reddish tinge, and cleft chin. "I like sports, women, movies, fast cars, money, and nice clothes. I'm an architect with a master's degree from UCLA. My grandfather was an oil sheik from Abu Dhabi and my family is rich and wealthy. Rich because my family is worth millions, wealthy because it has been calculated that the oil reserves that my family own will last for several more lifetimes if not longer and I'm here to fill my American duty. I'm thirty-five years old and I've been building buildings for ten years."

"Juror number eleven."

"Present," said a trill voice that melodically filled the room. "I'm an American-Asian and my father is black." She had deep-set, trance-like alluring ebony eyes that showed a penchant of slant; her naturally round rosy cheeks were in perfect harmony with her flat semi-flat nose and full lips and perfectly round chin. Her light-brown skin glistened under the room like a miniature sun. "I deal cards at the Bicycle Casino in Bell Gardens. I like to gamble on table games and gambol towards life in casinos. I'm good at it and I make money. I'm twenty-five-years-old and I love life. I studied liberal arts in school, and I have a bachelor's degree. My dream in life is to own my own casino."

"Thank you all for your participation. I'm juror number twelve," said Demetrius. "I am Mexican- French. I own a prominent new and used car dealership in Bellflower. I employ thirty employees. I have served in the jury system for seven years. I have served on grand juries. I am a people person. If I have any skills in life, I would say I'm a life coach, a coordinator of people. I like reading all sorts of material and books. I didn't go to college because I couldn't afford it. I've been working to help support myself and others ever since I was thirteen. I'm also very interested in politics. I campaigned locally for Bill Clinton. In fact, there's a young black Chicago member of the Illinois Senate by the name of Barack Obama who will be the first black president of the United States of America under the Constitution of the United States, which came into force in 1788."

Thus, the federal jury of the case concerning the largest cash heist in American history gelled as a team. They were fully aware of the importance of their forthcoming decision. They settled in and began the work that they were supposed to do—decide the fate of two men who claimed that they had nothing to do with it. They had listened to the arguments of both sides. The facts and evidence were on the table.

Demetrius knew that the whole process would be decided under a democratic process that characterized a system of government that is "of, by and for" the people. "Of the people" implies that the government is composed of regular citizens. "By the people" denotes that the government is elected by its citizens. "For the people" implies that the primary objective of the government is to act in ways beneficial to the people. The

"Of the people" component is established when people run for a public office. The "by the people" component happens when the people are allowed to elect suitable candidates. The "for the people" component bit happens when the government does what is required to keep the public informed on important matters. Some of the principal characteristics and basic tenets of a democratic process are that citizens of a given country get the chance to vote, both figuratively and literally, and that every citizen is allowed to live a life of their choice and is free to say and do what they want within the guidelines of the law.

Allen Pace III and Henry Jones, Jr. were no doubt citizens of the U.S. democratic system and held certain inalienable rights under the Constitution. But, were Pace and Jones allowed to live a life of their choice? Are they free to say and do what they want? The answer to that question is HELL NAW. Living free within the guidelines of the law is a fundamental right, but breaking the law carries its consequences, and Lady Justice didn't hold the sword of retribution as a symbol for any other purpose but to payback law breakers, the scales warrant the weighing of evidence, and the blindfold bade impartial objectivity. These twelve people in the jury lounge were on the verge of making history.

In this case, even the money couldn't tip the scale of justice in the favor of the defendants. The money couldn't be used as a shield; the money couldn't remove the blindfold so the law could see fallacy. Many times, the law has been manipulated by emotional and irrelevant pleas to the jury, but the scales of justice outweighed the whole lot.

Demetrius had been serving as a juror for seven years now. In his first call for service, he was assigned number fifty-six in the potential jury pool. Demetrius had served on grand juries in the past. Many lawyers, both prosecuting and defending, got to know him through his tenure of service and respected him as a fair and impartial juror. Demetrius thought it was a moral obligation to serve the people as a juror. Demetrius owned his own new and used car dealership that he built from the ground up. He had started on the ground floor as a salesman straight out of Hawthorne High School at a small used car lot on Lakewood Boulevard in Bellflower. He was real go-getter of an eastside Los Angeles background and an excellent people person. He talked fast but was a good listener and always waited his turn to talk. He rarely cut people off in mid-conversation. It seemed like he was always selling something or thought about how he was going sell something to someone else. He loved control but wasn't a control freak. In most of his life endeavors, he wound up leading the pack and now here he was leading eleven people to decide the fate of two of the craftiest men in bank robbing history.

"What cold hard facts do we have against the defendants?" asked Demetrius in a cool room in the downtown Los Angeles court building. "Is Allen Pace III and Henry Jones, jr. guilty of aggravated robbery?" asked Demetrius.

A black female juror assigned juror number four in her fifties spoke up first, "Nothing against Allen Pace III but Henry Jones, Jr., his father testified that he laundered $177,000 through his laundry business. He testified later that his son, Henry Jones, jr. confessed that he robbed Dunbar, and the prosecution made a connection between Pace and Jones as friends who worked together for over a year."

"May I have a show of hands for the following series of questions?" asked Demetrius.

"Do you think Pace is smart enough to rob Dunbar of all that cash? May I have a vote by the raise of hands?"

Two raised their hands, including Devereaux.

"So, most of us don't believe he's smart enough, interesting; we can't convict unless we all agree. The prosecution had no real defense against his intelligence."

The black man assigned juror number seven spoke up, "The cartographer said the trip could be made and Travelzoo said it couldn't. If Pace did this, it was highly planned and coordinated."

A white male juror assigned number three in his thirties spoke up, "He had a year and a half to gather all the information he needed. He looks like he's smart enough."

"Remember our instructions," said Demetrius, "facts and evidence only, although we know, all of us, how something appears will always have an influence no matter how slight. Do you think he fucked everybody's wife, and is that a valid reason to finger him?"

A white female juror assigned juror number eight in her early thirties spoke up, "Jealousy can definitely play a role, but I think they were too close. They probably fucked each other in orgies."

"Well, what about those goddamn money wrappers? The witness who worked there, Murray is his name, verified their authenticity and the initials," said juror number one.

A white male juror assigned juror number six in his forties spoke out, "If you're gonna steal millions, why would you leave the original money wrappers. I know if I stole it, I'd take those straps off first thing."

"Hindsight is 20-20," said Demetrius. "$20 million is not only heavy as hell, but it's a lot of spending loot. It'll probably scare the shit out of me. By the way, that evidence is as cold as a nuclear warhead still in the silo."

"All shit," said American born Mexican male assigned juror number nine in his thirties, "Anybody could have picked those wrappers up off the street."

"You're right, sir," said Demetrius. "When your girlfriend turns'em in and says under oath, she got'em from her boyfriend, Gene Upshaw. She probably didn't pick those motherfuckas up off the street."

Another white male assigned juror number one in his sixties spoke up, "That Gene Upshaw is a boob or the smartest guy on the planet or both. The prosecution tied him to a money laundering scheme of over a half a mil between him and Travis Tollson, who turned state evidence. Rumor is going around that he could get full immunity for turning state's evidence. How's that for ratting out your friends."

Another white female juror assigned juror number two spoke up, "I think that broken taillight haunted this group. The FBI was able to match it to the U-Haul that Gene Upshaw rented and turned it in at a later date. If Pace was at a party on September 12, 1997, that Gene Upshaw sure wasn't."

"How's that for poetic justice," said Demetrius. "If it wasn't for Gene Upshaw, they probably never would've solved this case. And not only that, we have to be very careful about putting the right people behind bars."

"Aww shit," said the white male juror in his sixties, "Can't you see, if one of them did it, they all did it."

"Hold on," said Demetrius, "Let's not jump to conclusions. I can see a slight chance where these particular six didn't have to be together if they were there at all."

"Gene Upshaw's ass sure was there," said the white male juror in his sixties. "Reading that trail is like reading a road map."

"I know this for sure," said Demetrius. "We all have to agree to get a conviction. If we make an erroneous decision, we'll have to live with that decision on our conscious for the rest of our lives. When you make that decision, just make sure it's the right one in all your heart, then you can live with it."

In the following couple of days, they talked, haggled, muttered, some cried, they asked for verification of the facts and more evidence, and then finally came close to a unanimous decision. The jury lounge got hot. When the jurors first entered the room, it was cool, and a few complained about the coolness. The black office-style chairs on casters slightly squeaked when the jurors rolled back and forth to study facts, figures, evidence, and admonitions of the case after lunch. The temperature started rising, as the barometer steadied at 68 degrees. Sweat beaded on the brow of many jurors, and they didn't complain because their mind was on one thing—making a decision.

"I hate to see another black man go down for a crime without a murder," said juror number seven. "We've gone over the facts for three days now and my brother looks like he got caught with his hand in the cookie jar when nobody was looking."

The black female juror number four painfully spoke, "Every one of those kids has a mother. My kids are around their age. So much money was taken, and it took them four years to get to this point. We have to decide to put our babies behind bars. As much as I hate to do it, I don't see any other way because no matter how I try to deny it with my heart, my head tells me that my babies are guilty."

The white male juror number one in his sixties spoke out, "Gene Upshaw is the weak link. I'm a Viet Nam vet and had tours of duty that I had hand-to-hand combat with the Viet Kong. I've heard soldiers cry for their mama, shoot themselves in the foot to get the hell out of there, I've seen soldiers shit and piss on themselves because they didn't know where the next booby trap or bullet was coming from. It takes a certain kind of man to be a soldier, or a robber, and Gene Upshaw is a punk on the battlefield. He's the key player in this whole fiasco. With all the evidence against him, I'm gonna vote guilty."

"The law is the law, facts are facts, evidence is evidence. Getting sucked into the emotional side is fallacious. The law and fallacy don't mix, but it's hard to separate once it gets under your skin," said Demetrius. Let's just take it from the bottom. Who all believe that the busted tail light belonged to the rented U-Haul? Please raise your hand."

All twelve jurors raised their hand.

"Who believes that Gene Upshaw was a friend or associate of Pace?"

All twelve jurors raised their hand.

"Who believes Priscilla Potts' testimony that Gene Upshaw gave her money to buy property?"

All twelve jurors raised their hand.

"Who believes that Pace was smart enough to pull this whole thing off and get away with it for two years?"

Nobody raised their hand.

"We asked for high school transcripts for Pace," said juror number one. "I don't know how we got them, but we got them. This kid got As and Bs in some tough basic subjects—math and English."

Juror number eight spoke out, "During the trial, it was mentioned that Pace's mother is an elementary school teacher. He could have had plenty of help with his homework."

"Who believes the testimony of the accomplices that Pace was the mastermind?"

Nobody raised their hand.

"Who believes that Travis Tollson sent Gene Upshaw $100,000 from L.A. to Vegas five times via Western Union?"

All twelve jurors raised their hand.

"Henry Jones, Sr., his testimony was crucial; he testified he received $177,000 from his son, Henry Jones, Jr. over a two-year period."

"That was some cold shit, but I believe it," said the black juror in his sixties.

"Who believed Henry Jones, Sr. testimony?"

All twelve jurors raised their hand.

"Who wants to see these defendants go free?"

All twelve jurors raised their hand.

"Who believes that Allen Pace III and Travis Tollson are guilty?

Ten jurors raised their hand.

"Well," said Demetrius, "We almost have a consensus; may I ask the reason for your dissenting feelings?"

A white female juror number eight in her early thirties who was not very vocal until this point spoke out, "They don't know who really robbed Dunbar, Mr. Devereaux. Every ounce of the prosecution's evidence is circumstantial and all of us believe Pace wasn't smart enough to pull this shit off. I believe that blacks have been given a raw deal in this country ever since it's been a country and even if he did it, I have a soft spot in my heart for the Robin Hood story. You know, taking from the rich to give to the poor. Besides, although I may look white, my great, great grandparents were black. Somehow, I sympathize with Pace and his Merry Men if he did it. Although it's a crime, he made a lot of poor people happy, even if it was for just a moment. Somewhere deep in my heart, I wish he would've gotten away with it. It's not like he's using the money to bomb the White House. Call me radical or a leftist if you want. To me, those young men are heroes. They saw an opportunity and seized it. They scared the shit out of a few employees who were working for peanuts anyway. I know, if everybody started taking shit the way they said they did, it would be total chaos; but only a handful of people ever would have the courage and smarts to get away with that much money. If they had more solid evidence, I'd convict him in a heartbeat for the sake of the law no matter how I feel personally."

"She's got a point," said another white female juror number two about the same age. "They need more convincing evidence to convict Pace. People'll run with you when trouble is far off, but when it's in their face, they choke like a baby who has swallowed too much milk. They ain't got shit on Pace and they probably never would have if it wasn't for those other guys. If we convict him, we'll be getting him off the street, a relatively good man, who wanted to get rich quick or never be rich at all. I can realize the motive and the opportunity, but if he did it according to the law, he's guilty. But I can't put a man away so easily who I don't think is a hardened criminal. Not a soul was hurt in that heist and just for the hell of it; they could've killed every last one of 'em."

"Whoa," said Demetrius. "Houston, we have a problem. I really appreciate your sincerity and truthfulness. What do we do now?"

Everybody looked perplexed, tired, and mentally beaten down. The heat was taking its toll. Nobody said a word for a long while.

The black male juror in his sixties spoke, "I guess this is where we really earn our money."

The white male juror number one in his sixties spoke, "Ladies, in my opinion, the law is a science encased in intent and reasonable doubt, but they try to mix art in it, and the good ones can. Pictures don't lie and they say that one picture speaks a thousand words. Maybe if we look at more photos we can establish a connection with Pace to Gene Upshaw because that dude, Gene Upshaw, is guilty as hell, and in my opinion a coward, too."

"He's right ladies," said Demetrius. "The law is the law, and the judge was very strict on studying and following the admonitions. We don't want to piss her off, do we? Let's get all the pictures they have and then go from there."

Both girls nodded in agreement.

They pored over a hundred pictures over and over again. They picked out pictures of Pace and Upshaw and set them to the side. They saw them together at parties, outside of EE and AMT, outside personal residences, and riding in cars together. At one point, both girls' wiped tears from their eyes. For three hours, they viewed photos like they were looking at family photo albums, bringing back past memories and drudging up long past forgotten emotions.

"Our decision boils down to three things: Pace's intelligence, the money wrappers, and the taillight," said Demetrius. Pace's high school transcripts reflect his intelligence despite who did his homework; the money wrappers despite if they were picked up on the street; the taillight that was directly connected to Gene Upshaw. Now, I'm going to ask a series of questions that must be answered yes or no. No matter how hard it is to choose, you've got to answer yes or no. Was Pace smart enough to mastermind the Dunbar Heist?"

Ten hands shot up, including Demetrius'. Juror number two and juror number eight dissented.

Demetrius reeled into a note pad.

"Who believes that the money wrappers turned in to the FBI are the original money wrappers of the stolen money?"

All twelve jurors raised their hand.

Again, Demetrius reeled into a notepad.

"Who believes the taillight is connected to the U-Haul truck rented by Gene Upshaw the day before the robbery?"

All twelve jurors raised their hand.

This time, Demetrius didn't reel into his notepad but slowly and deliberately wrote, and he appeared to be in deep thought for a while. "Intelligence, that's our hurdle, that's our mountain we have to climb," said Demetrius as he turned aside.

Juror number seven spoke, "I played little league baseball and we were cheated out of a game to go to Williamsport, Pennsylvania. Later, a guy on that same team didn't complete high school to sign a professional baseball contract. He played in the minor leagues for seven years before he made it to the American major leagues. Gary Ward is now a millionaire. Intelligence can be measured by neither a high school diploma nor a college degree."

"Duly noted," said Demetrius. "But anything is better than nothing. Our duty as jurors is to tie a knot of guilt or unravel that same knot into innocence." He paused then continued, "IQ and intelligence are misleading but a fair barometer on a natural fact. We must weigh the facts within the facts. We must put intelligence under a microscope to either convict or set free a fellow human being. And let's not forget the attorney of the defense's message: "For I am involved in Mankind. Therefore, send not to know for whom the bell tolls, it tolls for thee."

"That man is one of the best lawyers in the country," said juror number one. "If I ever got in trouble, I'd pay him to be my lawyer. I've never heard of a lawyer calling his client 'too dumb' as a defense. This whole case rotates around the 'intelligence' of a so-called mastermind and the burden of proof is the prosecution's responsibility and that responsibility has been shifted to us."

"I admit," said Demetrius, "that burden has now become very heavy, and we have to carry it together."

"We can carry intelligence to where it needs to go," said Juror number one. "So, let's make this decision now and forever."

"Juror number two and number eight, all I ask of you is to be fair to yourselves," said Demetrius. "Look at the facts and evidence again within your own volition for as long as you like, under no pressure. Convene among yourselves. The rest of us are here to answer any questions that you may have."

The two jurors rose with pictures and transcripts and separated themselves from their peers into an isolated corner of the room to ponder and converse. While ten read newspapers and magazines and scribbled in books, two sat between themselves conversing, haggling, crying, squirming, and after several clamorous outbursts they calmed and called over Demetrius.

"Do you believe in God?" queried juror number eight to Demetrius.

"God is real. God is with us. God is our savior," answered Demetrius.

"Do you believe in the devil?" queried juror number two to Demetrius."

"You can't have one without the other," said Demetrius, "There's a balance in the universe."

"Have you ever broken the law no matter how great or small?" asked juror number eight looking defiantly at Demetrius.

"Yes."

"Are you prejudice against blacks?" asked juror number two looking at Demetrius with tears in her eyes.

"No."

"I'm a Buddhist," said juror number eight.

"I'm a Christian," said juror number two.

"I'm a Muslim," said Demetrius, "No matter what religion we are, there's only one God. Religion is how we choose to serve that one God through our practices, morals, rituals, and ethics. We must realize we live in a country where you can practice any religion you like. I believe religion is a platform we stand on and God built that platform. No matter what the platform, God shines and rains on the just and the unjust and we're all here to serve God not only in spirit and truth, but also to decide not 'just us' but justice."

"I've seriously weighed the pros and the cons and the cons outweigh the pros. With me the scales of justice have settled to that," said juror number eight.

"I need a little more time alone," said juror number two, "Right now my pros and cons are in perfect balance."

"I understand," said Demetrius, "And may God be with you."

Juror number two sat in silence by herself with the weight of the world upon her shoulders for a long while, while everybody else in the jury did their own thing. Although juror number two detached her link from the chain making it incomplete, the court of the most powerful nation on the planet was asking for justice and a completed chain.

She asked herself: *Did Allen Pace III work at Dunbar? Yes. Did Allen Pace III know the accomplices? Yes. Did Allen Pace III have experiences with guns?" Yes. Does Allen Pace III have a domineering personality? Yes. Did Allen Pace III have an opportunity to rob Dunbar? Yes. Was Allen Pace III smart enough to rob Dunbar....? Yes.*

The pros were an overwhelming answer to one of the most perplexing questions in juror number two's young lifetime. After an hour, she waved over Demetrius. My heart says no, but my logical mind says yes. He's guilty.

Demetrius returned to the heartwood-oaken table and scribbled scrip on the compromised verdict form. It took three days to get to this point and jurors were spent. As many cases as Demetrius had been involved in, in terms of a dissenting juror, this one was most complicated thus far. In his hardest of hearts, a consensus of opinion for guilty verdict surprised him for the mere fact they never saw the defendant at the scene of the crime, besides he had what Demetrius thought was an almost air-tight alibi. Demetrius stepped out of the hot jury lounge and got the bailiff's attention and returned to his seat in the jury lounge.

Back in the courtroom, the lawyers and defendants were patiently waiting for the judge to enter the courtroom. Deputies walked back and forth completing chores and duties preparing for the judge.

"All rise, please," said the bailiff, "Court is back in session."

"You may be seated," said Judge Bird.

"Judge, the jurors have reached a verdict," said the bailiff.

"Okay," said judge Bird, "We have everybody. Bring the jurors back to the courtroom, please."

February 27, 2001, had been a long Wednesday for the jurors of the 1997 Dunbar Heist. A sudden knock at the jury lounge door startled most of the jurors. Demetrius answered the knock with a smile. Every juror heard loud and clear, "We're ready for you now." All the jurors rose simultaneously and formed a single file line and seated themselves in their assigned seats in the courtroom.

When Demetrius was in grade school, he had a childhood dream of being a lawyer. By far his favorite movie was "The Verdict" and his favorite actor was Paul Newman. He had a video tape of the movie and would watch it often. He actually cried when the best actor award went to Ben Kingsley for "Ghandi" in lieu of Paul Newman for "The Verdict." His love for the theatre immensely affected his everyday life and now he himself was like an actor on stage sitting as acting foreperson for one the most important non-murder criminal trials in the history of America. Again, he looks over the courtroom atmosphere and notices every picture and emblem on the walls, and then he looks at the faces of the attendees and emotionally reflected to the 1983 Academy Awards. Is this déjà vu?

With that moment stamped on his brain in history he spins backward to the 1983 presentation awards in each category of his interest. Best director—Richard Attenborough for "Ghandi"—his picture was nominated but didn't win. Best Actor—Ben Kingsley for "Ghandi"—his actor was nominated but didn't win. Best supporting actor—one of the cast, James Mason, was also nominated for "The Verdict" —but didn't win. Lou Gossett, Jr. won for "An Officer and a Gentleman." Best adapted screenplay—his motion picture, "The Verdict" was nominated but "Missing" won. In fact, "Ghandi" and "E. T." won in most major categories. Meryl Streep won best actress for her role in "Sophie's Choice" and Jessica Lange won best supporting actress for her role in "Tootsie." He remembered how disappointed he was that night that his picture didn't win anything. But now, as he sat in jury seat, number twelve, his team would win a verdict for the United States of America for the largest cash heist in American history. As he sat and waited, the smell of black roses filled his nostrils, a heavenly smell that's hard to describe that he knew from helping his mother in the garden when he was a boy, something like the smell of Jasmine incense. He knew, symbolically, that black roses meant the 'end and the beginning or the beginning and end' of something. The faces he saw waited in anticipation for a verdict they knew not of. Concerning the case, he thought that conscience makes cowards of us all, and the pale cast of thought of the accomplices, how they turned awry to expose Allen Pace III and Henry Jones, Jr. to their sins that would be remembered.

All sounds were like muffled whispers as Demetrius sat in silence. Noises permeated through the courtroom that barely reached Demetrius' ears. The gavel sounded like the peal of great bells at Amersham in Buckinghamshire that got everybody's attention. The judge dressed in black sat at the bench like an old crow with great wisdom. Two flags stood aplomb on either side of the judge's chair like toy soldiers standing sentry. In a mental world of his own, Demetrius focused on the flags and their symbolic meaning. He loved serving his country and reflected on the rich history of the two flag's historical and symbolic meaning. The 'Bear Flag Revolt' consisted of a small group of American settlers in California who rebelled against the Mexican government and proclaimed

California an independent republic. According to historical accounts the American army officer John C. Freemont arrived at Sutter's Fort, now modern-day Sacramento, with a small corps of soldiers and additionally persuaded a motley mix of American settlers and adventurers to form militias for a rebellion against Mexico in the spring of 1846. Shortly thereafter, in June of 1846, a band of about 30 Americans led by William Ide and Ezekiel Merritt attacked the Mexican outpost of Sonoma—just north of present-day San Francisco—and surrounded the home of Mexican general, Mariano Vallejo, arresting him and his family without bloodshed.

Having taken the Mexican general, Commander Ide and Commander Merritt went on to proclaim California an independent republic. With a cotton sheet and some red paint, they constructed a makeshift flag with a crude drawing of a grizzly bear, a lone red star, resembling Texas' star that was already a member of the union with the same red paint wrote "California Republic" at the bottom. Thus, this was the birth of the California flag that stood on the left side of Judge Bird. Old Glory, The Star-spangled banner, our national flag, the Stars and Stripes are all names attributed to the flag that stood on the right side of Judge Bird.

Demetrius' gaze now shifted to the Unites States of America flag, and he reflected upon its historic and symbolic significance. That powerful symbol was adopted in 1777 on June 14 for the original thirteen colonies, and adopted July 4, 1960, for the fifty states. From December 3, 1775, until July 4, 1960, the United States flag has gone through evolutionary changes. Historically, the American flag symbolized nationalism and the rejection of secessionism, a marking of American territory, to fight and die for, freedom of speech, a spirit of veneration, and a connection with God. For example, in 1907, the U. S. Supreme Court ruled and upheld that the U. S. flag is prohibited in the desecration statutes from marking on it, defacing it, commercially advertising it, showing "contempt" for the flag in any way by publically burning it, trampling on it, spitting on it, or otherwise showing a lack of respect for it. In one of the most important battles for independence on that historical date of Jan. 1, 1776, George Washington was granted control of the Continental Army, which was laying siege to Boston, which had been taken over by the British Army. George Washington ordered the Grand Union Flag above his base at Prospect Hill. The flag had 13 alternate red and white stripes and the British Union Jack, the canton, in the upper left-hand corner. Consciously, this historical knowledge flooded Demetrius' mind as the sound of the gavel again snapped him out of his reverie.

Judge Bird's facial movements were absent of any emotion. The lawyers from both sides shuffled papers and concentrated on scrip made by their swerving pins. The gallery was full of people: reporters, writers, family, friends, and associates. Now, every sound was amplified but an underlying quiet settled and set the tone.

"So, foreperson Mr. Devereaux," said Judge Bird, "The jury has reached a verdict."

"Yes."

"Alright," said Judge Bird, "If you'll please hand the verdict forms to the bailiff, thank you, sir."

The bailiff sauntered so slowly towards Judge Bird after she took the verdict forms from Demetrius and gently handed it to Judge Bird. Judge Bird reviewed the verdict form that she herself helped devise as she has done so many times before. Like a trained high-stakes poker player the expression on her face remain unchanged, "Okay, let the defendants please rise. Madam Clerk, you may publish the verdict, foreperson, what say you."

Henry Jones, Jr. was found guilty and considered to be only a minor player in the

Dunbar Heist. Now, all eyes and ears were on Allen Pace III, the Dunbar Heist Mastermind. Mastermind of the largest cash heist in American history.

"Circuit court of Los Angeles, The United States of America vs. Allen Pace III; Aggravated armed robbery, 24 counts of money laundering. We the jury hold that the defendant, Allen Pace III, in this case, is guilty as charged so say we all of aggravated robbery in the first degree and guilty on all counts to all persons of the jury, judge, and others on this date of April 23, 2001."

"Alright, you may be seated," said Judge Bird. "Would you like the jury to polled, Mr. Sharpio?"

"Yes," said Allen Pace III's' attorney.

"Madam Clerk, please poll the jurors," said Judge Bird.

The clerk now spoke with a slightly louder voice without a microphone, looking directly at each juror. "Juror number one—is this your verdict?"

"Yes," he said with an identifiable somber voice.

"Juror number two—is this your verdict?"

She didn't answer immediately. A tiny tear formed in the corner of her eye, "Yes."

"Juror number three—is this your verdict?"

"Yes."

"Juror number four—is this your verdict?"

She, too, cried but her tear rolled down her cheek, "Yes."

"Juror number five. Is this your verdict?"

He paused, "Yes."

Juror number six. Is this your verdict?"

"Yes."

"Juror number seven. Is this your verdict?"

He looked at the defense's table for a moment or two, "Yes."

"Juror number eight. Is this your verdict?"

Juror number eight was visibly shaken. She had developed bags under her red eyes, "Yes."

"Juror number nine. Is this your verdict?"

"Yes."

"Juror number ten. Is this your verdict?"

"Yes."

"Juror number eleven. Is this your verdict?"

"Yes."

"Juror number twelve. Is this your verdict?"

Knowing that saying this word would 'seal the deal' and lock up and link history to Allen Pace III at least until the foreseeable future—the infamous so-called mastermind of the Dunbar Heist, one of the most intelligent men on the planet, a man that should have gotten away with $18.9 million in cash—Demetrius took a deep breath, "Yes."

A loud burst of sobbing and crying shrieked through the courtroom. Writers wrote. Family and friends consoled each other with hugs and words of encouragement. Women cried. Many had already surmised the outcome, but now the law; the federal law had spoken with a ferocious voice. It was over—four years of investigations, sleepless nights, fun, folly, brilliance, and flaw were elements sealed by the ramous ribbons of the lucent law.

Judge Bird looked at Pace with her well-known poker face semi-beset with closely cut white hair before she made her post-verdict statements, "Thank you Madam Clerk. Ladies and gentlemen of the jury, I wish to thank you for your time and consideration of this case. I also wish to advise you of some very special privileges enjoyed by jurors. No juror can ever be required to talk about the discussions that occurred in the jury room except by court order. For many centuries, our society has relied upon juries for consideration of difficult cases. We have recognized for hundreds of years that a jury's deliberations, discussions, and votes should remain their private affairs as long as they wish it. Therefore, the law gives you a unique privilege not to speak about the jury's work. Although you're at liberty to speak to anyone about the deliberations, you're also at liberty to refuse to speak to anyone. A request may come from those who are simply curious or from those who seek to find fault with you. It will be up to you to decide whether to preserve your privacy as a juror. Thank you for providing a very important public service by serving as jurors in this case. Your jury service is complete and you're free to go and the bailiffs will help you out. Again, thank you all."

As the jurors were escorted off the premises, the defendants sat seemingly in another world. Pace looked like he wanted to cry, and Jones looked like he wanted to get up and run for the hills. The loud sobs reduced to whimpers and solitude seemed to cover the courtroom with a veil of foreboding anticipation. Detective Warren and Agent Malone sat in a quiet, inconspicuous corner of the courtroom in an ominous silence as a tiny smile creeped across Warren's face. Malone looked resolute. Sharpio spoke a few words to Jones's attorney who sat in deep thought. Ms. Sugar smiled wildly and her assistant, Shopmaskus, pumped hands with a few people from the gallery.

"Okay," said Judge Bird. "Are we ready to proceed?"

Both sides verbally agreed. The defense first; the prosecution second, shuffling a pile of loose papers.

Before-sentencing protocol allows anybody in court to make statements or speeches.

"Before we go to the podium, Henry Jones, Sr. would you like to speak?"

"No, Your Honor," he said.

"Mr. Allen Pace III, would you like to say something?" asked Judge Bird.

Allen answered in a weak voice, "No. No ma'am."

"Does anybody want to speak?" asked Judge Bird.

Everybody remained seated, and then an elderly woman rose slowly to her feet. She looked like it was hard to walk, but she also looked determined to speak. Her wooden supporting cane, she leaned on heavily. A couple of deputies rushed over to help her, but she motioned that she could manage. Her silver and ebony hair glistened under the courtroom's lights. It was easy to tell that her eyes weren't far from tears. She took a long look at Allen, then Henry before she turned to the podium.

"I'm Grandma Pearl. I've been knowing Allen since he was born. He was always the leader type. I remember going over to see him when his parents brought him home from the hospital. He was so cute. As he grew, he got along with the other kids so well. I remember watching him play with balls in the street with the other kids. He would manage all the time to get my grandson Mark on his team. You see, Allen and Mark have been friends since Allen was four and Mark was three. I know in my heart that Allen or Mark is not mischievous or bad people. I believe that the devil got ahold to both those boys just long enough to get them thinkin' that they could fool God. It's in the Bible that the love of money is the root of all evil. O Lord, vanity of vanities all is vanity. My boys were so full of pride, and they were doing so well without that money." Grandma Pearl started crying, "I'm all right, just let me finish. I know the laws the law, but those boys will try to help you before they hurt you. I know it in my heart because I know them. Thank you for listening." Family members watched Grandma Pearl laboriously walk away from the podium with tears in their eyes, but they let her be until she found her seat.

"Will the defendants go to the podium, please," said Judge Bird. "And it may seem you don't have any objection to the standard court costs. Again, is there anything anybody wants to say?"

If anybody wanted to say something, they didn't. Grandma Pearl said enough for everybody. The gamut of emotions and message were touched by her few words.

Sharpio said 'no' for both, in response as both defendants held their head in a bow.

"The jury has found you both guilty, Mr. Pace and Mr. Jones, in aggravated robbery. I will withhold sentencing until June 18, 2001, approximately two months from today."

"Would any of you like to appeal?"

We'll take care of that Your Honor," said Sharpio.

"Is there anything else I need to cover?" she viewed both sides. "Thank you everybody."

# Chapter 36

Approximately two months later, the courtroom buzzed like bees on steroids waiting for the official sentencing. On the day of sentencing, Henry was the first to be called and the judge looked tired. It was because, by this time, the entire case had taken several months to finish because Allen and Henry had vehemently denied any involvement. Due to overwhelming convincing evidence, and the way it tied all the defendants together in a tight bundle. The jury had deliberated for three days and came back with guilty verdicts for both Henry and Allen.

Judge Bird sat in the high black bench chair with her familiar poker-faced style, "Henry Jones, please stand; having been found guilty and working in complicity with six others. The 24 counts of money laundering will run consecutively to the aggravated robbery charge. I sentence you to 17 years in a federal prison without parole. You and your accomplices terrorized and tied up innocent people at gunpoint. I believe you were working under orders of another so I will not levy the full twenty-four years allowable by law. We're all happy that no one was hurt or killed. I believe that seventeen years is a long time. Time enough for you to reflect upon your actions and we pray to the Lord that you rehabilitate your attitude and never think about taking unearned money ever again."

When the judge saw Allen, she ignited like she was a thoroughbred in the gates at the start of the race in the Kentucky Derby.

"Allen Pace III, please stand."

Allen slowly rose with a blank stare etched all over his face and a wavering imbalance in his stance.

Judge Bird peered at him with elliptical eyes as wide as the Atlantic, "You've taken this court through a nightmare, not to mention, your decision to include your peers and what you took your coworkers through four years ago. The prosecutor is asking for 27 years. The only reason that's not going to happen is because nobody got hurt during this historic robbery. Your attorney is asking for 21 years. You have no remorse for denying your role in the robbery. You and your co-conspirators tied up and terrorized several Dunbar employees. You were the trusted employee who knew about the money's whereabouts."

Allen was standing silently wearing a green jacket and sandals.

The highly anticipated moment had come. Allen's baby's mamma, his parents, some friends and associates, and Detective Warren and Agent Malone were there. Judge Bird kept a straight face as the gallery awaited the future, accepted respected words as an interpretation of long-established law. Judge Bird looked at Allen for a long while, and then said, "I've checked historical records for my own edification. The Dunbar Heist of September 13, 1997, is the largest cash heist in American history of $18.9 million in Los Angeles, California. I found that $18.8 million had been taken from Loomis Fargo & Company in Jacksonville, Florida single-handedly by an entrusted employee, Phillip Noel Johnson, on March 29, 1997. He was a truck driver and $17.3 million was stolen by Steve Chambers from a regional vault of Loomis Fargo & Company on the evening of October 4, 1997, approximately four months after the Dunbar Heist in Charlotte, North Carolina. There is no evidence to these three events being related, but it's sure worthy of thought. Combined, these three heists amounted to $55 million, and they occurred within seven months apart in the same year. As I said earlier, there was no conspiracy detected in these three events. With that said, I'll continue with the sentencing. Mr. Allen Pace III, you were an entrusted employee with the Dunbar Company, and you knew about this money and you got everybody else involved. Again, the prosecution requests for 27 years and your attorney, Mr. Sharpio, asks for 21 years. Under federal guidelines, you can get as much as 24 years. Therefore, I sentence you to twenty-four years in a federal prison and serve 18 years without parole. I think this a very long time and a very serious sentence for denying playing a role in the robbery. You are ordered to pay back $18.9 million and if any of the $10,000,000 is recovered, you must pay back Lloyds of London, the insurer of the money. Do you have anything to say?"

Allen, holding his head down, said, "No. No ma'am."

"Well then, if there are no more questions and nobody has anything to say, the sentencing is complete. Thank you all for your service."

All was done. All the i's were dotted, and the t's were crossed, except for the $10,000,000 that vanished into thin air and a few million dollars spent and burned.

Later in post-trial interviews outside the courtroom, Ms. Sugar said, "It sends a message to the community that if you commit a crime of this magnitude, there are going to be stiff penalties for it."

"How long have you been working on this case?" asked the reporter.

"We spent approximately four years working with the FBI, IRS, and the Los Angeles Police Department detectives," said Ms. Sugar.

Sharpio was interviewed by a reporter, "It could have been worse. My client could have gotten additional years. Allen Pace III was loved and respected by his family, friends, and relatives. They spoke up for him and that may have had a bearing."

Reporters surrounded Agent Malone, "The investigation will continue until every dime of the stolen money is recovered?

Detective Warren was approached by reporters, "Why did it take so long to convict the Dunbar Heist robbers?"

"Allen Pace III got lucky for two years. When you break the law, it has a way of healing itself. Evidence and facts have a way of standing the dross and test of time and still shine like a diamond. We're going to continue to investigate with the FBI, IRS, and our very own Los Angeles

Police Department to find anything or anybody in connection with this case to find that missing money."

"Wouldn't you say that Allen Pace III is a historical mastermind to have thwarted some of the smartest investigative minds on the planet?" asked a reporter.

Detective Warren seethed at the eyes as they squinted to tiny slits, "As I said, he got lucky. It was just a matter of time. Evidence eventually popped up all over the place—the tail light was found at the scene, the money wrappers seeped through the cracks and crevices, and the money laundering cleaned the robber's clock instead of getting cleaned itself. A mastermind would have picked up the broken taillight, discarded the money wrappers, and never sent over ten thousand dollars over the wire whether he had control of it or not. And, even if he would have cleaned up those areas, I believe that the robbers would have been caught by some other device. The law is a mighty force, and if you break it, it will eventually break you. And as a result, Pace got the harshest sentence of them all. The law will always correct itself. The bigger they are, the harder they fall. I'm a lawman and I will fight crime until the end of time."

Mark's first few visits while in MDC came from his attorney, Michael Brennan. Based on attorney/client privileges, they sat eyeball to eyeball in a separate room. The counselor furtively slipped Mark a small slip of paper.

"I have good news, young man," said Brennan, "Due to your minor involvement in the Dunbar Heist and with your cooperation and the fact this was your first offence and your family's statements, I was able to obtain a downward departure from 10 years to seven years so you can get out of here sooner to resume raising your family."

"Thanks for your hard work," said Mark. "I'll do everything I can to comply while I'm locked up."

The nightmare continued for Grandma pearl and Florence, so Grandma Pearl moved not too far away to Lennox, California to mitigate police annoyance. Everything they found in the robber's name, they confiscated, including cars, motorcycles, jewelry, and a host of other consumer goods. Occasionally, the cops and federal employees would go by Mark's relatives' homes and completely search the premises for the unaccounted for money. They would thoroughly question everybody they could, including off-the-wall questions to the kids. All cars, on-site and off-site storage units were searched from box-to-box, drawer-to-drawer, shelf-to-shelf, and from garment-to-garment. They watched and searched from time-to-time and at random for a whole year. This activity turned Mark's family and friends upside down on a perfunctory basis. The local police would pull over and search family, friends, and associates on any given day.

One day, the FBI came to the neighborhood with several flat-bed tow trucks and confiscated cars, motorcycles, bicycles, and any consumer good that income didn't justify. Whoever complained had to show receipts, notes, and legitimate credit information along with proof of income. Looking for the missing money and to recover every dime that was available was their objective. Without the associates' knowledge electronic bugs were placed everywhere because one day Queenie ordered a Pac Bell phone service and the serviceman brought it to her attention. He told her that he couldn't remove it, but at least she was aware. Life was arduous, tedious, and pure hell for family members or anybody who had ever associated with Dunbar Heist Gang according to the FBI files.

# Chapter 37

Florence and Mark would talk frequently, and she and the kids would visit at first, once a month, and as time wore on, the visits were fewer and further in between. She told Mark about the FBI shakedowns. Florence could take a punch, Mark thought. Florence kept reminding Mark of all they went through, and she wouldn't send him divorce papers. But Mark constantly thought of all the orgies they all engaged in. His wife, wife's sister, sister-in-law, Allen; and the fact that his wife and her sister-in-law were casual lovers and the times they would have a threesome. With that thought, Mark felt comfortable that sex wouldn't break him and his wife up. But after about three years, Mark was transferred to Beaumont, Texas. He never saw his wife, but they would talk on the phone a couple times a week.

The Federal Prison experience for Mark wasn't like most would think. To Mark, it was a Club-Med experience. As long as you didn't 'drop the soap' and were straight, you didn't have to dodge those butt fuckers squeezed in the state prisons. To Mark, the only bad deal he could conceive of was the Repayment Penalty of the $18.9 million. Anytime he earned income over the poverty level, he paid Uncle Sam the difference. To Mark this was the perfect opportunity to self-educate. He figured he'd never be rich, but what the fuck he was once and fucked it off. He found ample time to study the scriptures. He fell in love with the King James Version of the Bible. One of the verses that Mark took to heart was Amos 5:6-9— "Seek the Lord, and ye shall live; lest He break out like fire in the house of Joseph, and devour it, and there be none to quench it in Bethel. Ye who turn judgment to wormwood and leave off righteousness in the earth, Seek Him that maketh the seven stars and Orion, and turneth the shadow of death into the morning, and maketh the day with night: that calleth for the waters of the sea, and poureth them out upon the face of the earth: the Lord is His name: that strengtheneth the spoiled against the strong, so that the spoiled shall come against the fortress."

In a daydream, as the seven-year jail sentence was coming to a close, Mark was in the prison hallway mopping. He was thinner, weathered as the prison guard approached, "You got visitors, McCrary."

Mark settled in a seat and picked up the phone to talk. The kids were older. Florence looked much older than her age also. There is a heavy tension between her and Mark, "You said you were going to wait for me. I'm not mad at you."

"Seven years is a long time," Florence squeezed out.

"We more than three-quarters-of-the-way through," said Mark with a slither of hope. "With good behavior they say I'll be out in months, and—"

"I'm sorry, it just...happened."

"Kids, hug your father," said Florence crying. "We got to go."

They all held their open palms up to the glass, and held them there for a long while, then Florence rose revealing a large pregnant belly—a knife to Mark's heart. He cried tears of blood. As he watched his grown-up kids leave, the whole room seemed to swallow Mark whole.

"McCrary let's go," the prison guard barked.

Mark's body was heavy, so he sat there for a moment.

"McCrary!" shouted the prison guard. Mark slowly rose with the weight of the world on his shoulders.

He didn't receive one other visitor in Texas, even after the day of his release. "They hate Him they rebuketh in the gate, and they abhor Him that speaketh uprightly." It was the seven stars of Orion that uplifted Mark. That constellation of stars that is situated in the middle of the night sky November to February that so inspired the building of the Pyramids. After coming across one of Dr. Ben's (Yosef Ben – Jochannan) books—"Black Man of the Nile," and taking time to read it, Mark was inspired just as much as his churchgoing background and the sermons he so enjoyed as a child. The connection of Dr. Ben and the Bible inspired Mark to study all of Dr. Ben's books. The study of The Bible, Dr. Ben's books, and the dictionary took up most of Mark's time in what society called a prison, but in Mark's mind this institution was freedom. As time passed, Mark still had a decent relationship with Florence, but towards the time for his release date, he knew something was wrong. One day, he called home after not hearing from Florence on their rhythmic basis, and Malcolm told Mark that Florence was in the hospital having the baby. Markie said that his mother told them not to talk about the baby.

In his cell later, Mark managed to write a letter with tons of effort:

*Grandma, Somehow, I've found peace today. It's taken a few years to find peace, but I have it now. Thank you for your letters and the books you've sent me. I'm reading every day. I know that my greed led me to do terrible things. I am a changed man now. Keep praying for me...I may get out within a year, optimistically. And I am hoping you will let me stay with you until I get back on my feet...*

Later that day, Mark mopped the rec room. A reporter's voice cut like a sword through the low hum of the above waning fluorescent light, "So, Detective Warren talk to us about the cracking of the biggest cash heist in American history—The Dunbar Heist."

Mark looked up from his duties and honed in on the broadcast. Warren sat in a dark suit with a blue tie looking distinguished but still looked like something was missing, like he had an itch that he couldn't scratch, like he was still hungry for something he wanted to eat—famished. "In truth, me and my partner Malone were the ones who didn't give up when it came to accountability, but it's not a happy ending for us—"

"What do you mean?" asked the reporter.

Detective Warren looked directly into the camera with intense eyes, "Well, out of the $18.9

million stolen on the night of September 12, 1997, only $8 million has been accounted for—"

"So, you're saying there's over $10 million floating around?" said the reporter in exasperation.

"Yes, yes, that's what I'm saying. We tried," said Detective Warren unsatisfyingly.

Mark's eyes twinkled, he mumbled, an opportunity. But he knew from the FBI files rendition that only a few had privy to—that Detective Warren was lying because the FBI's calculation of the total amount of cash taken was really $19.3 million and he said that $10 million had not been accounted for. In reality, they really only got back $1 million in cash and properties, and they told the public it was only $18.3 million, so it was then that he knew that around $15 million was still floating around out there somewhere. He could have been wrong, but he couldn't see how. To Mark, it was water under the bridge because he was focusing on the future not the past. Since he had really not counted every bill to the dollar in the entire two-year period, at that moment, he realized that there was still $15 million unaccounted for from his perspective. He had burned only about ten thousand before him and Gene decided to go to Vegas. And he himself had spent roughly a-quarter-of-a-million dollars, but he gave the rest to Allen, at his request, to invest.

As Mark reflected on the handling of the cash, he knew that Allen, Travis, and Gene became very close because after the heist, Travis started spending more time with his paternal family, and one of them or all of them finally handled $18 million at their discretion. But there is one thing for certain—we told on each other about who was involved and who the mastermind was, but they don't know where roughly $15 million in cash is and only three of us know what happened to that money, so the media is not telling the public the truth, because they didn't know the truth. Everybody had spent money in their own way. Maybe, just maybe, that's why Gene and Travis fought it out until the last blow, and Gene ratted; and they were faking a knockout, to get up off of the canvas again and float like a butterfly and sting like a bee.

On the other side of the country, in a different detention facility in Arizona, Allen watched the same telecast. The Federal Prison Camp in Arizona would be his home for a long time. After four years, Allen had somewhat settled into the federal prison system. He knew that he was better off with the federal instead of the state. He also knew that he needed a plan to get through the remaining years of his incarceration. As more time passed, he began mastering his first love—chess. He would imagine playing chess with Bobby Fischer, the living legend and Grandmaster. From his study of Ancient Kemet, he realized that a true grandmaster Imhotep had multiple skills that were far more than a chess player. So, he read everything he could about chess and the famous Bobby Fischer. He learned that it's really not known who invented chess; they believe it originated somewhere in India. But after careful inferential study, Allen surmised that the game originated in Kemet.

With bags of time on his hands, he would go to the federal prison library and study for hours every day. In fact, he relished his library time more than his gym time. Allen wanted to understand chess inside and out. He gathered every book he could find on chess, and he found as much information on Bobby Fischer as he could. He learned that Bobby Fischer was born on March 9, 1943, and still alive. Allen ordered "My 60 Memorable Games" by Bobby Fischer. He cried the day the book arrived. The book divulged a collection of his games from the 1957 New Jersey Open to the 1967 Sousse Interzonal. As Allen read through the book, he was intrigued to find that out of the 60 memorable games

Fischer played, he had nine draws and three losses, and the objective and painstaking analysis held Allen's interest on a consistent basis.

He reflected that Judge Bird hadn't been so lenient with him. Her words were: "You were the mastermind of the group. You had created the opportunity while motivating your accomplices to accomplish this undeniable act of greed by force and fear and after reviewing all the evidence against you, I sentence you to the maximum penalty the law will allow—24 years in federal penitentiary without the possibility of parole until 18 years served." In his wildest dreams, he thought it was the perfect crime if everybody had been on the same page, but there were tragic flaws in his plan because he could mastermind a theft, but he couldn't mastermind people's thoughts, emotions, relationships, or greed. Seven years had been a long time, but somehow it seemed like yesterday when he had that conversation with Gene about Priscilla and how he had trusted Gene to take care of the situation—mistake; once a mastermind always a mastermind, so he sat at the table playing a game of chess with himself and behind him is the countdown calendar that loftily suspends his hope. Determination and excitement flutters across his lips with a smile and then his entire face brightens as he captures the queen. To him, the Queen represents 24 years that has hidden 10 million dollars for the King, so they think—that comforting thought solidifies his determination and appeases his patience—JUST WAIT!

Detective Warren continues with the television interview, "We tried everything, but the money seems to have vanished into thin air. My old partner told me one time, "Never to underestimate your opponent..."

"Looks like your old partner was right," acceded the reporter.

Allen's lips curl into a grin that got bigger and bigger.

He thought back to the Catalina Islands—Allen was on a sailboat. The boat came to a stop. Allen looked into the water. Allen said, "Alright fellas, lift and lower, lift and lower." Molly came from behind, kissing his shoulders.

# Chapter 38

Mark's interest had changed while in federal prison. Since he had to be there for around seven years of his life, he wanted to know everything about its history. They just transferred him from MDC to FCI Forth Worth, Texas. He was truly grateful that he was not in a state facility. Every so often news would trickle down or rise up to the federal level of how murders, rapes, and killings would occur often in a lot of state penitentiaries. As long as he did his daily duties and kept his nose clean, there were no problems. He would wake a lot of mornings at 4AM and lie there and pray for an hour, shower, shit, and shave so he could spend that time with himself. When he had free time, he would go to the library where he spent a lot of time. Many times, he joked with himself on how Malcolm X must have felt self-educating himself in prison. Unlike Malcolm, Mark wasn't inspired by another inmate. Truthfully, he thought that his inspiration was Grandma Pearl and a Black Jesus he imagined.

Mark knew that the roots were already there, he just had to nourish them. Since the robbery, many years ago, he noticed how people would break their word, and how that pressure captivated him many times. He decided to work on himself from the inside out. Every breath he took and every move he made would be to strengthen his moral character and not so much his physical muscles. He would lift weights sometimes in the gym, but he spent more time in the library at a ratio of 10 to 2. He found that Language Arts were a very interesting and vast field. He really thought of the art of language as a vast field of flowers, and if he knew the right flowers to pick, he could pick the most beautiful bouquets in the world, maybe black roses. Again, without a doubt, he was always interested and fascinated by preacher's sermons, so he decided to study Theology.

As he studied, he found that building a vocabulary was one of the hardest things on earth. To build a strong foundation in Language Arts, he had to define and memorize the eight parts of speech. C I N V P A P A (See I Envy Papa) was the foundation. C - conjunction, I- interjection, N – noun, V-verb, P-preposition, A-adjective, P-pronoun, A-adverb. This Mnemonic device would brighten the dark allies that each part of speech would take him down. Day after day, Mark would read the dictionary and thesaurus. He would practice delivering sermons in the mirror every day. He studied Copi's "Introduction to Logic", Napoleon Hill's "Think and Grow Rich" and Niccolo Machiavelli's "The Prince," and Leo Tolstoy's "War and Peace."

From his childhood experiences, being by himself came naturally. He didn't need a crowd or other's approval to feel needed and wanted. He studied the history of the federal prison system and what he found out astonished him. He realized in the total scheme of things that the federal government's prison system was relatively young. He learned that The Federal Bureau of Prisons (BOP) is a United States federal law enforcement agency and a subdivision of the United States Department of Justice. The BOP is responsible for the administration of the federal prison system. The system handles inmates who have violated, or accused of violating, federal law. On March 3, 1891, the 51st U. S. Congress passed the Three Prisons Act. The passage laid the foundation for the federal prison system, even though the federal bureau of prisons did not come into being until 1930. Back in 1776, the only facility to harbor federal lawbreakers was the Walnut Street Jail in Philadelphia. After The

Three Prisons Act was passed, this authorized the building of the first three federal prisons: United States Prison at Leavenworth, United States Prison at Atlanta, United States Prison at Mc Neil Island. Until 1907, prison matters were handled by the Justice Department's General Agent. The General Agent was responsible for Justice Department Accounts, oversight of internal operations, and certain criminal investigations, as well as prison operations. Moreover, there were sweeping changes made in 1907: the General Agent's office was abolished and its functions were distributed among three new offices: Division of Accounts (which later evolved into the Justice Management Division, Office of the Superintendents of Prisons and Prisoners (which evolved by the 1930's into the Bureau of Prisons), Office of the Chief Examiner (which later evolved by 1908 into the Bureau of Investigation, and later by the 1920's became the (Federal Bureau of Investigation), FBI.

As Mark went through the compelling history of the Federal Prison System, he became more enthralled by the following: According and Pursuant to Pub. L No. 71-218, 46 Stat. 325 (1930), The Bureau of Prisons was established by the U.S. Congress within the U.S. Department of Justice (which was created in 1870, to be headed by the Attorney General), whose office was first established in the first Presidential Cabinet under President Washington and created in 1789, along with the Secretaries of State, Treasury, and War. The newly formulated Prison Bureau was under the administration of the 31st President, Herbert Hoover (1929-1933), and his administration was charged with the management and regulation of all Federal penal and correctional institutions. At the time this responsibility covered the administration of the 11 federal prisons in operation. By the end of the 1930s, the system had already expanded to 14 institutions with 13,000 inmates. By the end of the 1940s, the Federal Prison System had 24 institutions with 24,360 incarcerated.

Mark was fascinated but not surprised to see how the Federal Prison System had grown to date—over 200,000 inmates and over 100 facilities. He was also fascinated about the reverse percentage breakdown of inmates—over 50% white and just over 30% black and over 90% male. After Mark's research, comparing state to federal numbers, he found that the numbers were reversed concerning black and white inmates. As the years wore on, Mark studied in relative peace. He didn't make any waves or ripples; he just took advantage of this time, this opportunity. Five years literally passed by in the bat of an eye. The staff would try to start trouble with Mark more than inmates, but he got through that without long-range problems. In June 2006, Mark was released from FCI Forth Worth. Nobody came to meet him, but he headed straight to Los Angeles to live with Grandma Pearl.

Mark was assigned to Westside Center on Cotner Avenue, halfway house, for six months and a thousand hours of community service upon his release from federal prison six months ago. The Halfway House was designed to make a smooth transition from incarceration to normal societal living. He was assigned to do his community service at The Los Angeles Boys & Girls Club on 324 N Mc Donnell Ave. He stood at the podium after delivering a lecture about his lessons in life, "That's my story, thanks for listening." The children clapped profusely as Mark looked in the distance for a lead.

A year-and-a-half later, Mark returned to the halfway house for a friendly visit and coincidentally met Henry, "Don't tell anybody we're on the same case together or what I was in for."

Mark couldn't believe his ears, "I didn't tell anybody what I was in for. Unless you tell them, that's none of their business". Henry continued repeatedly, "And don't tell anybody we're on the same case together."

"No problem," replied Mark. Of course, Henry didn't plan to meet Mark and vice versa, but Mark sensed something strange about Henry. Mark knew that ten years could change a man, but Henry was skittish. Like he was trying to protect or deliver something. Like he was trapped and still locked up. Like he had something to hide. Mark was glad that he took his Uncle Phillip's advice and put the robbery experience behind him.

One day, shortly after Mark saw Henry, he saw Gene over at his sister-in-law's house. They spoke more in depth about their past and a lot of unanswered questions were answered.

"Why did you tell on everybody when we said if we got caught, we'd be quiet?" asked Mark, with no hesitation or remorse.

"They didn't get me on robbery; they got me on money laundering charges because I sent Henry and Tyronne $50,00 and a $100,000 over the wire because Henry and Tyronne was living in Vegas trying to buy homes at the time not knowing that any amount over $10,000 would be investigated. Besides, I gave my girl Priscilla a $100,000 of my money to invest in real estate with her cousin James. Later, I changed my mind, and they wouldn't give it back. After all kinds of exotic furniture started popping up and no deeds, I got angry and demolished the furniture and took it out of the house. Later, I kidnapped Priscilla and James, took them to one of my rentals in Sherman Oaks, and worked them over pretty good and tried to scare them to give my money back and stop fuckin' it up, and I dropped them off in The San Fernando Valley on a side street. I must have scared the shit out of Priscilla because she saved some money straps and took them to the police. I guess they were scared for their life. But I found out later, the large cash transfers plus the money wrappers got me locked up after a full investigation of them. Besides, they had pictures of all of us. Shit man, I was scared as hell. I felt trapped and alone, so I told 'em, I told 'em everything I knew."

"So that bullshit that they had on Masterminds and FBI files was a fabrication and lies about the broken taillight about cracking the case with a busted taillight and the straps being found on the money."

"You and I both know the media is designed to make fools out of the public," said Gene.

Mark then realized that money is a motherfucka, even if you earned it legitimately, people are greedy, and money will fuck them up every time if they don't control money instead of money controlling them.

He knew that $15 million was unaccounted for, minus whatever the group had already spent in Vegas or otherwise. There's no way of him knowing the exact amount. He also knew that Gene might know the whereabouts of the missing money, but that was no concern of his now. To be dragged again into the big money game without the proper state of mind would, personally, be self-defeating. Over the years, he had plenty of time to think about it and he'll work and earn every penny from now on, and if he ever had an opportunity to get in the big money game again, it would be on his own terms. So, he wouldn't ask Gene anything about the disappeared money, "So How is life treating you now, brother?" asked Mark.

"After the halfway house experience, I trained to drive big rigs. I'm driving over-the-road tractor trailers as we speak. I'm working on owning my own trucks. What about you, bro?" Gene said, asking for Mark's story and friendship.

"I'm thinking about owning my own private investigation company and going to theology school and be a preacher on the official side," explained Mark.

"Good idea," said Gene. "You've always been knee deep into the church and boy could you sniff out a ruckus before it happened."

"You wasn't too bad yourself," said Mark. "Remember that time at the Strip Joint in Carson when that young guy had the gun in the small of his back and he was talking shit in the line and you frisked him and found that thirty-eight and took it until he cooled off. That motherfucka would have shot somebody that night."

"That dude was crazy high off some drug," ceded Gene. "But remember that time at the AME church when that older guy wanted to shoot the preacher for fucking his girlfriend and you frisked him and found a twenty-two in his hip pocket?"

"That was easy," said Mark. "I'd heard them arguing the week before. I always wanted to ask you this. Why did you slam into the wall the night of the robbery?"

"Shit man, I was scared and happy at the same time. A weird feeling, but truthfully, I couldn't even feel my feet for a moment."

Gene rose to his feet, "Here's my number, Bro. If you ever wanna just talk, holler at me. I gotta go get ready for work tomorrow."

"Good looking out, my brother," said Mark, "And if you ever wanna burn money again, let's burn it on the barbeque to get a richer taste."

Gene smiled and tiny tears flashed in the corner of both eyes.

A year later, Mark waited for the bus while the sun beat down warmth on the bench. Mark reveled in the sun and thanked God for his freedom. He climbed aboard the uncrowded bus and found an unoccupied seat for himself. He was still amazed that America elected a black man for President; Barrack Obama was featured on the bus TV talking about America's budget deficit. Mark wore a FUBU jacket over a dirty apron and some old tennis shoes. His worn and chaffed hands showed telltale signs of a dishwasher. He watched young people kissing older folk as he stared off into the distance searching for something without hope.

An older woman spied his worn-out shoes, "Those shoes are talking to me, baby."

Mark ignored the comment as the waning sun reflected faint light off of the silver crucifix he wore around his neck. He pulled the overhead line, and the bus came to a stop. He got off and walked farther down the street. He saw a familiar blue Camaro parked inconspicuously on the side of the street. He recognized Detective Warren proudly perched in the driver's seat with a bottle of unopened vodka.

Detective Warren waited until Mark was in earshot, "I'll catch you slipping motherfucker if I have to crawl through hell."

Of course, Mark paused, trying to stay calm, then a fire kindled inside of him, thinking better of it and he slowly walked towards his grandma's house. When Mark got to Grandma Pearl's house, he stopped for a while looking back over his left shoulder. He still heard Detective Warren's words in his head, and he spoke an aside to himself: *Doesn't that motherfucka have anything else to do? I've paid for my mistakes. Do I have to pay for the rest of my life?* He knew that question was aphorismus in nature—a question that nobody on earth could answer. He shook off the burdens of the day, turned, and walked into the house. Grandma Pearl was in the kitchen leading a fellowship group. It's a diverse group in age and ethnicity—Asian, Caucasian, Mexican, and Black, ranging from twenty to seventy years old. Mark decided not to interrupt but listened from the living room:

An older black woman with all-white hair, dark skin, a bit hunched at the back, around 5'2" tall, and large breasts stood and addressed the other nine women, "My baby grandson needs prayer. He's tempted by all this evil. His mama caught him selling weed last week—said he needed the money to buy him some Jordans. He's only thirteen."

Grandma Pearl stood, "My grandson was like that, too, greedy as they come," the women nodded and agreed with some amens. "But he's different now."

The older black woman piped in, "The power of prayer."

"Amen to that," confirmed Grandma Pearl. "I prayed for him the entire time, he confided in me, and he came out changed, praise Jesus. He will not be tempted by the devil anymore. He's stronger now."

The younger black woman, in her thirties, listening to experience speak, nodded her head, "He came through the fire and he's stronger for it," she continued. "Can I tell you a story my grandmother told me when I was a little girl?"

"Sure baby. I'll read a scripture first. We need to hear about other's experiences to increase our own understanding. Besides, the Lord did say, 'In all thy getting get understanding'— Grandma Pearl opened her Bible—my NASB version reads in proverbs 4:6-8 it is written, then she began reading, '...6-Do not forsake her, and she will guard you; Love her, and she will watch over you. 7-The beginning of wisdom is: Acquire wisdom; and with all your acquiring, get understanding. 8-Prize her, and she will exalt you; she will honor you if you embrace her...."' she reached for another bible and read, "In the King James Version in proverbs 4:6-8 it also says, "'6-Forsake her not, and she shall preserve thee: Love her, and she shall keep thee. 7-Wisdom is the principle thing; therefore get wisdom: and with all thy getting get understanding. 8-Exalt her, and she shall promote thee: she shall bring thee to honour, when thou dost embrace her.'"

"Thank you, Grandma Pearl, for the reading of the scriptures," said the younger black woman. "My grandmother told me this story when I was a little girl that I think is appropriate for all. This is what she said: "'A couple was visiting in Africa, and they came upon a very old gift shop with an unusually beautiful teacup in the window. Since they collected teacups for years now, she wanted this one for her collection, so they went inside to buy it whatever the cost and surprisingly when the teacup was handed to them, the teacup vividly spoke to them with these words: "'I tell you that I've not always been this beautiful. It took a painful process to get here. There was a time when I was just clay and my master pounded and kneaded me and I screamed and swore, but he patiently smiled, "Not yet." And when he put me on the shelf it was too high, and I was to dizzy being afraid of heights. Again, I screamed for him to take me down. He said smiling, "Not yet." Then he took me down and put me in the oven. It got so hot, I thought I was going to die, so I tried everything to get out, but my master smiled and said, "Not yet." Then he took me out of the oven just in time and put me on a table and started painting me with a brush. I felt jabs and stabs and he was swirling me, and I started to gag and choke. Again, he smiled and said, "Not yet." Then again, he popped me in the oven and this time he turned the heat up twice as high. I thought I was surely gonna die. It was so hot I pounded on the oven's door screaming, Let me out. I could see him smiling, but tears welled up in his eyes and rolled down his cheeks and he said, "Not yet." Then just before I was down to my last hope for life, he opened the oven and gently took me out, fresh and free; he placed me high on this shelf. Then he said, "There, I have created what I intended. Would you like to see yourself? He asked. I said, "Yes!" He handed me a mirror and I looked for a long time, "That's not me, I'm just clay." Then He said, "Yes, that for certain IS you, it took a process to get you here.

If I hadn't worked you when you were clay, you would have dried up. I had to subject you to the stress of the spinning wheel for you not to crumble. I had to put you in the heat twice in the heat of the oven for endurance so you would not to crack. I had to paint you so you could have some color in your life. Now you are everything I intended you to be from the beginning. Now I the teacup said something I never thought I'd be saying, "'Master, forgive me, I did not trust you. I thought you were going to harm me; I didn't know you had a glorious future and hope for me. I was too shortsighted, but I want to thank you for the suffering, for the process of pain. Here I am! I give myself to You—fill me; pour from me, use me as you will. I want to be a vessel that brings You glory within my life.'"

All of the fellowship members said HALLEJUAHS and AMENS! When the young woman finished telling the story, Mark thought about Allen and Detective Warren. As Mark listened tears of great understanding flooded his eyes, he was no longer bitter for going through the fire while in jail, but grateful. At that moment, he genuinely and inwardly forgave Allen and Detective Warren.

Grandma Pearl's voice rang out, "Let's pray that your baby will see the light like mine did…"

Mark peeped around the corner of the kitchen door and saw Grandma Pearl hold out her hands as the entire group connected hands and bowed their heads to pray. It was then that Mark interceded for his grandma and penetrated the circle between Grandma Pearl and the young woman, "Let us pray in your holy name heavenly father. Most importantly, we thank you heavenly father for allowing each and every one in this room to be in this room gathering more of your wisdom for it is you heavenly father who is the source of all wisdom and understanding. You are our comforter and redeemer, and you are Alpha and Omega, the first and the last, the beginning and the ending and everything in between. Therefore, we call upon you to bless this room and everyone in it with protection from evil and their loved ones and all of your children. Yes, heavenly father, we put you first so we may walk in your footsteps and goodness and mercy shall follow us all the days of our life and may your mercy surround us forever and ever. In your holy name we ask and pray, Amen."

During the prayer, there were many undertones uttered: yes, yes Lord, thank you, Jesus and they echoed throughout the room. Tears took over in Grandma Pearl's eyes as she hugs everybody. They all hug each other, and the guests leave with the spirit on their heart.

Later that night, Mark and Grandma Pearl sat watching The Wheel of Fortune and eating 'Hungry Man' TV dinners, "Baby, I'm going to beat you this time," said Grandma Pearl. "I'll guess the phrase before you do."

Mark lifted a spoon of food to his lips, "You know when you beat me, it's because I let you, right?

"You'd better quit," mused Grandma Pearl. "I'll win fair and square.

"Square is fair in life, but circles bring around what comes around," said Mark philosophically.

"I'm proud of you for changing your life," said Grandma Pearl with a tear in her eye, "You talk to the kids and read to find wisdom."

"Wisdom comes from God," said Mark, "It's like knowing the answer to two plus two and knowing when to use it. Fundamentals are the basis to everything. After all is said and done, it ain't easy."

"God is goin' to reward you, Mark. You'll see. He's going to put an opportunity right in your path."

Mark took a bite of food, "I know. I believe you."

Grandma Pearl turned away from the TV, "You'll see, all you've got to do is say, yes."

"Grandma, I love you."

She turned her attention back to the TV, "She needs to buy a vowel. That's what she needs to do."

The phone rang. Mark walked to the kitchen to grab it, and just before he answered, Grandma Pearl screamed in excitement, "Oooo, I'm about to solve it."

Mark responded, "Go ahead then!" He spoke into the phone, "Hello?"

A woman's voice penetrated the line, "You ever been to Catalina this time of year? The water is so clear you can see straight to the bottom."

Not being able to make out the voice, in curiosity, Mark wondered, "Who is this?!"

Instead of answering, the strange voice simply said, "I will seek opportunity. If not given opportunity, I will create opportunity."

A decade later, a daydream husked over Mark's mind. All six guys were there that pulled off the historically largest cash Heist in American history. He was now a fiery Baptist preacher, who had a large following and a successful PI business on the side for his popularity as a preacher had grown to monumental proportions beyond his wildest dreams and expectations. His controversial message of a Black Jesus connected to ancestral roots captivated many and affronted many. The reunion far exceeded that of a formal high school reunion. Every guy had a smidge of ecru hairs somewhere on their body. Allen had become a world-renowned chess player; Gene owned a fortune 500 trucking and transportation business; Henry owned a successful clothing, apparel, and accessories business where many Hollywood movie producers featured many of his designs and products; Travis "the troubadour" Tollson was an iconic rap star; and Tyronne owned a chain of successful restaurants that he named, 'Ophelia's Opportunity' as well as a world-renowned Master Chef. They were all sitting in Mark's church listening to him speak and hearing his forthcoming sermon.

Mark began to preach:

*"God is larger than life and there is no comparison to his existence. We were made in his image. He has feet, ears, arms, legs, a mouth, lungs, a head, and a heart just like we do. The primary difference is that He lives in the Spirit. We all have heard the term "Holy Spirit" or "Holy Ghost" uttered before*

*in our lifetime. "Holy" is so powerful, all-consuming, constraining, and infinite until it is indescribable and inexplicable, but can be understood if you trust it. Our ancestors discovered what we call a "Spiritual Realm" and they visited it often. Our ancestors were visiting the spiritual realm long before Jesus Christ set foot on the earth. We live in the "Natural Realm" every day, and we think we know the natural realm, because we have so much experience in it. I'm here to tell you that what you see is not always what you get in the natural realm. The spirit supersedes the natural, in other words, what's done in heaven will be done on earth—the spirit speaks the truth. If the spirit gives it to you, then nothing or nobody can take it from you. A book is not good enough. God himself speaks and says what no book ever could. We have conflict over what or who to believe in or have faith in on this earth. But the spirit is omnipotent and all-knowing and is the foundation of truth. Now what truly and really is the spirit? Some say Jesus Christ. Some say Buddha. Some say Allah. Some say Yahweh. I say the spirit dwells within you, and you must understand it for yourself.*

*Each experience that you have is a chapter written in your textbook or novel, many natural, some spiritual. When the spirit comes to visit, you must trust it, but one thing is for certain, you'll never forget it. In the spiritual realm what you see is what you get. Although the spiritual world is not three-dimensional, you can feel it better than you can see it—that strong or subtle feeling that you have when something is right or wrong, that cautioning that you should follow your first mind, those familiar words 'I told you so', or that dream you had last night, and much, much more. We need to understand what our ancestors understood. Our ancestors, the Kemetic people, put a lot of emphasis on astrology and astronomy. They studied the stars constantly and effectively.*

*Out of all the constellations named, Orion is referred to the most; first by the Kemetic people, the Greeks, and then the Romans. Let us think closely and clearly, if the Great Pyramids were one of the Seven Wonders of the World and were built and situated according to Orion's belt, I believe our ancestors were trying to tell us something that very few understand. Just as they left many clues behind by way of hieroglyphics and paintings on walls, they also left clues behind by way of monolithic structures. Rhetoric and propaganda will always be among us. Deception and lies are a part of the lisle thread of life. The spirit leads, guides, and protects you. The good spirit will smash lies or deception to smithereens. The spirit is a dichotomy of subtle and strong, easy or hard to understand, good or bad to wield, heaven or hell to live, wise or naïve to choose. Bad spirits are copies and charlatans of the original spirit. How do I know if a spirit is a copy? You shall tell them by their fruits. You can't plant an apple seed and get a cherry— common sense. Common sense or your first mind will guide you. The simplest way is the best way. Being honest with the spirit is the best policy. Honoring your mother and father even under provocation is healthy for the spirit. The good spirit can transform the bad spirit through perseverance and understanding. Establishing good morals is the key to hearing and following the good spirit. Moral keys unlock and open doors to physical and mental freedom. Greed is destructive and tears down a good moral house. Teamwork is the way of the world and trust is a basic element of living and thriving and let the good spirit decide what is right or wrong."*

After the sermon, the six met in the church breakroom. Allen, Gene, and Travis left for minutes then returned with two large duffle bags in either hand, and a six-pack of Corona beer in a paper bag and a jigger of Yak.

"Have a beer with your friend," said Allen to Mark.

Like old times, the guys sat around the table reminiscing.

"I have a present for you, my brother," said Allen smiling at Mark. He reached in a duffle bag and pulled out a bag of marbles and heaved a duffle bag on the table in front of Mark.

The five friends shook Mark's hand individually.

"There's $3 million in that bag and the marbles are the ones that I've ever won from you," said Allen. "You will always be my friend and I always will take care of our friendship. What's mine is yours. And it is a tantamount truth that I will seek opportunity, and if not given opportunity, I will create opportunity.

THE END